A Collection of Aromantic Fiction about Love, Connection, and Empowerment

BEING ARO

EDITED BY MADELINE DYER AND ROSIEE THOR

PAGE STREET YA

PAGE STREET YA

First published in 2026 by
Page Street Publishing Co.
27 Congress Street, Suite 1511
Salem, MA 01970
www.pagestreetpublishing.com

Distributed by Macmillan, sales in Canada by The Canadian Manda Group.

30 29 28 27 26 1 2 3 4 5

ISBN-13: 979-8-89003-442-7
Library of Congress Control Number: 2025948333

Cover and book design by Rosie Stewart for Page Street Publishing Co.
Cover illustration © Sam Prentice-Jones

Printed and bound in China

CONTENT WARNINGS

KIMBERLY MA MEETS HER MATCH – none

THE BINDING – compulsory romance, arophobia, violence, gore, torture

LOVESICK – illness, contagion, grief and loss, death, blood/injuries

PRESERVATION – descriptions of animal cruelty, blood

JOUST FRIENDS – none

THOMAS MARLEY'S FAKE BRIDE – compulsory romance, control, violence, blood/injuries

SWORDMAIDEN – violence, misogyny

FLYING SOLO – arophobia, compulsory romance, forced mind-sharing (off page), suffocation, medical stay

PAPER REBELLIONS – book banning, institutional queerphobia, death of a loved one

DO YOU SEE ME? – discussions and mentions of death, generational trauma

DAUGHTER OF TIME – death of a parent (off page, before story starts), animal entrapment

INDULGE THE OTHER – gore, torture, invalidation of identity

CONTENTS

INTRODUCTION

JULIE SONDRA DECKER

"I think your story needs some romance in it," a reviewer said after providing a test read. "At least a romantic subplot. Something."

"Why?" I asked.

"Because the need to be loved is a primary driving force for every human."

I was perplexed. The story did involve several kinds of love, just not the romantic kind. But when I persisted in seeking justification for this feedback, it all boiled down to this exasperated revelation:

"Romance is what makes stories interesting."

This was not the first time I'd heard the opinion that readers simply expected romance to figure into every story, and it was not the first time critics had implied that a character without such experiences would be boring, weird, and utterly not worth reading about.

Unsurprisingly, as an asexuality and aromanticism educator and activist, I've also heard that assessment applied to people in our communities—or at least, to the idea of them. It's not a genuine reaction from knowing us. It's derived from their concept of us as definitively missing something vital. Something they can only conceive of as an absence. One detractor even wrote—in what he surely thought was a well-considered, reasoned presentation—that my asexuality was "probably a genetic issue," but that my aromanticism was fundamentally more disturbing, and rendered me—I quote—"very weird, spooky, hardly human."

It's unsurprising that those who think the lives of aromantic-spectrum people lack something essential would also feel that stories about us are not worthy of being told.

I am pleased to offer this collection as evidence that they are wrong.

Just like in reality, our stories aren't simply narratives that lack romance, nor do they always describe a person who is "complete without romantic love." A story about our lives can also involve the aromantic experience of living in a largely romantic world, and what we do with that expectation. How we cope if we do have romantic or sexual relationships on the aromantic spectrum; how our friendships are misunderstood as either the precursor to romance or as necessarily shallow; how we handle being pursued by those who misinterpret or desire us; how we exist when our love must be analyzed and chopped into pieces before we can understand which pieces we intrinsically want. All of that is nuanced and worthwhile and *interesting*!

More than enough to justify a story (or twelve) about it.

I grew up asexual and aromantic in the 1980s and 1990s with

no internet community to discuss my reality and no stories that named the experience. I was luckier than most; I was very sure of what I wanted (and didn't want), and never felt broken or left out the way many people in our communities describe. But it certainly wasn't easy, and I wasn't completely immune to peer pressure or negative feedback. What bothered me the most was that I rarely found lives like mine represented in the world around me.

Unmarried women were labeled as tragic, cautionary tales. Happy endings were punctuated by marriage. Lack of romantic connection was a red flag for identifying characters who were evil, stubborn, or damaged, and rehabilitating them involved "learning to love" a romantic partner. Even in science fiction, an alien or robot character could begin to understand humanity only through falling in love. I didn't *mind* reading stories that incorporated romance, but its omnipresence was tiresome after a while, and its portrayal as a prerequisite to fulfillment and even *personhood* was disturbing.

Growing up, writing was my refuge. It was how I figured out what my feelings were when they were confusing, and it was how I cemented the truth of my experiences when others would tell my story differently. I turned to language to put the stories I needed out into the universe, knowing others might need them too. I wrote about my life; about the nuances of my experience as an aromantic, asexual woman; and I was pleased to find that—contrary to my beta reader's assessment—my story was fascinating to people. And importantly, it was *not* only similar people who enthusiastically consumed it. Everyone—aromantic and not—benefits from knowing that aromantic people are part of our world.

Without stories about us, we lack context. Those who don't share our experience are led to believe aromanticism is at best a phase, at worst a dangerous flaw to be mended. And those on the aromantic spectrum often see that stories about humanity don't include their experience, sometimes leading to confusion and anxiety—a reasonable reaction when we're described as "spooky" and "hardly human." And on top of being left out, sometimes when we break through to the mainstream and insist on our relevance, we're beaten back with statements like "Why do you need these labels? Just be a person!" or "Everybody wants to be special these days." The detractors may not think so, but these sentiments limit discussion and authentic exploration of identity. We are *not* yet at the point in society where unnamed, unseen identities are universally embraced, and ignorance abounds when we don't even have language to discuss them or forge connections. Things that exist have words. Stories are how our world talks to itself. If we're not included in those stories, we think we don't get to be part of the conversation.

In this collection, we see people living the aromantic experience from multiple avenues. We meet people who must reject their society's traditions to seek fulfillment; we follow stories of less common partnerships; we learn many different approaches to understanding gender, community, sexuality, and humanity.

Every one of these is an authentic representation of an aromantic experience—even the ones that contradict each other. And that fact shouldn't confuse us; it should inspire us. There is no single aromantic experience. And the sooner we have diverse stories, the sooner we'll see how much flavor our less typical lives bring to the recipes of humanity.

INTRODUCTION

"Aromantic" isn't necessarily easy to define. In my attempts to educate on this subject, I settled on "people who feel little to no romantic attraction," but what helps at least as much is having stories about what it is *like* to be aromantic. And seeing aromanticism in context—seeing it braided into a life, even a fictional one—makes it far more meaningful and *real* than seeing it on a vocabulary list in a textbook.

Without hand-holding us through aromantic education, this book offers us a gentle education on aspects of aromanticism we didn't consciously understand (or if we did already fully grasp these things, we'll be delighted and relieved to see them authentically explored). In one example, a character at first doesn't realize asexuality and aromanticism aren't the same thing. That was me when I was young; romance and sex were unappealing, so they all went into one big bag of "nope" for me, and I didn't find out until much later how nuanced that understanding can be. Sometimes learning about aromanticism is learning what it is *not*.

We encounter characters who are confused, and characters who are sure of themselves. People who are just embarking on an aro coming-of-age journey, and people who have known forever. People who describe queer camaraderie with other stripes of the rainbow, and people who find rejection there. People who are disgusted by romance, and people who could take it or leave it. People who need—and find—allies who listen to them. People who revel in the importance of their non-romantic relationships.

We may see very specific aromantic narratives in this book that some of us will have *never* encountered in someone else's thoughts before. Some of us may have our very first experience of saying

"I can't believe I'm not the only one." Stories in this book may validate feelings we have no name for, and give words to those who lacked the language to have the conversations they want. We will see aromanticism treated as one element of a person, not a flaw that must be mended for a plot-relevant reason or a hurdle for someone else to overcome to get their happy ending. *We* are the main characters this time. We get the endings that make sense with *us* at the center.

We have always been here. It's time we have some reading material that reflects that.

KIMBERLY MA MEETS HER MATCH

ANN ZHAO

THANK YOU FOR DONATING TO THE HATCHBURG HIGH ROBOTICS CLUB!
HERE ARE YOUR HATCH MATCH FUNDRAISER RESULTS.

MA, KIMBERLY J.
Grade 11

MOST SIMILAR: YOUR GRADE

NAME	PERCENT MATCH
Nathan Green	97.2%
Hannah Li	96.9%
Ellis Clarke-Hughes	93.4%
Mabel Kim	90.2%

Sara Zayed	88.6%
Jason Tang	85.0%
Chandna Rajan	84.7%
Amanda Petrov	81.3%
Bridget Murphy	78.9%
Andrew Xi	76.1%

MOST SIMILAR: OTHER GRADES

Name	Grade	Percent Match
Georgie Moore	12	98.3%
Rowan Powers	9	97.6%
Brian Chen	10	95.4%
Theresa Pope	10	93.1%
Emily Zhang	12	90.9%

MOST OPPOSITE

Name	Grade	Percent Match
Grace Quinn	11	0%
Hayden Robertson	9	1.9%
Eva Olson	12	2.6%
Michael Wang	10	3.8%
Lydia Tanner	10	4.5%

In spite of myself, my pulse races as I read through the printout.

My results have most of the same names as years past. I feel my chest tighten seeing the top result: my ex-boyfriend, Nate. We only dated last year because we matched, and, well, he's my ex now, so. I don't know if I agreed to go out with him because I actually liked him or because the algorithm said we should. And honestly, we're *really* better off as friends.

Beside me, I hear a whispered "Ugh, of course."

My cousin Brian immediately folds his sheet in half and puts it aside. I don't have to look to know that the top result is a kid in his grade he doesn't like—they matched last year too. I look around at the others as they react to their own results. Those of us working the Hatch Match table this morning are the first people in the whole school to see our matches. Nina, a freshman, blushes furiously; Mohammad, a senior, maintains a neutral poker face. Mrs. Belmont, our advisor, smiles serenely as she observes.

Right now, it's nearly 7:00 a.m. This morning's robotics team volunteers, along with me and Mrs. Belmont, are set up on a folding table in the school cafeteria. Once the first buses arrive, we'll be busier than the Dunkin'® drive-through during finals week.

I look back down at my sheet. The rest of the list for my grade is unsurprising; the other two lists have some new names. Zero percent with Grace Quinn is weird; we take a few of the same classes, and that alone means she shouldn't be that different from me. But hey, maybe she's got a whole life I don't know about.

I can't believe I had to pay for this. I'm literally running the whole fundraiser.

The robotics team at Hatchburg North High School hosts the school's most popular, and most unusual, annual fundraiser. Most clubs sell chocolate, partner with chain restaurants, or do car washes. We run a school-wide student-built compatibility algorithm analyzing personality questionnaires handed out during homeroom, and then we make people pay to see their results. With 2,500 students at our school, most of whom are eager to find their matches, it's an easy moneymaker.

As robotics team treasurer, I'm the one in charge of Hatch Match this year. I may not be the one to code the compatibility algorithm—that's the job of whatever computer geniuses we have from year to year—but I've done pretty much everything else. This black-and-white printout in front of me is the culmination of months of work.

"Anything interesting?" asks Mrs. Belmont, peering over my shoulder.

In addition to being the robotics advisor, Mrs. Belmont is one of our deans. She, as a member of school admin, is the reason why we get away with making the whole student body do the questionnaire.

"Not much," I say. "Brian's on it."

At the sound of his name, Brian looks up and unfolds his sheet. "No way."

"*Yes* way," I say. "Face it, we're more alike than you think."

"Yeah, sure," he says, rolling his eyes. Then he looks back down at his printout. "Hey, I've got something interesting. A zero percent match. Someone in Kim's grade named Grace Quinn?"

I frown and look at my sheet, where the zero glares back at me. "She's on yours too?"

"Weird," Brian says. "But apparently, you and I are pretty similar, so I guess it makes sense?"

"Hold up," Mohammad says. "I've got a Grace Quinn on mine too. Do you know her?"

"Yeah, she's, like, a normal person," I say. "We've had some classes together. I think she does theater?"

"Well, she must be the complete opposite of a robotics team member," Mrs. Belmont quips.

Footsteps and voices grow close, and that effectively cuts off our conversation; the first buses have arrived. Soon, our table is swarmed. Nina's zooming back and forth between us and the printer at the speed of a track star.

My friend Hannah arrives a few minutes in. Disheveled and cranky, like every morning, she hands me a five-dollar bill wordlessly and yawns.

"Good morning to you too!" I chirp.

"Shut up," she replies.

I chuckle and hand her the printout of her results. "See you in class."

The next person to approach me is, to my surprise, Nate. I know he's my ex, and things are supposed to be weird between us because we're exes, but I'm actually happy to see him. At least he, unlike Hannah, is a morning person.

"Hey," he says, grinning when he sees me. "Do you take Venmo® this year?"

I shake my head. "Just cash or check, still."

"What kind of high schooler has a checkbook?"

"Don't ask me," I say.

He thumbs through his wallet. "Shoot. I only have two dollars."

I slide over my own results page. "We're pretty closely matched again. Just look at mine to see basically your results."

"I mean, I just wanted to donate to you guys," Nate says. "Maybe next time?"

"I'll sneak you your printout on Monday if you bring me five bucks then," I say.

"Oh, sweet," Nate says. "Thanks!"

He walks off, and Brian nudges me. "Awkward."

"It's really not," I say. "Did you even listen to our conversation? We're fine. It was more awkward when we dated."

Last year, after Hatch Match put us as super compatible, Nate asked me out, and we dated for a couple of months. Half the time, it felt like we were basically just hanging out as friends, where our "dates" were just us sitting or walking somewhere and talking to each other. It wasn't hard to make conversation; we'd known each other since middle school band, and we had a few things in common. But the other half of the time, it was the weirdest experience of my life. Nobody told me that kissing is kind of gross at first. You get used to it, but gosh. All that saliva? Very weird. A biohazard, even.

But the thing is, life got busy for us. Baseball season started up for Nate; robotics competitions consumed all my time. As we saw each other less, I realized I really just liked being friends with him. So we broke up. And now we're friends.

I shake off my thoughts and help the next person in line. After that, things begin to really take off, and I don't have time to think about my interaction with Nate. I lose track of how many people I greet and exchange money with. Word seems to have spread that I'm the mastermind behind the fundraiser this year because everyone compliments me on the survey questions and the formatting of the printouts. (All I did was change the typeface from Arial to Calibri.)

It's the same scene every year. The freshmen and sophomores are the most into it, screeching with excitement whenever they see their friends (or crushes) on their lists. The upperclassmen are a little over it, expecting to see the same names as before, although there is an element of surprise, given that we recalibrate the algorithm and update the questions every year.

A few minutes into the rush, Mrs. Belmont goes to the bathroom, leaving me alone to deal with the money. And despite how busy I am counting bills, Nina taps my shoulder. "Kim?"

"Yeah?" I don't even turn around to look at her, still leafing through a wad of cash.

Her voice drops to a whisper. "I know we're not supposed to read the results, but I keep seeing Grace Quinn pop up as a zero percent match on, like, every single printout."

I pause my counting and look up at her. "What?"

Brian overhears and leans over. "Yeah, I've been seeing Grace on all of these."

I gulp. "That's not good."

My eyes scan the cafeteria. People are clustering around with their friends, looking over their lists. I hear it now: "Grace Quinn, Grace Quinn, Grace Quinn," uttered over and over in the echoing cafeteria.

"Brian, quick, before Belmont gets back," I say. "Can you find Grace's results?"

He obliges, though he looks reluctant to do it. "Holy crap."

"What?" Nina and I both ask.

"Zero percent match with everyone," Brian says. "The names on this list are just the first people in the junior class in alphabetical order."

How on earth did Grace Quinn fill out her questionnaire?

By the middle of the day, everyone at school is buzzing with the mystery. We've made way more sales than we expected since everyone wants to see if they're also completely incompatible with Grace. That's about where the good news ends. We can't edit the printouts to take her name off because they're generated as PDFs. Grace is nowhere to be found; she didn't show up to AP Lang, a class I have with her in the morning. For privacy reasons, we shredded everyone's Scantrons and deleted their answers after the algorithm was done matching people, so we have no way to tell how this happened.

I know where Grace sits at lunch because I know where every Asian AP student in my grade sits, and she's not at her usual table. I'm starting to think she just happened to not show up to school today. But a couple periods later, I walk into the locker room for PE and see her hunched form on a bench: wavy, dark brown hair brushing loose over her shoulders, a T-shirt in our school colors on, and a pair of headphones still around her neck. And she looks *mad.*

I walk up to her. "Hey, Grace!"

"I don't want to talk about Hatch Match," she immediately grumbles.

My eyes widen, and I recoil in surprise. "Okay. Sorry. Um, I'm actually helping run it this year, so—"

Her posture straightens. "Great, so can you take my name off of people's results?"

"Um . . . I don't think so."

Her expression darkens. "Why not?"

"The printouts are computer-generated, and there's no way to edit them because they're PDFs—"

"You guys are STEM people. I'm sure you can figure out how to edit a PDF."

"Well, it's just—"

Now she looks positively furious. "Could you not have stopped collecting payments when you noticed? Rerun the program? Now the whole school is talking about me."

The bell rings to remind us to get to our PE classes. I turn back to look at her. "Okay. I have to go. But I promise I want to figure out what happened. Maybe a bug in the algorithm, I don't know. Can we meet up after school?"

She sighs. "Fine."

Grace offers me only the time it takes to give me a ride home—an oddly kind gesture given that I'm responsible for ruining her day—which will afford me about fifteen minutes, maybe twenty if the school's parking lot is really backed up, to figure out what could have gone wrong with her results. I'm certain something happened to her answers; I'm just not sure what happened or whose fault it was.

I find her in the back of the junior parking lot leaning against a gray sedan with a dent in the bumper. Despite the February chill that's common here in Illinois, she wears merely a light jacket. She unlocks the doors, and we get in and start to creep out of the parking lot, which, thankfully for me, is quite backed up.

"So," Grace says. "You want to talk."

I decide to cut right to the chase. "How exactly did you fill out your questionnaire for Hatch Match?"

She sighs. "Here we go."

"I just want to know if it was something on your end or ours. If our algorithm is broken, we need to figure out what went wrong with it so this doesn't happen again."

"Your algorithm isn't broken," Grace says dejectedly. "It was all me."

"What did you do?"

She grips the steering wheel as we slowly inch through the line of cars. "Your survey had choices A through D for every question. I bubbled in E for everything."

It takes a moment for my mind to register what she's said. We use these standard Scantron forms. They're really old-fashioned, and we could definitely create a secure online form that would work more easily, but Mrs. Belmont likes the tradition of paper forms. Since they're standardized, we can't customize them to have fewer multiple-choice options, so the entire E column is redundant.

But clearly, the E responses were able to make it into our system.

"What did you think would happen?" I ask. I don't understand why such a stunt was necessary, and she obviously isn't enjoying the attention from it.

"I thought you'd throw away my answers," Grace says. "Does nobody check the results before you give them out to people?"

"We've been doing this for years," I say. "Our program has never given us a reason to worry it could act up."

Not in my memory, at least. It was all made by some coding whiz that went to Hatchburg years and years ago. The coding whizzes since then have been the ones to maintain it.

"That seems overly trusting of the process," Grace says.

I ignore this comment. "So you wanted us to throw out your answers. Why?"

"I didn't want the attention."

"Well, that backfired."

"No shit, Sherlock."

Who even says that anymore?

"What kind of attention did you not want, exactly?" I ask.

Grace sighs. "Freshman year, five different people slid into my DMs after I wound up on their 'most compatible' lists."

"Is that . . . bad?" I ask.

She sighs. "You don't get it, Kim. You've had a boyfriend. You're popular, at least among the people in the honor roll. You're somehow on the boards for, like, five clubs."

"It's actually four." Robotics, scholastic bowl, math team, and knitting club. (Look, sometimes you need to do crafts instead of crunch numbers for a change.) "And Nate and I broke up almost a year ago."

"Whatever. Also, half the guys in our classes are into you."

I frown, a sinking feeling suddenly expanding in my chest. "They are?"

She views my expression with curiosity. "Yeah. You didn't know?"

I shake my head. "Are you sure about that?"

"I hear people talking about you," Grace says. "I'm, like, sort of invisible at the lunch table sometimes."

"That's . . . interesting to know."

"Look," Grace says. "The point is, you're a social butterfly and top of the class, and I'm just trying to get by without being noticed. You're so used to attention that you don't even realize that people are into you, and my *worst nightmare* is someone trying to hit on me."

I have no time to think about the implications of what she's saying. Things that I didn't know anyone thought about me. Instead, my curiosity takes over. "But *why*?"

At this point, Grace looks like she's had well enough of me, which is probably fair. "It's literally just not something I'm interested in. I don't like people . . . like that."

Oh. I think I know what she means.

"Are you ace?" I ask.

Taken aback, Grace replies, "You know what that is?"

"Well—yeah, of course!" I exclaim. "LGBTQIA. That's the A."

I don't even know when I learned it. Even if I wasn't bi—which I am—isn't it something that everyone growing up in a sort-of-liberal town's public school system finds out at some point?

"Oh. Um. I was prepared to do a lot of explaining." She flips on her blinker; we've finally reached the front of the line of exiting cars. "Yeah. I'm aroace. *Just ace* isn't really about romance per se. Although it's all kind of muddled together for me. I don't want any of it."

I've vaguely seen aromantic and asexual people talk about it online, though I haven't really read up on it.

"I've identified as bisexual for the past year," I say. "That's kind of the opposite of being aroace, isn't it?"

Grace frowns. "Uh, no. Not really. You can be bi and also aro, or ace, or both. It's a spectrum."

"Oh. Um. Sorry."

I have a feeling I've already messed up this conversation.

But now I see exactly why Grace wanted so badly to stay out of Hatch Match. I probably would, too, if I hated any sort of attention, let alone if I particularly hated the romantic kind.

"But wait, why couldn't you just take it as a friendship matching game, like we advertise?" I ask.

"Tell that to the rest of the student body," Grace replies. "Everyone treats it as a matchmaking service. Which, like, it is. And it was just so annoying, and tiring, and I just didn't want to deal with it all anymore. Last year, I tried to give really weird answers so nobody would match well with me, but then I got matched with a bunch of *freaks,* and it just made my DMs even worse!"

"Like who?" I ask.

"Like Josh Paulsen."

I immediately cringe. Josh Paulsen is a boy in our grade who thinks the moon landing was faked and posts flyers about it all across the school. He's pretty much always in detention. At this point, I have to wonder if detention is really that effective.

A car behind us honks. We've missed at least one opportunity to turn left. Grace swears under her breath and exits out to the road.

"Um, I'm really sorry you've had to deal with that," I say. "I don't think any of us thought about it that way, which is super shortsighted of us."

Grace softens. "Oh. Thanks."

"Uh, yeah. Of course."

She takes a right onto the main road and then says, "Well, there's your answer, anyway."

"Yeah. Thanks for telling me. And, uh, trusting me with everything."

"No problem. But my friends all know about me. It's not a secret at all."

"Oh. Sorry."

I don't know why I apologized for that.

We're quiet for the rest of the ride back to my neighborhood.

Right after Grace drops me at home, my mom texts me to head to Brian's house because she and my dad are working too late to make dinner. Which is fine by me, though I wish she'd told me about three minutes ago so I could avoid having to walk there in the cold. Xiǎoyí (Little Aunt; my mom's youngest sister and Brian's mother) is a far better cook than either of my parents, and this gives me a chance to ask Brian what he thinks about making some changes to Hatch Match. He doesn't exactly have much of a say in robotics team decisions—while I'm on the board as treasurer, he's just a regular member—but his opinion is important to me, at least.

I've spent nearly as much of my waking life at my aunt and uncle's house as I have at my own. They live just a few streets away, a less than ten-minute walk from my house. Brian and I are only children, but because we live so close to each other and are only a year apart in age, we're basically like siblings. So he doesn't bat an eye when I barge into his room and drop my backpack on the ground.

"I know why Grace was a zero percent match on everyone's results," I announce.

He looks up from his laptop, perched on a tray table on his bed where he sits cross-legged, sipping on a mug of tea. (He's very high-maintenance.) "What was it?"

I explain the situation, keeping it vague why exactly Grace did this. Brian guffaws when I reveal that Grace filled out all E's on her Scantron.

"She told me she really hates all the attention from weird people that she gets after every Hatch Match, and she thought we'd throw away her answers," I say.

"Well, I guess we should've," Brian says. "We're engineers; we're supposed to check our work."

"I know," I groan. "I feel so stupid."

"In any case, you got your answer," Brian says. "So, like, we're good now. Right?"

"Right," I say uneasily. "But, like, the whole school is talking about her. That's not great."

"Maybe people will forget about it over the weekend," he suggests.

"Maybe," I echo, still uneasy.

Brian returns to whatever work he was doing; I take a seat at his desk and open my own computer. But instead of also doing work, I google *aromantic asexual.*

Since she revealed it in the car, I've had a gnawing desire to know exactly where Grace was coming from. Why she couldn't just fill out the survey and ignore the few random messages she got. We all get those random messages. Sometimes they're from people who really just want to be friends.

Well, okay, that was one time. It was Hannah. But Hannah is now one of my great friends. So there.

Anyway, I'm hoping old LGBTQ+ forums can give me an answer.

I read through the first page that comes up. It tells me what I already know—aromantic people experience little to no romantic attraction, asexual people experience little to no sexual attraction—but then it gets more complicated. Some aromantic people still have romantic relationships. Some asexual people still have sex. Some are totally capable of romantic and sexual attraction, but it doesn't happen a lot, or it takes an emotional connection with the person. There are about a dozen other words to describe more specific places on a whole spectrum of aromantic and asexual identity: gray, demi, flux, and so many more. I never realized all this was an option. There are so many more ways to *exist* than I thought.

In the next page I click on, there's a list of things you might feel if you're asexual or aromantic. A line catches my eye:

You're not sure if you want to be in a relationship because you actually want to or because it's expected of you.

Wait. I've had that thought before.

Did I go out with Nate because I liked him or because I expected I'd like him after I got my Hatch Match results?

Well, that's not the same thing. I do like people—I have crushes. The only thing that was expected of me was that I'd automatically like a person who answered a survey the same way I did.

When was the last time I really had a crush on someone, though?

I figured out I was bi just before I started dating Nate. Hannah came out as bi earlier that school year, and I asked her how she realized.

"It's pretty boring," Hannah told me. "I get so awkward and nervous around boys I like, and I realized I was doing that around a girl too. Then I thought about it, and I could totally see myself ending up with, like, someone of any gender."

After a few weeks of thinking about it and talking extensively with Hannah, I decided I also felt the same way about people regardless of gender. I, too, got nervous and awkward around people of any gender, so that decided it.

But I haven't actually, as my twelve-year-old self would've said, *like*-liked someone in a while. Probably the last time was a few years ago. It's so embarrassing; when I joined robotics freshman year, the captain, Gregory, was a no-nonsense, ambitious leader who ran a tight ship—and he had a *very* chiseled jawline. I was so jumpy around him that I couldn't even tell if it was because he was intimidating or because I was into him. Looking back, though . . . did I seriously like a guy named *Greg*?! That's a very unfortunate last person to have had a crush on.

My eyes focus back on my screen. The page explaining aromantic and asexual thoughts is still on my browser window. That's right, I'm just looking at all this to understand why Grace didn't want to do the Hatch Match survey.

"Brian?" I say.

"Hm?" he mutters, still focused on his laptop screen.

"When's the last time you had a crush?"

His eyes widen in alarm, and his cheeks flush pink. "Uh, why are we talking about this?"

"I'm not asking who it was. Just, when?"

"I still don't want to answer that."

"My last crush was freshman year. Is that a long time to go without one?"

He frowns. "Did you not like Nate?"

"The whole reason why we broke up was because we weren't that into each other to begin with."

"Right, but you still liked him, right?"

"I thought I'd have the potential to, given our results, but—hey, wait, don't make this about me. Answer my question."

He averts his gaze. "Fine. I, uh, sort of like someone right now."

Well, *that* is interesting. I won't try to figure out who it is, but there's something else I want to ask now. "When was your last crush before them?"

"What's up with all these questions?" he exclaims.

"Just tell me!"

"Like, a few months ago! Is that not normal?"

"Well, that's what I'm trying to figure out! I haven't liked someone for two years now! What happened?"

Bewildered, Brian shrugs. "I don't know! That's your problem, not mine."

"Is there something wrong with me?"

He snorts. "There are many things wrong with you."

If I wasn't sitting several feet away from him, I would reach over to smack him. "You are so—"

"DINNER!" calls Xiǎoyí.

And that's the end of this discussion.

Maybe there is something wrong with me. Is two years without a crush long enough to be considered typical? If it's not typical, does that make me ace? It's "little to no" attraction. But what counts as *little*?

Or maybe there's something wrong with Brian. Two crushes in a few months is a lot, right?

On my walk home, I look up how often people have crushes. There's a study of college students that found that over seven months, people reported an average of five crushes.

Five in seven months?!

And I haven't liked anyone since Greg?!

Honestly, did I even like him? I was just thinking about how I didn't know if I was intimidated by him or if I liked him a lot. Maybe I didn't like him. In that case, I haven't liked anyone since . . . gosh. Since Andrew Xi in middle school. That was when all my friends were getting their first crushes. *Everyone* liked Andrew. He was so smart and so cute. Of course I liked him too.

Oh no.

What if that wasn't a crush either?

But I've thought of people as attractive. Lots of people. Pedro Pascal. Reneé Rapp. Simone Ashley.

Oh god, they're all celebrities. Another thing that one website said could be a sign.

I feel like this isn't the kind of thing I can puzzle out on my own. When I came out as bi, I talked to Hannah for hours about it. But Hannah's not aromantic or asexual. She can't help me.

Maybe I need to talk to Grace again.

Wait, maybe I'm just really suggestible. Hannah told me she

was bi, so I decided I was bi. Grace told me she's aroace, and now I'm questioning everything all over again.

But Brian told me he was gay when we were in middle school, and I didn't decide I was gay then. But also, he's a boy, so maybe that's something to do with it?

Okay. Yeah. I need to talk to Grace again.

Before I can second-guess myself, I shoot off a text.

Surprisingly, Grace agrees to talk the next day. I expected her to say no. It's not her job to keep on talking to me about things. She has her own life, after all.

It's the weekend now—and it's Valentine's Day, so all the good hangout spots are swarmed by couples. Which means we end up at an ice cream parlor. In February.

It's at least not at the peak coldness that we get when a polar vortex passes down here, but in temperatures hovering around the freezing point of water, the last thing I want is to eat something made of ice.

And yet, here I am, licking a mint chocolate chip cone in the downtown Hatchburg Kilwins—and shivering while I do so.

We spent the drive downtown chatting about basic things. Grace is skipping Chinese school for this; she assists her mom, who's a teacher there. That was how I learned her mom is Zhào Lǎoshī (Teacher Zhao), the strictest Chinese teacher I've ever had. With all the small talk, though, the massive elephant in the room just kept growing while we parked and then waited in line for our ice cream.

Finally, Grace eats a measured spoonful of ice cream from her cup and then, without pause, asks, "So why the hell are we here right now?"

I clear my throat. "Would you believe me if I told you I enjoyed our conversation yesterday and want to get to know you better?"

"I'd more willingly believe that the Earth is flat."

Ouch. "Okay, fine. I'm having a crisis, and I think you're the only person that I can talk to about it."

"Uhhhhhhhh. Okay."

"So, yesterday I looked up what asexual and aromantic are."

Grace eyes me suspiciously. "I thought you said you already knew what they were."

"I wanted to learn more. And I did. And then I started thinking about it, and then my cousin told me he's had multiple crushes in the past few months alone, and I don't think I've actually liked someone since freshman year, and maybe I didn't even like them at all, and—"

"So," Grace interrupts, "you're having a sexuality crisis, and you decided the only thing you could do about that was find someone of that sexuality to confirm or deny your suspicions?"

"Um. Yes?" Now that she puts it like that, I'm ready for her to fully walk out of this conversation.

Grace shakes her head and sets down her ice cream. "Well, you're not the first one."

"Really?"

"I'm in tech crew," she says, as if that explains everything. "Everyone's some flavor of queer there by the time they graduate. You don't think I've been asked about being aro?"

"Oh," I say. "So . . . it's okay if I ask?"

She shrugs. "We're already here."

I still can't really tell if she has an attitude because she's just like this or because I'm severely annoying her.

Regardless, I lay out everything I've been thinking about for the last twenty hours or so, in a bit more detail than my initial outburst. Something deep inside me tells me I'm probably oversharing, but Grace just sits and listens, nodding along. When I'm finally through everything, though, Grace says something I don't like.

"Look, it's up to you how to identify. I can't tell you if all that makes you aroace."

I groan and slump in my seat.

"Hey, I can't tell you how to label yourself," Grace says. "*But* . . . what you're saying sounds pretty familiar. I mean, it's really not the same for me. I knew since I was a kid that relationships icked me out. But dating a guy because you feel the pressure to? That sounds a lot like what my friend who's a lesbian went through. And someone in tech crew who's aro said they couldn't tell the difference between butterflies and a fight-or-flight response. You're checking off a lot of boxes."

I slump forward even more and put my head down. "I don't like that answer."

"Did you want me to tell you that you're not aromantic or asexual and that you're just being silly and that I don't want to speak to you ever again because it's really weird for you to info dump all this on a random girl from your classes that you publicly humiliated literally just yesterday?"

"That's sort of what I expected," I mutter.

"I mean, it's a little true. But fortunately for you, I'm a nice person."

I look at her aloof, frigid expression. I'm not very convinced by her statement. "Okay."

She sighs. "Listen, I figured this all out when I was twelve. You think I had anyone to talk to about it? I sure fucking wish I did. So yeah, I'm gonna try to help you out because I don't want people to feel as alone as I did. You should've seen me the day I realized being forever alone really can mean being alone, like, forever."

I feel all color zapping away from my face. "Oh my god."

"Yeah, well, it fucking sucks, and society is built for people who aren't like us, blah blah blah, but straight women married to emotionally unavailable husbands who moved them far away from their friends are just as lonely. Everyone has the ability to be lonely if they don't find a community. So, you know, here I am. Being your community."

I don't have the wherewithal to process everything she's saying right now. I might not for a while. I mean, I don't even know how to label myself. I don't know if any of this is even applicable, or if I'm just having a really weird day.

But Grace is extending a hand—metaphorically; I don't know if she'd ever, like, actually shake my hand—and I take it.

"Thank you," I say. "That, uh, means a lot."

"Although," Grace says, "I would really appreciate it if you did something in return."

"Sure. Anything."

Three days later, the robotics club issues a statement on our Instagram account. And we announce some changes:

The Hatchburg robotics team has become aware of a mistake in our survey collection that resulted in one student being listed on every Hatch Match results sheet. We sincerely apologize to the affected student and will take measures to ensure this mistake does not occur in the future.

We are also excited to announce that future Hatch Match surveys will take place at the beginning of the school year rather than Valentine's Day week to encourage students to make new friends at the start of the year. In addition, the survey will be optional, and we will provide alternatives for those wishing to contribute to the team's funds without participating in Hatch Match.

Because we love surveys so much, consider filling out the following survey if you have any ideas for future fundraisers (Valentine's Day or otherwise): shortenedurl.com/hatchburgrobotics26

Grace DMs me after the post goes up:

@grace.meiling

thanks for the notes app apology

@kimberlyma13

Canva, not notes app

@grace.meiling

yeah whatever

appreciate it

you guys should partner with jazz band and make your robot play

people love songs for vday on the piano

@kimberlyma13

I don't think you understand what our robots are capable of

@grace.meiling

okay

is your crisis still happening

@kimberlyma13

Um

Yes

@grace.meiling

want to talk?

i'm here

or whatever

Zero percent match aside, I think Grace might just end up being a friend.

THE BINDING

SOUMI ROY

Lanterns swayed from gnarled branches, their light flickering like breaths held too long, casting trembling shadows across the village square. Marigold garlands draped the altar stones that ringed the clearing. Eight individuals, each eighteen years old, stood barefoot on the packed earth before the altar stones. They were clothed in white linen kurtas. Red cords looped around their necks—like promises, like nooses. Waiting to tighten.

Gauri stood among them, trembling like a thief about to be caught. She wished the Bindings came less often, the way they had in her parents' time—annually, when an entire age group came of age in the same year. But now the ritual happened every month.

"Stop fidgeting," Priya hissed from Gauri's right.

Gauri couldn't help it. The air felt heavier inside the circle, like it knew that she was a fake. That she felt hollow.

She had known stories of the Binding before she could even walk—how the cords chose a person. How Lord Raveth whispered names into the scarlet silk. How a heart would glow when its match stood across the altar. A divine design.

But no one spoke of what happened when the thread stayed still. Not the elders. Not the pundits. Not the acolytes who dragged the Unbounds away.

You're just a late bloomer, Gauri'd told herself, again and again.

But the truth was simpler, sharper. Her heart hadn't stirred when Priya had kissed her under the neem tree when they were fifteen, or when Tarak had asked her to the Moon Festival last year. She had watched others burst with longing, with sighs, with nervous glances exchanged in the shadows of the banyan groves. She had pretended when she could, painted love on her cheeks like rouge, but it never took root in her heart. She had thought that if she tried hard enough, she'd catch up.

She had not.

There were no flutters, no ache, no yearning. Just a quiet confusion that she hid behind practiced smiles. But tonight, Gauri was no longer sure if she could.

Gauri's fingers stilled where they'd been unconsciously tugging at the hem of her tunic. Across the circle, Tarak gave her a near-imperceptible nod of encouragement, his cheeks red, the corner of his mouth lifting slightly—expectant.

"Now I know why you didn't kiss me back," Priya teased Gauri.

Gauri didn't answer. She couldn't, guilt blooming in her chest like a bruise. Priya wasn't like her. After Gauri, she had moved on to Neel. They had been together ever since. Priya knew what to expect with Neel standing in the same circle.

The village's head pundit stepped into the center, cradling a bowl of sacred ash in his weathered hands. "Speak your name," he intoned, voice carrying across the hushed square, "and the cord shall find your other half."

The circle tensed as one. Kiran, the blacksmith's son, squared his shoulders—of course he did. He always volunteered first, whether it was for the spring hunts or the monsoon preparations. "I am Kiran, son of Dava and Nira. I am willing to bind." His voice was steady despite the tremble in his lips.

The ash in the pundit's bowl stirred without wind. The red cord around Kiran's neck glowed faintly, warm embers against the white of his kurta. The cord pulled up like a living vine, reaching toward Ria across the circle. Gasps rippled. Ria's thread flared in response.

A match. A blessing.

Another voice rang out. Another match. Red cords twisted out midair, seeking each other.

Then Gauri's turn came, and oh, in the name of Lord Raveth, Gauri hoped—truly hoped—she would find a match. Her gaze darted briefly to Tarak, whose smile still remained reassuring. *If only he knew.* Gauri took a deep breath, tasting the bitter tang of fear on her tongue.

"I am Gauri, daughter of Seya and Jagan." Her knees trembled with the words, and she had to dig her toes into the earth to steady herself. Nonetheless, she kept her voice firm, just as she had practiced for all these years. "I am prepared to bind."

The red cord around her neck pulsed once.

And stopped.

The silence was deep and absolute, broken only by Priya's sharp intake of breath. The pundit's eyes widened, then narrowed, his mouth forming a tight line beneath his silver beard. No other thread moved. No eyes met hers—not even Tarak's, for he seemed to have found a sudden interest in studying the ground.

Gauri's cord sagged around her neck, the end coiling at her feet like a severed vein. Lifeless. Unclaimed. The ash in the pundit's bowl remained still, no movement to indicate the magic had found her match among the rest.

Then, after a moment, the head pundit cleared his throat. "Gauri is . . . Unbound."

The word fell like a rock down a well.

Something in Gauri's rib cage twisted. It wasn't sadness, nor shame. It was something worse—knowing. She had known this was going to happen. She had always known.

Her mother's eyes met hers for only a second—then dropped. She wrapped her shawl tighter, as if warding off a chill, but it was shame that curled in her shoulders, not cold. The lines around her mouth hardened. She did not speak. She did not look at Gauri anymore.

Her mother had been fading for years, pulled inward by something Gauri could never name. Her voice had grown quieter, her smiles rarer. Her touch no longer lingered on Gauri's head after blessings, only brushed past like habit. Part of Gauri had hoped—foolishly—that if she was Bound, maybe her mother would see her again. *Love* her again. But even in failure, even knowing what came next, she turned away. And that, Gauri thought, hurt worse than the thread going still.

"Let us go on," the pundit declared, his voice carrying a forced formality that barely masked his discomfort. And even though the ceremony resumed, something in the air had soured. The cords still glowed, another match flared to life, but the applause came soft and scattered. The villagers tried to smile, but their joy rang false, as if Gauri's failure had left a crack in the ritual that no one could quite mend.

Gauri kept her eyes on her mother, memorizing every angle of her—the way the shawl stretched taut around her shoulders, her downward gaze—knowing she was on borrowed time.

After all the pairs were decided, one boy was left, orphaned by her failure. He stood awkwardly as the pundit explained that he would be allowed to participate in the next month's ritual. Relief softened his features, even as he tried to maintain a dignified expression.

Maybe it was Gauri's fault. Maybe she'd always known she wouldn't be chosen. But that didn't dull the sting—not just of failing, but of not being offered a second chance. Not like this boy. She had already been tried, judged, discarded. Girls didn't get do-overs. Girls were expected to fit.

Two acolytes came forward with iron chains as old as the ritual itself. The ceremonial solemnity of their movements contrasted sharply with the fear in their eyes. They were barely older than the participants themselves, perhaps twenty at most. The younger one, Arjun, had taught Gauri to swim in the village pond when they were children. Now he couldn't meet her gaze as he held the chains.

Priya's perfect composure finally crumbled. "Gauri, no—" She took an impulsive step before her newly Bound partner restrained her. Her hands clenched into fists as she watched, paralyzed by tradition and horror.

"It's okay," Gauri whispered to her best friend, giving her one last smile. The acolytes didn't have to drag her. She followed them quietly out of the circle, past the villagers whose expressions ranged from pity to superstition to bitter vindication.

She followed them through the grove of banyans—where she had played as a child, had first learned its history; where she had practiced the binding words in secret—to the boundary of the forest, where ruins towered.

They brought her to the shrine—an old and forgotten temple, really—just before dawn. The sky was the color of dried blood, and the banyan roots cast long, spindled shadows.

The temple had no roof, only stone pillars swallowed by moss and time. Vines crawled across the floor like veins beneath skin. The altar in the center was smeared red with years of offerings, both sacred and sacrificial. Gauri didn't know which kind she was meant to be.

They chained her to one of the pillars. The iron cuffs bit into her wrists, the chains jingling when she was made to kneel. Gauri didn't fight them. What was the point? They were two well-trained men, and if she resisted, they'd drag her, kicking and screaming, and chain her anyway. And she wouldn't beg—not for mercy, not for understanding. She held still, jaw tight, eyes dry. Let them think her silent out of shame—only she knew it was rage that kept her still.

Arjun's fingers trembled as he secured the locks.

"For the Collector," the older acolyte ground out.

Arjun could only nod pitifully, his throat working as he swallowed back words—perhaps an apology, perhaps a prayer.

And then they left her, their footsteps fading into the predawn stillness.

Gauri sat quietly. She did not weep. She did not plead to Lord Raveth. She traced the red cord still around her neck, fraying at the edges now. She had tried, hadn't she? She had hoped for someone to bind with. For that hum of something—longing, devotion, desire. But her heart never echoed back.

By nightfall, the lanterns were lit around the outer ring of the village. Not for her comfort—no, the villagers never came this close at night—but to keep whatever came for the Unbound from venturing too far into the rest of the village of Veyra.

The Collector.

A legend told in hushed tones by children too young to understand what being Unbound truly meant. A beast of string and teeth, of unmaking darkness, who didn't feed on flesh, but on lack. On what was missing.

She thought of the day Priya had kissed her. Everyone had said a kiss would feel like magic, that her heart would skip. She remembered only the press of lips, and how she'd laughed after to cover the silence that followed. No spark. No awakening.

Even with Tarak, her feelings remained the same.

He was handsome. Kind. Intelligent. All the right things. She had said yes because she wanted to want it. She had danced with him beneath the lanterns, let him tie a blue ribbon—

her favorite color—into her hair. But when he had leaned close and whispered, "Can I bind to you?" all she had felt was panic pretending to be politeness.

She had tried. God, she had tried. Hours spent in front of her small mirror, practicing the expressions she had seen on others' faces—the soft gaze, the tender smile, the yearning. She had studied Meena's blush whenever Arjun approached. She had memorized the gestures but could never summon the feeling behind them.

A rustling broke the memory.

The elder pundit entered the ruin, his robes dust-streaked, his hands clutching a small clay jar. Up close, he looked smaller than he had during the ceremony—just an old man burdened by traditions he hadn't created but was bound to uphold.

He approached her slowly, eyes weighed down by ritual, not compassion. "Child," he murmured. "Raveth is watching."

Gauri met his gaze without flinching. The chains made a soft, musical sound as she straightened her back, refusing to be diminished even now.

He dipped two fingers into the jar and dabbed oil onto her forehead. It was cold, sharp with the scent of crushed camphor. A drop ran down her temple like an unwept tear. "Pray one last time," he added with a whisper, and for a moment, something like genuine sorrow flickered across his face. "Perhaps Raveth will soften his will. Perhaps the thread will move after all."

Gauri said nothing. What was there to say? That she wished she could fix herself? That she would trade her silence for one thread's shimmer, if only to be spared this?

The priest waited, but no plea slipped past her lips. She just stared at him. She wouldn't apologize for how she felt.

He turned away with a sigh. Gauri watched his silhouette fade into the dark.

Midnight seeped into the shrine. The moon, a knife-edged disk, hung low through the broken roof, casting silver across the altar. The vines trembled once, then stilled. Even the wind held its breath. Somewhere, the sound of a flute frayed into the air—perhaps from the celebration still continuing in the village, where Bound pairs danced and families rejoiced. Gauri sighed. Perhaps her absence had already transformed into whispered caution.

"I didn't choose this," she whispered, pressing her palm against the cold floor.

The moss didn't answer. The sky didn't shift. Only the silence turned viscous, thick with something ancient and listening. Something moved in the trees.

Gauri closed her eyes.

Let it pass, she told herself. *Let it stop.*

At first, it was only sound, the low dragging of silk across stone. A sigh rasped against a temple pillar—syrupy. Then came the scent, must and iron, like old cotton soaked in blood. And then—movement.

Gauri opened her eyes.

A shape emerged from the far side of the ruin, uncoiling from shadow as though born of it. It was tall, clad in robes the color of twilight that were stitched together from strands of red and black. Its arms were longer than they should have been, its head tilted unnaturally to one side, and its face—if it had one—was hidden behind a pale mask, cracked down the center and stitched at the mouth. It radiated a wrongness that was more eerie than monstrous. Mournful.

Gauri didn't scream. She just stared, too tired for fear, too hollow for pleading. "So," she said, voice hoarse, "you're the Collector."

The creature paused, head cocked like it was listening. Or deciding.

Then it moved closer.

Gauri expected pain. Teeth. Claws. An unending darkness.

What came was silence. And then, words.

Not spoken aloud, but pressed into the air like heat before a storm.

"*You weren't chosen.*" The voice was not cruel, or cold. It was ancient. "*You were left.*"

Gauri's hands clenched in their chains. "Because I'm broken."

The Collector took another step. Red thread trailed from its sleeves, writhing like smoke. "*No.*"

It knelt before her, one clawed hand reaching out. Gauri pulled herself back, instinctively, before remembering there was no use. She was chained to the pillar. To her surprise, the creature brushed a single fingertip along the red cord resting on her collarbone. The cord blackened and fell away, scattering into ash on the floor.

"*You are not broken,*" the Collector whispered, not with pity, but with acknowledgment. Its mask leaned closer, so close that Gauri could see the sheen of old silk sewn over the fissures. She stared into its eyes—through the eyeholes. Nothing was there. "*You are mine.*"

A shiver rippled down Gauri's spine. "What does that mean?" she croaked.

The Collector didn't answer in words. Instead, it raised a hand and touched its palm to hers. A warm sensation awakened across her skin—then flared.

Gauri hissed as a mark bloomed to life just below the line of her thumb, etched in thread-thin script. Not a heart. Not a sigil of love. But a spiral, split in the center. She stared at it, panting. "What did you do to me?"

"I unbound you—truly."

Something in her chest shifted with those words. Not broken. Not healed. Just shifted.

The chains fell from her wrists with a dull clank. Her legs trembled as she knelt there, free. "Why me?"

The Collector rose, its robe whispering against stone.

"*Because I was the first, and I hope you'll be the last.*" Its voice thinned, as if it were disappearing even as it spoke. "*Until the threads break, we are never truly gone.*" A pause. Then, softly, "*I was Unbound. And they sacrificed me to the altar, hoping it would make me holy.*"

She looked at the ash of her cord. Gauri couldn't remember the faces of those in years past whose cords had fallen away, their names lost to her, never spoken of again. "How many?"

"Too many."

The Collector turned around, its cloak trailing behind it. It did not look back, but before disappearing into the dark, it said, "*If you still want to die, stay here. But if you'd like to know how to break the Binding—join me.*"

And it was gone.

Gauri stood alone for a while, her wrists bare, her cord turned to dust, her palm marked with a symbol older than the village itself. And for the first time, she thought that maybe survival was rebellion.

So she chose to follow the Collector.

"Why do the villagers sacrifice the Unbound to you?" Gauri asked the Collector. The question had been twisting in her throat since the moment she'd decided to follow the Collector farther into the woods.

The Collector did not look back. It just shuffled along, soundless, between the trees that grew behind the shrine, where no trail existed and none dared venture. "*They believe I consume what their god cannot.*" A thread from its cloak twitched in the air. "*But I do not take; I free.*"

Gauri's eyebrows furrowed. "Then who are the sacrifices actually for?"

The silence thickened for a long moment before the answer finally came. "*Raveth.*"

Gauri flinched. Raveth was the patron god of her village, Veyra—the god of bounty, devotion, and sacred love. His shrines stood in every home and every field.

The Collector turned, and the mark on Gauri's palm burned. Not with fire—but with knowing. "*He feeds on love made hunger. On devotion and dependency. On hearts that cannot bear to be alone.*"

"This can't be." The words scraped out of her throat. Even Gauri had lit oil lamps in his name and scattered marigolds on his altar. "He blesses us. Protects us."

The Collector paused for a moment, threads shifting faintly around its form. "*He is draining you. Every year. Every thread tied to another is a vein opened in offering.*" Its voice was a soft echo in Gauri's head. "*Have you ever wondered why so many Bound in your village grow empty?*"

She thought of her mother, how her eyes had hardened when Gauri failed the Binding. Not out of cruelty, or even grief. Just resignation. A kind of numbness. And Priya—now that she was Bound, would she drift away too?

The Collector's voice hummed low. "*Or why the ones who fall in love most fiercely are the first to wither?*"

The elders always said Raveth's favor brought early rains and rich harvests. His blessing ensured safe births and sweet marriages. Maybe the rains, yes. Maybe the births.

But Gauri wasn't so sure about the sweetness.

Her father was in their house but never quite present. His words were always clipped, his touches mechanical. In hindsight, her parents, like all the other couples in the village, moved through a script they didn't seem to remember choosing. They shared meals, walked to the well together, and left offerings side by side.

Bound. But not connected.

Together. But not whole.

Never free.

Now Gauri understood that it wasn't love that had made them tired. It was being fed to something that never stopped eating. "Raveth cannot taste us," she said. "So he casts us out."

"*But the priests feared that. They thought we were curses. Disruptions. Yet they offered us anyway. Hoping he'd take even the empty. And when he would not . . .*" It raised one hand, long clawed fingers splayed. "*That job was left to me.*"

The deeper they went into the woods, the stiller the air became. The villagers called it the Woven Woods. They said it was cursed. That the trees swallowed those who went in too deep, only spitting out their hearts. Gauri's breath fogged, even though the night was warm. The moon stayed suspended among the branches.

Red threads hung between the trees like cobwebs. Some were taut, woven from trunk to trunk. Others dangled loose, drifting like strands of hair. They brushed against her skin—cool, curious, alive.

She should have felt afraid.

Instead, Gauri felt watched. Not by the Collector, but by something softer. Grief. Memory. Presences too faint to be bodies. They whispered:

"I never wanted to marry."

"They called me cold, but I wasn't."

"I wasn't enough."

This wasn't a place for the lost. It was a sanctuary for the forgotten.

And there, nestled in the roots, was a stone slab softened by moss. A place to rest, Gauri assumed. She sank to the floor, her legs folding beneath her. "What happened to the other Unbounds? Have any of them ever tried to break the curse?"

"*Yes,*" the Collector said, voice low, almost reverent. "*They went back into the circle. Not to bind again, but to sever.*" It paused. "*One screamed the truth as the cords rose. Another carved runes into the altar stones with his own blood. One simply walked into the fire meant for the offerings—and smiled as it didn't burn her.*"

Gauri felt the weight in those words.

"*Some came close to breaking it, succeeding in making Raveth's hunger waver, the threads falter. But they all failed. Raveth unmade them. Erased their names from every tongue, their faces from every heart. Even their parents forgot. I had to stitch them out of time to keep them from unraveling.*"

This was why she didn't remember any Unbound, any disruption during the ritual. This was why no one could tell what happened to them. Gauri felt her heart breaking, anger rising.

"*The Woven Woods hold what remains.*" The Collector's voice hung in the stillness like incense smoke. "*Protected by forgotten magic. But even that frays. I am the only one who remembers, the only one left who can walk freely. Who can still speak the truth the others could not.*"

"Of course they didn't win." Gauri let out a sharp breath. "After all, Raveth is a god—"

"*Raveth is a belief, grown ripe on feeding,*" the Collector corrected. "*His hunger has become too strong, the Binding too heavy. It was never meant to carry this much weight—this much longing, this much need. Now it feeds too fast. Demands too much.*"

Gauri looked down at her hands, the mark pulsing faintly. "So the altar is now overripe," she said quietly. "It's time to strike." Then she looked up, fists clenched. "But what if I fail?"

The Collector was silent for a moment. Then, "*You'll fade, too,*" it said simply. "*And Raveth will drain Veyra dry—until every heart is hollow, every love a lie worn thin. And when there's nothing left, he'll move on. Village by village.*"

"And we don't know when the next Unbound will come." Gauri's stomach twisted. She wasn't afraid of fading—or dying. She had made peace with that the moment her thread remained still. But she was terrified of what would be left behind—of Priya's laughter going quiet, of the next generation turned to stone behind their eyes, of the world falling into silence as Raveth fed endlessly.

She couldn't fail. The cost was too steep.

The ones before her had dreamed of freedom, of being themselves. But dreams on their own were never enough. And Gauri knew she couldn't do this alone.

"Force won't break the Binding," Gauri said. Her voice was steady, though her heart thundered. "It feeds on belief. That's why others failed—they tried to cut through devotion with fire, rage, resistance, but I have a different idea."

She paused, scanning the shadows between the trees. The air was thick, still—watching. She could already feel the weight of what she was about to summon.

"The villagers' belief is a fortress," she continued. "But even stone can crack." Though not by will alone. Belief was not a thread she could sever with strength. It clung. It remembered.

The Collector tilted its head, slow and serpentine, as if realization was dawning. "*Go on.*"

She looked toward the Collector, the mark on her palm faintly pulsing. "I can't do it alone. Raveth doesn't just sit on the altar—he festers in them. In every bowed head, every red cord drawn tight. If I'm to unmake him, I'll need a weapon rooted in memory, not might. And you'll need to teach me how to wield it."

When Gauri returned to the village square—trained, steadied, marked by all she had learned—the Binding circle was already lit. Barely a fortnight had passed since her own ceremony. Perhaps it was her "failure" that had left Raveth unsatisfied, urging the pundits to move the ceremony forward. A way to patch the rupture. To appease the hunger.

The altar had never looked so small before. Lanterns glowed like watchful eyes, golden light flickering against the early twilight. The crowd—parents, elders, pundits, and the still-hopeful—circled like vultures dressed in linen. At first, Gauri stayed at a distance, cloak drawn tight, hood shadowing her face, the Collector's mark glowing on her palm.

Her parents were in the crowd, as were Priya and Tarak with their matched partners. Everyone had come to witness the ritual as it demanded. Gauri waited until the head pundit stepped in and commenced the ceremony. Smoke curled from the bowl of ash in his hands. Names were spoken, and the red cords around the teens' necks rose like serpents into the air, seeking. The ritual was working. Raveth was feeding.

It was time.

She stepped forward and let her hood fall. "Did you already forget me?" Her voice rang out, steady and cold.

Gasps rippled through the villagers.

"She was taken. She should be—"

"Dead?" Gauri finished, striding forward.

The crowd parted like the sea, fear shimmering in their silence.

Gauri stole a look at Priya's face as she stepped into the circle, seeing on it a blend of horror and relief. As for her parents, they simply looked away—as expected. The pundit's voice wavered mid-chant, but he didn't stop. Not yet. His gaze flicked toward his acolytes.

"Seize her," he barked. "She defiles the rite!"

Gauri almost laughed. If they only knew the ritual was already unraveling from the inside. The Binding ceremonies came faster now. The threads burned brighter, then faded just as quick. It wasn't just belief fueling the ritual anymore. It was desperation. Addiction.

And that was why the Collector had waited. Why it had sent her back now, when the cracks had widened just enough.

Two of the acolytes stepped forward, Arjun among them. Their hands twitched toward the sickles at their waists. Gauri raised a hand, the spiral on her palm glowing like an ember refusing to die—and the acolytes froze mid-step.

The ground beneath her feet seemed to breathe. It pulsed low and steady. The pundit raised his voice louder, more desperate now, drowning in ceremony. "Let the hearts be revealed. Let the threads find their mates. Let Raveth witness our devotion—"

"Raveth is not a god," Gauri shouted despite her knees threatening to buckle. "He is a belief made monstrous."

And she'd make sure that it crumbled.

The mark on Gauri's palm widened, the spiral unfurling like silk pulled from the dark, until it became a blade. It wasn't the color of steel or bone, nor did it look like it was made of either. It was made of memory. Every name the village had forgotten. Every Unbound the altar had tried to erase. Every whisper Gauri had heard in the Woven Woods now wove itself into the hilt.

And she wasn't alone. Not anymore. The weight of every forgotten life steadied her grip.

The villagers scattered, some backing away, others dropping to their knees and covering their eyes. The teens inside the circle stood frozen, including the boy who was left when Gauri was declared an Unbound. He looked at Gauri, as if unsure whether to run or stay.

The pundit recoiled. "Blasphemy," he hissed.

"You told us this was love," Gauri said. "But it was just obedience." She raised the blade. "You told us we were chosen. But you only chose those he could feed on. You told us those who couldn't love like you were broken."

Raveth was already stirring. Gauri felt it—the pressure beneath the altar stone. Not a sound. Not a shape. Pure, raw hunger. Vast, formless, and to her surprise, sacred. The god wasn't watching from above—he was woven into the ritual. In the cords. In the chants. In the silence of everyone like her afraid to say, *I don't want this.*

One pair of threads, hovering midair between two trembling teens, began to entwine. The Collector had told her Raveth wouldn't let go without a fight. Gauri stepped between them.

"Don't," the pundit begged, eyes fearfully fastened to the sword, as if he'd seen it before. "You'll destroy everything."

"I know," Gauri sneered. "But some things shouldn't survive."

And she cut.

The blade passed through the cords like they were butter—and the red ropes screamed a high, thin wail before dissolving into nothing.

The teens staggered. One of them clutched her chest. The other sobbed once—not in pain, but in relief.

"I didn't want it," he whispered. "I just didn't know I could say no."

The pundit lunged forward. "Stop her!"

"Why?" Gauri asked. "Because I won't let you feed him?" She turned to the crowd next. "Do you even remember who you offered last year? Five years ago? Ten?" She herself hadn't, not until she'd brushed against their strings in the Woven Woods.

There was no answer.

"They're in the Woven Woods. They're still there." Gauri's voice was heightened by the adrenaline in her veins. "Your children. Your friends. The ones who wouldn't bind. The ones who said no. You didn't lose them. You gave them up."

The altar cracked, a line down its center leaking a dull red glow. Raveth pulsed, desperate. Unraveling, but still clinging on. Gauri stepped to the altar and placed a hand on its surface. "You think you need him," she whispered. "But it's he who needs you."

With those words, her mark glowed white-hot, and the blade began to shudder in her other hand.

"*This isn't a battle you are meant to win with a physical fight,*" the Collector had said during her training. "*It's a rot you are meant to expose—so it can finally bleed out.*"

Gauri raised the blade and plunged it into the altar.

The sound was not a scream like when she cut the cords. It was a release. The crack bled light—and then, there was darkness. Raveth—the belief, the hunger, the lie—shuddered and fell silent.

Gauri didn't remember what happened after, if she had dropped her blade or if it was just gone. All she remembered were the changed looks on the villagers' faces, their relief, how her parents had run to her, hugged her and sobbed. It had been a warm feeling.

Weeks after the altar was gone, a circle of wildflowers had begun to grow in its place. Red threads still dotted the soil, but they were dead roots now. No one had dared start the Binding again.

The village had changed in ways small and slow.

The chants in Raveth's name had stopped. So had the monthly gatherings and the worshiping of Raveth. For the first time in her memory, no new cords had been woven. No matches were made by magic. People talked more and asked instead of assumed.

Gauri's parents had not said much at first. But her mother touched her hand more often now. Her father began to hum again as he carved wood. They smiled at each other more. Not because the ritual said so.

Because they chose to.

And the Unbound—those the village had lost over the years—began to return from the Woven Woods. They were older now, with no memory of pain. All they could remember were fragments, like names they hadn't spoken in years and a sense of being preserved.

None of them remembered the Collector.

Only Gauri did.

Sometimes, she walked beyond the edge of the village and followed the old path to the Woven Woods. The trees still whispered, but faintly now. Once, she found the spot the Collector had taken her to. There the moss had curled into a sleeping shape. She pressed her fingers to it, hoping the mark on her palm would pulse in response, but it didn't.

The memories were still hers, though. The silence the Collector had carried. The way it had knelt before her and said, "*You are not broken. You are mine.*"

Gauri smiled faintly. No one else remembered the one who saved them. But she would. And when the wind stirred the branches of the Woven Woods, she liked to imagine its voice stitched into the leaves.

A thread brushing her wrist.

Just once more.

LOVESICK

TAKA OWEN

The ending began the day Esther got sick.

There were a few minutes—ten, maybe more—when I didn't know the extent of it. I thought we were mostly safe, hidden away three floors up in some abandoned office building. I'd managed to get my breathing back under control and had even sat down, squashed into a corner against flaking plasterboard. My muscles were still shaking. With exertion or terror, I couldn't say. At some point between the first viral outbreak and the rapid collapse of everything I'd taken for granted, they'd become one and the same. The new age of: *If you're scared, you should be running.*

At least I wasn't on my own.

"Okay," Devon said, trying to force a smile as she rummaged through her battered first aid kit. The wound on my arm was still burning with pain from the disinfectant. "What about this one?"

She hummed a melody. I huffed; a hollow thing that failed to become a laugh.

"Bit on the nose," I managed. "'Eat You Alive,' Limp Bizkit."

"Got it in one," she replied, pulling out a bandage. The overcast light pressed against the window like a bruise, blooming through the grime on the glass. The dimness caught on the short tufts of her hair and left her face looking washed-out. Pale against bluish shadows. Behind her, the open-plan office was dull and dead, tables turned over, papers scattered and abandoned weeks ago. When we'd come up the stairs earlier, taking two steps at a time in our panic, I could've sworn I'd seen dried blood on the walls, dark with age.

I tried to smile—to pretend, right along with her.

"That one was too easy. You gotta make it harder for me."

She gave me an amused huff. "Challenge accepted."

Devon was calmer—or, at least, she seemed like it on the surface. I'd learned to read her at the edges the last couple of years. Her fingers were shaking as she wrapped the bandage around my arm. She'd been learning from Thea—before Thea got sick, that is—who'd been a paramedic before all this. Now, there were just the four of us. Devon was nineteen, just a few months older than me, but she was the closest thing to a medic we had. There were times when I thought it was cruel—that burden of being the one person standing between us and death, or worse fates. I hated myself for not being able to help more. That I'd not also learned all that stuff from Thea when she was still around, along with everything else I missed about her.

But there were times, like now, when someone had to make a decision. When Esther was hurt way worse than I was, but Devon was out here patching me up instead. And I was just stupidly, *painfully* grateful that I wasn't the one who'd had to make that call.

A groan came from the other room—one of those little conference rooms that hadn't been used for its intended purpose in months. We both went dead still, listening. But no other sounds came, other than the quiet cadences of soft voices. Soothing.

"At least," Devon said after a moment, the words barely a scrape against the air, "we don't have to worry about you."

I swallowed down all the things that neither of us were saying and tried not to think about Esther in the other room. About Aaron, who sat in there with her, clutching her hand. About how much blood there'd been on her clothes, and how Devon had still triaged *me* first, and what all of that meant for Esther's chances.

I felt far too aware of everything—the carpet bristles against my skin, the throbbing pain of the wound, the smell of the disinfectant. Trying to distract myself, I made another attempt at a laugh, but it came out way too alarming, a choked gasp. "Probably don't even need to bother with the bandage and all that, am I right?"

Devon stared at me, serious and unflinching.

"Don't say that," she said. "Just because you're immune, doesn't mean you can't still get infected the regular way—"

"Yeah, I know. I *know that*." I stared at the wall, hating the heat that was rising in my cheeks, the guilt sinking in my gut. The wrongness of it, because I should have felt grateful. To be immune, in a situation like this? To not be afraid of the *one thing* that was haunting everyone else in every waking moment, and every one besides?

To know that, even if everyone else succumbed to this, I would remain *myself.*

Alone.

Devon sighed. Her nails scraped against my skin as she tucked away the edge of the bandage, securing it.

"Sorry," she said, quiet. Friend to friend. There were days where I felt like she was the only person who really knew me anymore. "It's just—"

"No, it's okay," I said, looking back at her. "I shouldn't have said that."

Devon's eyes met mine, and there was something there that I couldn't quite grasp. Piercing, like she could see something hidden within my gaze. I frowned, opening my mouth to ask—

Movement in my periphery. I flinched back, instinctive, pulse pounding and ready to run. But it was just Aaron standing in the doorway. I tried not to notice the blood smeared against his skin—and that was the first warning sign. Right then, I should've known.

"What is it?" Devon asked beside me. For a moment, Aaron didn't speak, like he was trying to figure out the words. "Aaron—"

"I'm giving you both of our supplies," he said, just coming out with it like it wasn't a *bombshell.* I looked him over, frowning. He wasn't injured. He didn't look *sick.* "Head out as soon as you can. If you keep to the backstreets—"

"What are you on about?" I said, standing. "You're coming with us—"

But Devon grabbed my wrist, cutting me off—and in that moment, she must have seen it. I saw it too. His hand, clenched into a fist. Wet—no, *dripping* with red.

"What have you done?" she asked him.

He lifted his chin, defiant. "This is my choice," he said. "This is what I want."

Dread crawled in my gut like it was something alive. "You infected yourself."

"Yeah," he said. Simple devastation. "I did."

When the virus first came about, the government put out a bunch of those public service announcements so that people knew what symptoms to look for. Dizziness. Sudden increases in heart rate. Mood swings. Erratic or obsessive behavior. I'd stood in the kitchen, pamphlet in hand, and joked that it sounded like how people described falling in love. Mum hadn't taken too kindly to that one. I'd realized I was aroace about a year before, and she'd not reacted to it well. Something about me being too young to know, about late bloomers, but it was mostly just her trying to reassure herself that I was still human. That I wasn't going to miss out on *the most wonderful thing a living person can experience.* The whole thing had sounded about as appealing to me as that pamphlet in my hand.

I'd hoped that she'd come around. But she'd died, along with everyone else that I knew.

The virus entered a new stage. *Erratic and obsessive* turned to *violent and aggressive.* Rabid. Those who were infected started attacking other people, trying to draw blood, *biting* them. Of course, that was how it spread, like every zombie movie ever—

infected bodily fluids got into your bloodstream, and you were done. Some people did call them zombies. Some called them the Infected. Some said they were just sick. But whatever they were, they weren't human anymore.

I hadn't been the only one who was immune—there'd been three of us in Manchester. The plan had been for us to be escorted down to Cambridge, where this research facility was desperately working toward a cure. At that point, things had started to get bad but were still mostly in order. Contained. It went downhill pretty fast after that. The scales tipped, and there were more people infected than not. We started getting blackouts, then we lost electricity entirely, and after that, everything fell apart in a cascade. The world I knew—the world I thought I was stepping into, just as I turned eighteen—collapsed right in front of me.

The other two in our group who were immune didn't make it. There were other things, after all, that could kill you when everything went to hell. But the rest of us kept going, even as the escort group got smaller and smaller. Jill. Mark. Parveen. Eric. Julian. *Thea.* At night, sometimes, when my thoughts were racing and I missed them so much that it ached in my *teeth*, part of me would think that the virus had mutated and I was getting sick after all.

You'd think it would be a postapocalyptic fantasy, right? Being immune, having a whole group of people trying to get you across the country to find a cure.

Trust me. It wasn't.

Aaron and Esther had been dating since the start. They were only a couple of years older than me and Devon, and they *adored* each other. Sometimes, it was a little much. As time went on, and Devon became one of the closest friends I'd ever known, the two of us would joke about them making out at the most inopportune times. *Straight people, am I right?*

I wasn't laughing anymore.

"Why would you do that?" I lurched forward, not even sure what I was planning to do. But Devon's grip was tight on my wrist, holding me back. It felt like I'd fallen into another universe, where this made sense to everyone else except me. Zombies, I could understand—but *this*? "Aaron, you can't—we *need you*—"

"I'm not leaving here without her," he said—and his voice was firm. Steadfast. He'd already made his decision. And he couldn't back out now, even if he'd wanted to. Infections didn't run in reverse. The virus was in his blood, and that was it. "You guys can make it without me, I know you can—"

"You don't know that," Devon said—angry, but quieter. Calmer. Everything that I couldn't be.

"You're *killing yourself*!" The words clawed their way out of my throat, raw and bleeding. "That's what this is!" I stared at him, feeling nothing but utter desolation. Losing Esther was bad enough, but *both of them*? After losing Thea, and how awful that had been, I couldn't fathom how Aaron could be so okay with forcing us to go through that all over again, two times over. "How can you do that? How can you choose that, after everything?! You're going to *die*!"

"We don't actually know that," Aaron said, cutting me off, and through the bristling briars of my horror, I wondered how long he'd spent trying to convince himself of that. How long he'd spent lying next to Esther and lying to himself until he believed it. "We know the Infected communicate with each other. They stay in groups, like herds—"

"Like packs," I corrected, stepping forward, yanking myself out of Devon's grip. Something was wrong with my lungs. Each breath came short and ragged, amputated. "They hunt people in packs."

"Avery—" Devon said, reaching for me again, her fingers brushing my arm.

I pulled myself out of reach. "The virus takes over your mind until there's *nothing of you left*!"

"I'm sorry," Aaron said—and the worst part was that he looked it. Like this was genuinely hurting him. But he chose it. He *wanted it*, to be taken over by this thing, and I couldn't accept that. "But I go where she goes. And if that's death, then . . . I'm okay with that. I don't—" His voice cracked, splintering. He looked up, blinking away tears, before he looked back at us. "I don't want to live in a world without her. And I know you don't get it." His gaze was brimming with emotion. Those same eyes, within hours, would be glazed over and lifeless. "But someday, Avery, you'll fall in love with someone, and you'll realize that there are some people you can't go on without."

It wasn't his fault—he didn't know. But it was the worst thing he could have said because I couldn't say the same thing back at him. How he'd never understand how devastating this was—for anyone, but especially for *me*, knowing that I would always come second to someone else's more important relationship. And even when life as we knew it was breathing its last, dying gasps, I couldn't escape it.

What about me and Devon? I wanted to scream at him. *You'll die for her, but you won't stay alive for us—*

But I didn't say anything. I just clenched my fists so hard at my sides that I felt one of my fingernails break the skin. It was all too much—the silence too loud, the dim light too bright. All the anger and horror and *loss* were building in my chest, blooming like blood under a bandage, and it was only a matter of time before the pressure of it broke apart my rib cage, and it all came pouring out. Viscera, cascading out into the dust.

"Avery," Devon said again, voice shaky—and this time, when her fingers found my wrist, I let her take it. "Come on. We need to go before they turn."

I didn't want to go. I didn't want *any of it.* I wanted to grab the stopped clock off the wall and yank the hands back, reversing time to before Esther got infected. To before we left Manchester. To before I stood in my kitchen with a pamphlet in my hands, laughing at a list of symptoms that would take everyone I cared about and turn them into something I no longer recognized.

"You'll be okay," Aaron said, like a prayer. Like an apology. "I swear, you'll make it without us."

Neither of us said anything. And by the time we'd packed up all the supplies, Aaron had disappeared back into the room with Esther, and we had no idea what condition either of them was in. For a long moment, Devon and I stared at the doorway cast in shadow, wondering if we should risk checking on them.

I imagined it—the pair of them on the floor, sleeping peacefully. The pair of them on the floor, dead. Their eyes opening, inhuman and bloodied, before seeing us and *lunging*—

After a few moments, Devon shook her head.

"We shouldn't," she murmured before slinging her rucksack on her back and heading toward the door.

And so, we left without saying goodbye.

We didn't talk about it for days. Neither of us wanted to dwell on the fact. By that point, we'd already lost so many people, and grief had grown tiresome, scratched like an overplayed VHS tape. Too many scars, too many healing wounds. When you were bleeding out already, another cut didn't make much difference.

We carried on walking and didn't do anything stupid. Kept to the shadows, stayed alert, watched out for any packs of infected people. We crossed through overgrown fields and haunted towns that seemed to go on forever, passing the skeletal remains of life as we knew it—empty houses, the rusting shells of cars. It was harder, sleeping with two less people to keep watch, but we made it work. It helped that it was Devon—that was the only thing I was able to cling to at night in the darkest moments. That, despite everything, I still had my best friend. And she still had me.

"How about this one?" I said, giving my best attempt at humming a melody. I was lying next to her on a grass bank as she scoped out the route ahead through a pair of binoculars. We'd been aiming for this abandoned motorway for days, figuring it would be the easiest route into Cambridge. The southbound carriageway was largely clear of cars—but there was a group of the Infected down there. They were just lazing around, soaking up the heat of the hot tarmac and skulking about between the nose-to-tail vehicles on the northbound side. Almost unthreatening. Almost. They seemed docile, but we weren't about to risk getting too close and having them spot us, so we were killing time while we waited for them to move on. Compared to Devon, my ability to hold a tune was—well. There wasn't really a polite way to put it. Long story short, she choked on a laugh.

"Once again, I'm gonna ask for some *lyrics,* because I have no chance of getting that."

I grimaced. "Okay, how about: *distant songs of luminance, fall-out fireflies at dusk.*"

"Huh." She frowned, clearly thinking, and then hummed to herself for a moment. "I don't—oh, wait. Is that 'Uranium Candles' by Desert Empire?"

I grinned at her, warmth kindling in my chest despite everything. "Yeah, that's it. Man, I loved that album."

"*We're all just slaves to limerence, to a home of rot and rust,*" Devon sang, her voice rough and gorgeous. She could've easily been in a band, before. "*But as the world slips through our fingers, know I'll never let you go.*" She glanced at me. "Good choice."

"So, when's your new single coming out?" I asked, flashing her a smile.

She smiled back, tight and sad—and in that moment, I knew she had to be thinking about everything we'd lost. The world we'd grown up in that we'd never get back. That was what that song was about, really—yearning for a past that was long gone, like burning ashes fading to dust. Obsessing over a time we could never return to.

"I wanna say I wish I could listen to that album one more time, but—" I gestured to the group of literal zombies that were blocking our way. "Maybe a concept album about the apocalypse isn't the best idea right now."

Devon hummed, looking studiously through the binoculars again. For a moment, neither of us said anything. It probably should have been an awkward silence—or maybe a charged one, if Devon had been with some other girl. But instead, I just felt comfortable. Safe and not alone. But something was on her mind, I thought. She didn't hum me another nu-metal song.

"Do you think they're down there?" Devon asked after a moment. I swallowed, that fresh, heavy grief beginning to rise to the surface. Leviathan, awakening from slumber. I didn't need to ask her who she meant.

"I don't know," I replied, frank, as I watched the pack down below us. Their movements were disturbing to me—the way they walked, the way their heads would snap up at the slightest noise. Uncanny. Not quite human, not quite animal. I thought of Aaron and Esther being like that and felt sick to my stomach. "Honestly—I hope they're not. The virus might have killed them outright. That can happen. And whatever Aaron said . . . that's no kind of life."

For a moment, Devon went quiet. Then, she swallowed. "Yeah. You're probably right."

There was something she wasn't saying. I frowned, turning to look at her.

"What is it?"

"Nothing," Devon said. "It's just—I dunno. I hate that he did what he did. But—" She broke off, before turning to look at me, her gaze piercing. Like she wanted to pry at the edges of my face and see what I was made up of underneath. "Don't you kinda wish you had someone like that? Someone you loved so much you'd die for them? And they'd die for you?"

"Uh," I said, intelligently—but honestly, I didn't know what to say. "No? Not really. I mean—" I swallowed, my voice turning firm—because this, at least, I knew. "I don't want *anyone* to die for me."

Too many people already have, I didn't say. *And it's the worst thing that's ever happened to me.*

Devon was watching me, her gaze strange with something I couldn't read.

"Did it . . ." she started, faltering. "It made you think of Thea, didn't it?"

And I knew what I should say—because yes, of course. Losing Aaron and Esther made me think of everyone we'd lost. It made me burn from within, almost childishly, with how unfair it was. How selfish it was for Aaron to give up like that. To think that we could make it on our own. That we didn't need him. That us losing him would be fine compared to him losing Esther. I guess, to him, it was. But he didn't give us a chance. Didn't give us the *choice.*

But, when it came down to it . . . Devon was right. Because I *had* thought about Thea, rather than any of the others. Maybe because we'd lost her most recently. Maybe because she'd meant so much to me. I knew the truth, though—it was because she'd wanted so badly to live. She'd raged against that dying of the light, clinging on to the world with broken fingernails that were still chipped with the last remnants of nail polish. Bright and bold as she'd always been, even in her last moments. Compared to Aaron, who'd been so prepared to die, it felt wrong. For him to have survived this far only to throw it away like it meant nothing. Like the only person worth fighting for had been Esther. Like Devon and I weren't worth the pain of going on.

If Thea had been given the chance he'd had, she'd still be here now.

With anyone else, I'd have glossed over the question. Said that I'd thought of everyone in that moment when Aaron had stood before us in the doorway, hand dripping with blood. But I wasn't talking to anyone else. I was talking to Devon, and I was so sure she knew everything I hadn't said. That she had thought of Thea, too, when she'd realized what Aaron had done.

"Yeah," I breathed. "Of course it did."

For a long moment, Devon just stared at me. Whatever she was hoping to see, she couldn't find. Her gaze turned uncertain—and then she looked away.

"Right," she said. "Yeah. Of course."

Uncertainty bristled in my chest, building. Maybe I'd been wrong. Maybe she thought that I didn't care about everyone else we'd lost, and that wasn't true. "Devon—"

She stood up, ending the conversation. "I think we need to find another way round. These guys aren't moving."

I should've pushed it, then. I should have said something.

But I didn't. I just let it drop, following her back down the hill and into the shadows.

TAKA OWEN

Thea was the only person I came out to properly, after everything went to hell. Devon obviously knew I was queer, but I hadn't really gone into it more than that. I'd never really liked coming out—there were just too many people who didn't get it. Who didn't *want* to get it. Even queer people. Sometimes there would be no problem, but other times people would be outright against it, saying that we didn't belong. That we weren't queer enough, that we were taking up space—and that always felt worse, somehow, than when straight people were awful about it. Because queer people were supposed to understand. Were supposed to be *family*.

But Thea had asked me about music.

"Babes," she'd said, clutching my hand. We'd been sitting on the concrete floor of the abandoned remains of a small train station, waiting for the others to come back with scavenged food. A golden beam of sunset had streamed through the window we'd broken only hours before, and for the first time in months, I'd felt warm. "I have to know. What *is it* with you and Devon humming at each other all day?"

"Well, what are we supposed to do?" I'd countered, laughing—but she'd ended up asking me why I liked metal music so much. I'd told her it was because, more than anything, a lot of metal songs weren't about romance. They were about being angry, about screaming at the sky, about the nuclear apocalypse, about *so many other things* that made much more sense to me.

"I'm aromantic," I'd told her, knowing I could talk to her about that. She was trans, and she'd spoken to me and Devon about queer stuff before. But also, I just felt safe around her. She was the kind of person who'd listen, and then see you exactly as you were. She got me in a way that I don't think anyone else ever will. "And it's just—it's so tiring, y'know? Everyone thinking life is all about romance. And it's everywhere, right? In adverts, in TV, in music—"

"Oh, babes, tell me about it," she'd said. "Even with our folk. It's always *Love Wins*, which is wonderful for all the gays, lesbians, and bisexuals, whom I adore, but—"

"But when you're trans or aro," I'd said, relieved that I could actually say it, "it doesn't really mean much."

"No," she'd said, and it had felt like coming home. "It doesn't."

When Thea died, weeks later, she'd grabbed my hand. Her blood had smeared against my palm like a promise. Like blood sisters. Like a stain I'd never be able to wash out.

"*I'm so sorry, kiddo,*" she'd said as I choked on sobs. "*But you're gonna have to be brave, okay? For me.*"

I missed all of them. Every single person we'd lost. But losing Thea had felt like someone had pried my ribs open and stolen my lungs, and I hadn't been able to breathe right ever since. I'd stitched myself back together, of course—I'd had to. But that part of me was never coming back. I could never be the same again.

Devon kissed me two days later.

We were running, hearts pounding, hand in hand as she dragged me through the streets on the outskirts of Cambridge. The Infected were fast but uncoordinated, and it gave us the edge that we needed to be just ahead of them—but only just.

The easiest way to confuse them was to get inside, especially a building with lots of floors and rooms—but then it all became a question of timing. Getting into an office building wasn't always easy, unless someone had already broken the door in, and so sometimes you were better off just running. That's how Julian had gotten infected—trying to get a door open, paying the price when he couldn't.

This time, no doors were opening, and we were running on fumes. The Infected wouldn't get tired, but we would, and we couldn't afford to slow down. Not now, when we'd gotten this far.

For a few minutes that stretched on for years, I was so sure that we were going to die. Then Devon veered left without warning and pulled us straight toward the fence of an abandoned construction site. There was the smallest of gaps in the fence, and we shouldn't have been able to fit through—but adrenaline does things to you that mean you don't take no for an answer, and within moments we were on the other side. We didn't stop running—if we could get through, the Infected could too—but in a matter of seconds, we'd gotten into the builder's cabin and shoved a stack of shelves against the door. We sat with our backs pressed against the wall and listened, clutching each other. The sound of our breathing, the pounding of my pulse, and the distant howls of the Infected outside were the only things I could hear.

Seconds ticked by, and we were so scared that we couldn't speak. Then I felt Devon's hand on my cheek, terrifyingly tender, as she turned my face toward her—and that was the only warning I had before her lips were pressed against mine.

It took me a moment to process what was happening—part of me still thought I was about to die. And then reality crashed over me, shattering glass. My muscles tensed, a whole different type of panic rushing through me, and before I could think about what I was doing, I was shoving her back, heart pounding in my throat and dragging up a rush of horror with it.

"What?" I asked, gasping, as Devon stared at me, her expression rapidly breaking from bewilderment into something painful and unreadable. "You—*what?*"

"You don't feel the same," Devon said, simple devastation—and the horror of the realization ran both ways. Because this was my worst nightmare—something borne of the old world that I thought I'd left behind. I'd feared losing my best friend to the literal zombies, but not to *this*—

"We can't do this now," I said, just desperate to not have to face it because I knew how it would end. I stood, wiping the taste of her from my lips with the back of my hand as I stared through the murky window. The building yard was empty. "It's clear. We should keep moving—"

"Are you serious?" Devon said, voice breaking, cold and deadly as the cracking of ice underfoot—and that wasn't right. Because she was supposed to be the calm one. I was the one who let my emotions get away from me. Not her. "Avery, won't you even *look at me*?"

My hands clenched at my side. I tried to breathe normally. Tried to clamp down on the sick feeling that was rising in my throat, churning with bile. Tried to ignore the urge to run, to *get away*. If only I could turn back time. If only—

But it wouldn't change how she felt about me.

"I can't do this," I said. "I'm not—I can't give you what you want—"

"What are you on about?" Devon got up and moved next to me, grabbing me by the shoulder and turning me to face her. And just looking at her broken expression was like swallowing shards of glass. "You've been dropping hints for days, haven't you? I thought—"

"What? No, I haven't," I said, fear swarming in my gut. "That's not—Devon, I don't feel like that about *anyone.*"

At that, she went still. Disappearing behind her eyes. She stared at me, assessing.

"You said you were gay," she said, not quite accusatory.

"No, I said I was *queer,*" I corrected. "I'm not—I'm aromantic, I don't—"

"No, no, no," Devon said, taking a step back. "That can't be right. You had a crush on Thea; everyone knew that—"

"What? No, I didn't. She was like my sister—"

And Devon just *laughed,* a bitter, twisted thing. "Well, it sure didn't look like that—"

"She was my *friend,*" I said, desperate, scrabbling for control as my stomach twisted into knots—because had I been leading her on? Making her think there was something there when there was never a chance of anything? "Just like *you're* my friend—"

"But I'm not her, is that it?" Devon said, choked and raw. She'd taken another step back, away from me. "You could at least just say that, y'know, rather than coming up with some piss-poor excuse—"

"Devon. You're my best friend," I insisted, trying to stay calm and failing. "I didn't mean to make you think that I—that I don't—I *care* about you, more than anything—"

"But not that much. Okay." She looked away, blinking rapidly, before turning back to level me with a burning gaze. "Seriously? After everything we've been through?"

Suddenly, she was a stranger to me. And she was devastated, I knew, that was why she was talking like that. But I couldn't stand it. Not after Aaron and Esther. I'd lost so many people to the virus, but here was this other, insidious thing that I was also immune to, something that had taken people from me as well. This lovesickness that everyone expected me to feel, to want, to *crave* like the Infected craved blood. And here was Devon, showing symptoms. Turning before my eyes.

"What is wrong with you?!" I snarled, anger suddenly screaming out over the shrieking hurricane in my chest. "Why isn't what we've already been to each other this whole time enough for you?!"

"Because it's not as much as how I feel about you," she spat. "Is it?"

I blinked, tears turning the cabin around me into watercolors. Devon's face became an expressionist painting, and I couldn't make out the meaning.

"I'm your friend," was all I could manage—and for some reason that was the worst thing I could have said to her. "I'm your *friend*."

But Devon just shook her head. She was turning toward the door, pulling the barricade of shelves away.

"Devon, wait—" I said, voice breaking.

"*Don't*," she snapped, and then pressed herself against the door, a horrible choking sob splintering in her throat. "I just—I can't be here with you right now."

"No, please, just listen to me—"

I reached out for her, my fingers brushing against her wrist. But she was already pushing down the handle, and within seconds, she was gone, stumbling out into the open, the door slamming behind her.

I should have gone after her. I should have run out there and grabbed her, pulled her back in. Instead, I just pressed my head against the window as she crossed through the building site, disappearing behind the shell of a half-finished shop front. And all of a sudden, I felt nothing. Numb. The cabin was another universe, cut off from the rest of reality, and I was *alone*—

I stepped backward until I was pressed against the wall and slid down it, breathing ragged, mind empty, *reeling*. I couldn't think. I couldn't speak. All I could do was sit there as the tears spilled from my eyes, unbidden. Weaving trails in the dust marks that Devon's fingers had left on my face.

I don't know how long I sat there for. Too long. The light had shifted by the time I got up, midday shadows stretching into golden hour, soft rays streaming through the small window and cutting across the floor. Devon hadn't come back. I should've known then. But I just got up, out of my mind, like a zombie, and my hand found the door. My feet took me down the metal steps of the cabin, across the yard. Following her path from hours before.

It took me a long time to find her. She'd gotten to the other side of the construction site and made it out. It was more luck than anything else that I even saw her. Something caught my eye as I passed by a smashed-in shop window—the contours of a body, a dark shape against the floor. Normally, I'd have moved right on—but I was still existing outside the world, pressing against the glass. I picked my way through the broken window, and traced the trail of fresh blood across the floor that led me directly to her.

She'd been attacked, that much was obvious. Probably tried to get through the window and hadn't quite made it in time.

She was also dead.

Her eyes were still open, unseeing, her face pale in the bruise of shadows. How long had she been here? How long until she turned?

Not long, probably. It didn't matter. I knelt next to her, throat choked with a scream that wouldn't take form. All I could do was reach out, shaking fingers brushing against the coolness of her cheek. After a moment, my fingertips found her eyelids, and I gently shut them with a ghost of a touch.

A song came into my head—that same one by Desert Empire that Devon had sung to me. I tried to hum, but I couldn't get it right. I'd never been able to do it like she could.

"*Time can't be unwoven, but I—I still can't help but try,*" I sang off-key, each word like disinfectant on an open wound. "*And we never know the ending, but—but I—*"

I couldn't do it.

I knew what Aaron would have done. Knew what Devon would have done if it had been me on the floor. She'd have laid down next to me, humming that song, and waited for the end.

But I couldn't afford to do that. I had to keep going. Immunity was thrumming through my veins, whether I liked it or not. And so I stood and stepped back.

"Be brave," I whispered to myself, as the tears finally came, pricking at the edges. "Be brave."

Then I turned, glass shards crunching under my shoes as I climbed through the threshold of the window and out into the ending.

PRESERVATION

KEMI ASHING-GIWA

Dearest friend,

Of all the weapons I have wielded—and there have been many—you were my favorite. Do you remember that first dinner, the night I got back from prison?

A couple of glances over the lip of my bottle, the press of my ankle against yours beneath the embroidered tablecloth. We both knew what would happen the moment the dishes were cleared away and the rest of the Family drank themselves to sleep. Then it was just us; the flicker of candlelight over polished glass; and row upon row of taxidermied heads, peering down at us with dull eyes.

"What do you want from me?" you asked. Your voice was softer than a breeze, your smile as bright as the full moon on a cloudless night. It was all very well done.

I leaned forward in my velvet-lined chair and stared you dead in the eyes, my pulse picking up. "I want you to leave my family alone. I want you to go parasitize someone, anyone else."

You smiled then, and it was a beautiful, terrible thing. I'd worshipped you for far longer than I'd known you, from the first day I'd heard whispers about you at the Academy.

"You and I, we're going to be family soon," you said. "Why don't we start over?"

I shot up from my seat, so fast my chair toppled over. "Leave," I snarled. "Leave this house, leave this family. While you still can."

It was all part of the game—but oh, I'm getting ahead of myself.

The procession winds inexorably through the streets of the city. The Family is small, but their staff and sycophants comprise half the local population. The saying goes: You may loathe the Spires, but you'll love their money.

A small girl walks alone at the front of the silent parade. She is the single spot of blue in a sea of black. She knows her mother and father never wanted a funeral like this, never wanted their loved ones weeping in silence while chasing their coffins to the grave. They wanted a party, with good music and better food. They wanted their lives to be celebrated, not mourned. The girl tried to say so. But the Family didn't listen, didn't care. They loved her father and despised her mother for taking him away. For ruining him. Their regard for the girl falls somewhere in the middle, expressed as silence, cold looks, whispered words.

PRESERVATION

Peregrine Spire, the matriarch, tries to love the girl. But with each passing year, she finds less and less of her beloved brother in the child's face. The girl knows this because she overhears the whispers. She's gotten good at listening.

And waiting.

Of course, it was an act of violence that set me on my path to you.

A few months after I got kicked out of the Academy, Dear Old Aunt Peregrine shot one of her friends while hunting. Normally the issue would've been dealt with in the usual manner, but this particular companion was a distant relation of some lordling named Birchbridge, from the next planet over. His immediate family didn't care, were even happy to lose their miserly patriarch, but someone had to take the fall, and it wasn't going to be Dear Old Aunt Peregrine.

The Family—and by that I mean my father's excuse for one—reviled me for three reasons:

1. My father ran away with the gardener, a woman from one of the last few genuinely garbage polities in the system. To make matters worse, the pair kicked the bucket not eight years after having yours truly, leaving no one to care for me but my paternal relations.

2. I had a nasty habit of ruining every family gathering, because I never was able to shut up about *Irujus shouisa*, aka the tufted urju. There are only forty tufted urjus left in the entire system. A herd of twenty only produces one litter every century, and

only when there's enough territory. Which there isn't, not since the Company started mining in the middle of the mountain range the urjus call home. The species is predicted to go extinct in the next few decades unless immediate action is taken.

3. A few counts of ecoterrorism, you know how it is. Were there human casualties? Yes, but only after the Company built that reservoir in the middle of the western valley, which is where the largest herd has always laid its eggs. (Anyway, the casualties were nonlethal. No one died, and the few people who lost limbs got them regrown.)

There were other reasons, but those three were the main ones. The Spires had done their best to be rid of me, even before I blew up that dam and brought great dishonor, shame, etc., upon the family name. They shipped me off to the Jemiso Academy for Exemplary Youth on Xisomang Station, where I decided that my purpose in life was to save the tufted urju or die trying. Come to think of it, everything that has come to pass is the Family's fault because I never would've uncovered my life's calling if their savagery hadn't pushed me to it first. I suppose I ought to have thanked them more for that, but well, we aren't exactly on speaking terms, are we?

But I'm getting off track here.

Aunt Peregrine's friend was dead, and they needed a scapegoat. Being the only expendable member of the extended Spire dynasty, that sacred duty fell to me. I mean, I was the only Spire ever to be expelled from any institution, and I was going to prison anyway for the dam business. What was another few years? My sentence was shortened on account of my young age and Family connections; even with the additional charges, I'd be out before I turned twenty. I shudder to think what might've happened to me if I'd been a full-grown adult when they arrested me, or if my last name hadn't included "Spire."

Do you remember that video of Company security shooting the leader of the construction worker union?

Look at me going off on another tangent. Anyway. I had an alibi as solid as a stone in my pocket with the whole Birchbridge incident, and so for my cooperation, I could demand a price from Dear Old Aunt Peregrine: a paltry tenth of the Spire fortune, a mere hundred million credits. Enough to buy the habitat the Company had stolen and make them wish they'd never landed on this planet. Enough to hire guards to fend off poachers. Enough to maintain a permanent team of veterinarians. Enough to bribe politicians to help me keep the reserve safe. It's not a secret that there isn't a government in this system brave enough to stand up to the Company. The people who care about keeping our worlds livable have no one to rely on but each other. Thankfully, we are many. And the oligarchs in charge are few.

The Family is many things, but they always kept their word. I believed that they would uphold their end of the deal. So imagine my surprise when I discovered that perhaps I was unwise to trust them.

And then imagine how I felt, not long after, when I came home and found *you* in my place.

Rarely does the Family invite the girl to holiday with them, but this winter she finds herself among them for reasons she can only guess at. Long before she began running around with trigger-happy tree huggers, they considered her an embarrassment. By the time she turns fifteen, even Peregrine Spire no longer raises her voice to defend her niece when the cousins denounce her. And now, imprisoned within the Spire hunting lodge, the girl is subject to her older cousins' whims. Nowell and Finley and Alva and Gray are not particularly creative bullies, but they're proper little monsters.

One bitterly cold morn, Gray yanks the girl out of bed by the ankle and forces her on a brisk run around the estate.

"You can't be serious, Gracie," says the girl. Anger and resentment, but not surprise, twist in her chest. "There's practically a blizzard outside!"

"A sprint in the snow is good for the blood," Cousin Gray sings, pulling a sleek black energy gun from the foyer closet. There are several large carnivorous fauna on this side of the continent, and they do not discriminate when it comes to prey. "If I make it back before you, I'll throw all your tablets into the fireplace!"

That wakes the girl up.

She races after her cousin as best she can, but schoolwork and exclusively academic extracurricular activities do not a fine athlete make. The path, though regularly scraped clean and sprinkled with salt by robot servants, is still dangerously slick, and the sky is vomiting snow. A fall might very well end with her cracking open her skull, and the girl doesn't trust her cousin not to let her bleed out. The distance between them grows until Gray disappears into the swirling drifts. The girl's lungs fill with the imagined stench of scorched metal and burning wires. She cannot afford replacement work tablets on her own. She'll have to beg the Family. Perhaps that's what Gray wanted all along.

She doesn't give up, though. Hoping against hope, she forces herself forward, arms and legs pumping, shoes slapping against the frozen dirt. And then she sees it, as it steps onto the path—

Nearly twice her height with long, glinting tusks. Two sets of eyes, one gold, the other aquamarine. Four double-jointed legs ending in sturdy hooves. A pristine white mane glowing against the wintry landscape. A predator perfectly adapted to her environment.

The girl doesn't know the species, not yet, but the animal is majestic, breathtaking, almost ethereal—up until Gray's gun goes off. The girl collapses, but it's not her who's been shot. Gray lets out a wild hoot of triumph as he leaps up from his hiding spot.

"Why?" the girl cries, when she finally finds her voice. Shock and horror constrict her throat. "We don't need the food!"

Gray shrugs. "Just wanted to shoot something."

The girl trembles as he stomps past, crashing through the foliage without a care in the world. The animal trumpets, eyes blinking rapidly as her blood pools. Gray kneels before the body, a slender, unfamiliar instrument in hand. A glowing blade unfolds, throwing a sharp blue gleam into his eyes. The knife slices through the animal's beautiful tusks, easy as breathing.

Gray tucks the tusks underneath his arms and stands, his face freckled with blood. Finally, he gazes down at the girl where she kneels in the snow, sobbing breathlessly.

"You can't—you can't just leave her like that," she cries. "You can't just let her suffer!"

"You finish the job, then." Gray presses a hidden button, and the blade retracts, taking its eerie light with it. He tosses it to the girl and turns on his heel. "High time you fixed someone else's mess, rather than the other way around."

The girl stares up at him, her vision flashing red. She imagines two mangled bodies bleeding out into the snow. But she is nothing like Gray, nothing like the rest of her family. She stands, heart thrashing against her rib cage, and does what she must.

A few weeks later, the girl arrives at the House for the birthday celebration she neither wanted nor asked for. She knows this is merely an excuse for the Family to summon their friends and favorites, to show off their unimaginable wealth, to wring every drop of jealousy they can from their rivals. She will be left to her own devices and ignored, as always. There is no one to greet her at the door. She shoves open the massive slab of polished wood and steps into the entrance hall.

She notices it immediately, mounted above the grand staircase for all to see. She knows the species now—it's all she can think about these days. The head and neck and shoulders of the tufted urju Gray shot, straining out of the smooth emerald wallpaper as if to catch her final breath. It's poor work. Done by an amateur, and a brutish one at that.

The girl tears through the House until she finds Aunt Peregrine in her study, reviewing tax reports from the previous year.

"Please," she gasps. "Take it down!"

Peregrine stares at the girl, startled. "What are you on about, Eglantine?"

The matriarch grimaces at the taxidermied urju when the girl drags her to it. Gray trails behind like a scolded hound. The Family gradually gathers round, like vultures to carrion when it comes to conflict.

"It's a wretched thing, Gracie," Peregrine says, after a long moment. "Especially with the tusks sawed off like that. Take it down at once."

"But, Auntie," Gray whines, his voice high and brittle, "it's for my favorite cousin. She loves it! Don't you?"

The girl gives her answer, but the conversation has already turned to more pressing matters. She stands there, frozen and fuming, her chest slowly filling with painful resignation. She'd hoped to ask the Family for funds—just a little, just for her birthday—to support local conservation efforts. She's still going to ask; the stakes are too high not to, but now it's brutally clear that it's a foolish wish.

She will have to take matters into her own hands.

Cousin Gray, the heir, had brought you home for the winter holiday. You were the latest in a long string of favorites; Gray acquired and lost lovers like it was a competitive sport. I never understood all the fuss, all the drama that erupted whenever Gray found a new paramour, but like you, romance has never interested me. So what do I know? The important bit is that you, my dear Kameron Fleetfoot—Kam—were there to stay.

I still don't know how you managed to wrap him around your little finger. Gray isn't clever enough to appreciate wit, and he's too shallow to appreciate your singular beauty. What did you tell him? What awful things about me—probably all true—did you whisper in his ear? He was always going to figure out a way to cheat me out of my fair share of the loot, I knew that, but he wouldn't have made his move so soon without you.

Apparently, we were in the same year at Jemiso, but I hadn't the slightest recollection of meeting you, nor of ever laying eyes on your face at the Academy (not that I'd lasted very long there). And I made my distrust clear from the moment I saw you sipping *my* tea in *my* drawing room chair. I looked you up in the class roster, and I saw exactly what I'd expected. I called for a family gathering and sat everyone down in the parlor for tea—willowy Nowell, little Alva, mustachioed Finley, infuriating Gray, and, of course, Dear Old Aunt Peregrine.

I leaned over your (*my*) chair, stuck a finger between your eyes. "They're a liar," I said. "A fraud, a charlatan."

"Oh, that's very impressive, Eg," you replied, your mouth sliding into a thin smirk. "You have a thesaurus."

The Family tittered.

My face grew hot above my collar. "Other words, then." With a thought, I sent my findings to the implants of everyone in the room. "No one by the name of Kameron Fleetfoot ever attended Jemiso."

Gray laughed. It was not a happy sound, nor did he seem at all humored. "I should've put a stop to this immediately. I saw the recording from after dinner, when you threatened my Kam."

I drew back. "Pardon?"

Gray reached over and took hold of your hand. "How do you

think we gather blackmail material on our guests? There are cameras in every room including yours, you sweet fool."

Heat flooded my face. I ground my teeth together as genuine white-hot fury poured into my gut. Of course, *of course*, I was only a guest. Poor and poorly-bred, no less a parasite than you.

You intertwined your fingers with Gray's, your head bowed as you set down your (*my*) gilded teacup. "My father was a monster. And after mother died . . . . Well, he was fond of reminding my siblings and me that he'd brought us into this world, and he could just as easily take us out of it." When you looked up, your eyes were shining with unshed tears. "Things got ugly after I got accepted to the Academy. The plan had always been for me to stay home, but I had grown tired of his cruelties. I told him I was leaving him to rot; he told me he was going to finally make good on his old promise. And then . . . . And then . . . ."

"My poor child," Dear Old Aunt Peregrine crooned and then glared at me.

I rolled my eyes. "Even if that's true, I couldn't have known—" I began, but you cut me off with a piteous sniffle.

"After, I changed my name and fled to the Academy." You turned to Gray, the tears falling fast now. "And then you saved me."

"Gods," I snapped. "Gracie, you can't possibly believe that stupid little gold digger—"

"How dare you?" Gray shot to his feet. "I wanted to wait to deliver the news," he said. His voice was flat and hard, like the quick strike of a hand against a jaw. "But this is the last straw. We appreciate what you did for the Family, that unpleasantry with the Birchbridges. But you won't be seeing a single credit from us."

I whirled around to face Dear Old Aunt Peregrine. "Please, Auntie, tell me he's not serious."

"Oh, he's serious, and so am I," said Dear Old Aunt Peregrine, shaking her head. "Arson, tree spiking, blowing up dams—"

"It was only one dam!"

"Blowing up *a* dam, I can abide. But frittering away the family fortune on your ugly little beasties is going too far. Eglantine Spire, I won't allow it."

I fell into a chair. I hadn't missed how she'd dropped the first half of my surname, the only thing my mother had ever given me, but I let it go. "What if—"

"Don't bother finishing that sentence," said Cousin Alva, brushing golden shortbread crumbs from her blouse. "The moment the credits are in your bank account, they're going straight toward building your ridiculous little sanctuary. It was all you could talk about during the last winter holiday."

"And my birthday," said Cousin Nowell.

"And my wedding," piped up Cousin Finley.

My hands curled into fists. I took a deep breath. "If you don't pay me, I'll talk," I said, very quietly. "I have proof I was on the other side of the planet the day you blew off that man's head, Auntie. You all know that."

Gray sniffed. "Go ahead," he said. "No one's going to believe the woman who spends every waking moment stalking Company officials. And blowing up dams."

"It was *one* dam—"

"I love you, Eg, you know I do," said Dear Old Aunt Peregrine. "But like your father, you must learn the hard way. You are welcome to spend the rest of the holiday season here, but you won't be living out of my purse. Since you got yourself expelled, I recommend you start looking for a job. A real one, whichever will take you."

"I appreciate the offer," I ground out, "but it would be best, I think, if I took my leave now."

"Oh, thank the gods," said Cousin Finley.

"Good riddance, too," added Cousin Nowell. "Have fun with your vicious little friends. What'll you destroy next?"

"I suppose you'll find out, won't you?" I replied.

Then I stooped to give Dear Old Aunt Peregrine a kiss on the cheek, spun on my heel, and slammed the parlor door behind me. They couldn't hurt me anymore. I'd told myself so for years, but now it finally felt true. I *did* have my vicious little friends. You included.

As searchlights slice through the black sky above, the young woman's thumb hovers over the transmitter's blinking red button.

"Are you certain?" says the man crouching beside her. "Are you absolutely certain?"

"I am."

"There's no coming back from this."

"I certainly hope so."

"There are better ways to get your family's attention."

The young woman whirls around to face him. He wears the same nondescript clothes that she does, his face covered by an identical black mask.

"It's your plan," she says. "You want to back out now?"

"No. No." He laughs, brittle. "But I have everything to gain. You *have everything to lose. You're a—"*

"Don't." She cuts him off. "Don't, please. Once this is over, I'm one of you, right?"

He reaches out, grabs her free hand. "You've always been one of us."

"You're all the family I need," the young woman says.

She presses the button. In the far distance, a sound like thunder. A horrifying tremble under their feet. A rush of water.

You ended up replacing me in truth.

You had no connections to the Family, be it blood or business, but you were the wet-eyed, parentless pet that people like the Family always crave. Someone to comfort and compliment them without a single complaint because you'd never known better. Someone to look down on, to pity. Perhaps that had been me, once. Before Gray had butchered that tufted urju, and I finally grew a spine.

The Spires wrote you into the will just to spite me, as I knew they would.

They didn't give you a hundred million credits after Dear Old Aunt Peregrine joined my parents in whatever happens after. Nor did you receive even half the sum promised to me for serving as her scapegoat. But it was just enough. Enough to buy the habitat the Company had stolen and make them wish they'd never landed on this planet. Enough to hire guards to fend off poachers. Enough to maintain a permanent team of veterinarians. Enough to bribe politicians to help us keep the preserve safe. Enough to protect the tufted urju for the foreseeable future.

You signed over every cent to me, as I knew you would. Because the thing was, I *did* know you. I'd known you for years, in fact. We hadn't met at the Academy, no, but we'd shared a cell in prison.

A gloved hand slams between the young woman's shoulder blades, sending her to the gritty floor with a grunt of pain. She staggers to her feet like a drunkard, feels for the nearest wall, and slumps against it, barely able to see a few paces ahead with both eyes swollen half shut. Someone paid the guards to rough her up. Could be the Family, one of the cousins, probably Gray, who never forgave her for taking down his beloved trophy and burying it in the middle of the woods. Could be the Company. Not much difference, these days.

She made the mistake of fighting back. Things escalated. But it's not like she hasn't been beaten within a centimeter of her life before.

A dark shape shifts to the right. The young woman turns, the movement pulling at a cut along her jawline. She has to grit her teeth to trap a whimper. Someone sits up in bed. And suddenly they're standing before her, in her space, helping her onto a lumpy, stinking mattress. She'd much rather be sleeping on sun-warmed soil and soft grass, but criminals can't be choosers.

"This is a gross abuse of power," her new roommate is saying. "This is barbaric—"

"You should see what the others look like," she croaks.

Something dribbles down her swollen face. Please, please let it be blood, *she thinks. Snot or tears would be mortifying. She tries to wipe it away with the balled-up edge of a sleeve. When she looks at the red smear, she can't tell if it's new or if she was already bleeding through the cheap cloth.*

"You're a Spire. Aren't you?" Their voice is toneless.

The young woman really doesn't think she can take another tenderizing. "No."

"Very convincing," replies the roommate. "But I recognize the general shape of your face. Even with all . . . that. You've got the Spire jawline. And eyes."

An uncomfortable silence crawls between the pair.

"Barely a Spire," the young woman says finally. "Eglantine Ade-Spire, pleased to make your acquaintance. I'm the one who blew up that dam. I did it alone. Oh, and I shot that fellow. It was an accident. Mostly."

"The pleasure's all mine, and I know. I heard about what happened." Gentle fingers prod at her face. "You'll recover, I think. I'll trade my spare shiv for antibiotics tomorrow. But you'll owe me."

For a moment, the young woman can't find any words. She shoves down the strange urge to cry. "I think we're going to be very good friends," says the young woman. She tries to smile. A tooth is definitely loose. "And who are you?"

"Kameron. My friends call me Kam."

The young woman snorts. "I don't believe you," she says.

The roommate helps her lay down on the bed. "And why not?"

"Kam Fleetfoot blew up the Alchedine oil rigs," she whispers, turning her head into her shoulder so no hidden cameras can read her lips.

"I did no such thing. You'd have to be very stupid to do that," the roommate says loudly. "The cleanup would be a mess."

Only while the rigs were active, which they weren't when Fleetfoot struck. The only casualties that day were mechanical and financial.

"Kam Fleetfoot saved the Jasblure Rainforest," she continues. "Kam Fleetfoot single-handedly took down a poacher squad."

"Come on. Those were all group efforts. Which I took no part in."

"You're normally very, very good at covering your tracks. What did they get you for?"

"Oh, just some stuff with my dad, but they haven't got anything substantial on me. I'll be out of here soon." A sigh. "How do you know so much about the things I definitely didn't do, anyway?"

"Kam Fleetfoot is my hero." The young woman draws in one agonizing breath after the other. Tomorrow will be better. It has to be. "The universe doesn't like me enough to put me in a cell with them."

The Spires took their revenge, of course. You'd committed far worse "crimes" than I had for the sake of the system's environments, and though you'd taken great pains to conceal your involvement, no amount of care could've hidden all your secrets from the Family fixers. The police slapped a pair of magcuffs on you and ripped you from my arms.

But here is the beautiful weakness of the blue-blooded: Nothing matters, so everything matters. Reputation is the only part of their lives they have to work for. But I don't care about reputation;

the Family had already ruined mine. I don't care what people say about me, about us, about the friends we freed from their own legal predicaments. We're entirely out of money now, but money is made-up, and there are other forms of power, as you well know. And now you're on your way back home, to the sanctuary, to the tufted urjus we protect, to me.

Before you, Kam, I thought I'd be doomed to a life alone. I don't fall *in* love; but by the gods, I love deeply, with my whole heart. And I am going to do such wonderful things with you.

Forever your friend,

Eg

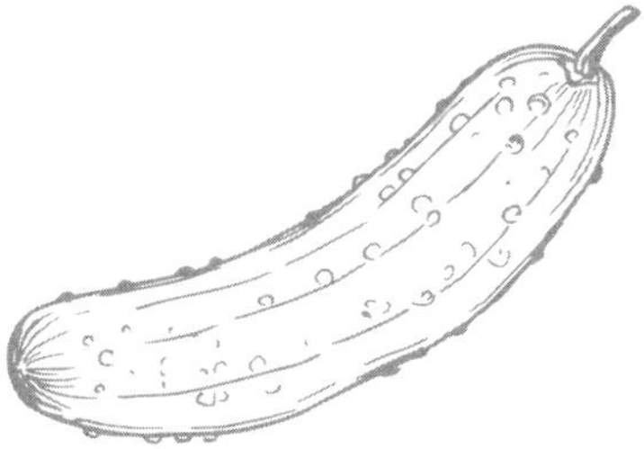

JOUST FRIENDS

ROSIEE THOR

The sun is shining, I'm dual wielding turkey legs, and I'm rocking a ye olde little guy fit that makes me feel like a hobbit about to embark on an adventure. To put it succinctly: I. Am. Thriving.

"Oh my god; oh my god!" Bailey squeals beside me, bouncing in her seat.

We're in the second-to-last row of the raised benches overlooking the jousting arena of the Coastal Oregon Renaissance Faire. Below, two silver blurs charge toward each other on horseback, but I'm barely paying attention. I've got turkey legs to think about.

"Ahh! I can't watch!" Bailey buries her face in my shoulder just as I take a bite, the motion smooshing my face into my food. A bit of turkey skin goes up my nose, and I cough.

"Sir Geoffrey has been unseated!" the announcer bellows, his voice amplified by the *totally* period-appropriate microphone and speaker system.

"It's over," I mumble. "You can look."

I couldn't be more wrong.

The knight, Sir Geoffrey, rises to his feet, his armor caked in mud, and rips off his helmet. He spits on the ground, then points at the knight still astride his horse. "You are no knight of the realm, Sir Tristan! You are nothing but a common knave!"

"There are ladies watching," says Sir Tristan. "Let them see you honorable in defeat."

"An even better reason to go on fighting!" Sir Geoffrey pumps his fist in the air as he steadies himself and rises to his feet.

"Ohhh!" Bailey leans forward, eyes wide. "Drama!"

I stifle a laugh. As if two men wielding giant lances and barreling at each other at top speed isn't dramatic enough already. Around us, the crowd *ooh*s and *aah*s as the two knights circle each other.

"Be careful, Sir Geoffrey!" shouts a woman in the stands behind them. She's seated just below a man in the highest seat—probably a noble lady, then.

"Never fear, Lady Gwendolyn. The sight of your fair face has bolstered my resolve. I shall fight on in your name!"

"Very well. For the heart of Lady Gwendolyn. May the best man win."

Sir Geoffrey draws his sword, but I don't bother to watch.

"Come on. This is boring," I say. If I wanted to watch patriarchal bullshit play out in front of me, I'd watch my mom's reality shows or, like . . . the news.

"Aww, really? It's just getting good!" Bailey pouts.

My stomach churns uncomfortably. "I don't know . . . I don't feel good."

"No shit. You ate like four turkey legs."

It was only three, but I'm not about to argue. Bailey gathers up her skirts—green to match her ivory bodice with botanical embroidery she did herself—nudging me over toward the exit. I follow her lead, heading for the gate and the dusty path beyond as the knights battle for their lady love in my periphery. I don't care who wins, but I linger at the exit for a moment, looking back with a sour taste in my mouth unrelated to the turkey.

"Archer?" Bailey tugs on my sleeve. "Come on. Better walk it off. You'll feel better after a little movement."

She's probably right. This is just some stupid show. And I really did eat way too much turkey.

"I'm serious, Arch. No more food for at least an—oh my god! There's a pickle priest!" Bailey shrieks, grabbing my arm and nearly flinging my half-eaten turkey leg to the ground in her haste.

I immediately spot where she's taking me. A guy wearing a large black cloak with a wide hood pulled up over his head is muttering pickle-flavored Gregorian chants. There's about a dozen people lined up to watch the spectacle. I can hardly blame them. The pickle priest is sporting one of those glittery pickle ornaments people hide at Christmas on a rope hanging around his neck. He lifts the pickle to his forehead, closing his eyes as he blesses the pickle in a deep tenor before handing it to the patron.

Bailey drags me through the crowd. I hit my boot on the side of a hay bale, and my hat nearly goes flying, but I catch it on one of the turkey legs like an absolute pro. When we first arrived, Bailey bought it for me, a leather cavalier hat with a big white feather. I was happy with my ensemble—a handmade tunic I embroidered with white flowers and foxes—but Bailey insisted. She had tucked my hair behind my ear, smiling slyly as she turned me to face the mirror and . . . yeah. She was so right. It tied the whole fit together, making me look like a gnomish troubadour. Little guy vibe activated.

I'm grateful for the extra layer to my disguise when we get in line just behind a girl from school. I recognize her immediately as Francesca from the volleyball team, but she barely acknowledges Bailey and ignores me completely. Mission accomplished.

This is my favorite thing about the renaissance faire: I can go incognito. There's a magic to these last few days of summer break before we return to the accursed halls of Willamette High, and I have to decide whether to come out or not—and to decide what to even come out as. Right now, with no one to perform gender for, I can just be myself. I dread having to define what that means for everyone else's benefit.

When it's just me and Bailey, there's no performing. She's never felt like part of my audience so much as a fellow thespian. We've always been two queerdos, making it up as we go along. All summer I've had the freedom to try whatever I want—clothes, pronouns, names—but when school starts, I have to be a person for public consumption.

"One pickle, please!"

Francesca reaches the front of the line by the time I finish my fourth turkey leg. A couple of boys from school, Noah C. and

Noah R., cut in front of us, draping themselves over her. I shudder involuntarily, but Francesca doesn't seem to mind, chatting animatedly with the newcomers. Beside me, Bailey bristles.

"Sorry, three, actually," Francesca corrects herself, accounting for their increased number.

I toss my finished turkey leg in the trash and nudge Bailey hard. It's just a couple more people. No harm, no foul. I silently pray to the patron saint of nonconfrontation that she leaves it alone. I really don't want them to look at me any closer than necessary.

"Excuse me, we were here first," Bailey says.

I let go of her hand, turning so they can only see a sliver of my profile.

Francesca laughs uncomfortably.

"Begone with you! Cutting shall not be tolerated, for it is not good and pickley!" shouts the pickle priest. "To the back of the line!"

The Noahs slump their shoulders before slinking away to line up directly behind us. Bailey grins at me, but I just shrink into myself. This is much, much worse.

"Seriously, Bailey?" Francesca huffs, turning around to face us. "Why do you have to be so difficult?"

"You're the one who was trying to cheat the system!" Bailey growls. "We were here first. We deserve our pickles in a timely manner too."

"Okay, but this is just delaying things *more*." Francesca rolls her eyes.

"It's cool," says Noah R. "Now we can interrogate Bailey about her new *boyfriend*."

They've seen me now, but it doesn't seem like they've recognized me. With three pairs of eyes scrutinizing us, my chances of detection are skyrocketing by the second. "I'm gonna wait over in the shade," I say in a low voice.

"Oh, come on. Don't be like that—"

I don't hear whatever Bailey says next as I slip away, shrinking under the immensity of their combined attention. In the distance, the crowd still attending the morning joust roars. I would give anything to be sitting in the stands instead, a single fish in a sea of spectators.

A few seconds later, Bailey joins me at one of the picnic tables. She's carrying two pickles, but she doesn't give me one when she slides onto the bench across from me.

"What the hell, Archie?"

If I didn't know better, I'd think she looked almost wounded. But it would take a much sharper blade than anything I can wield to pierce her armor.

I shrug. "Sorry."

"Yeah, that's not good enough. You just left me there."

I avert my gaze. "You didn't have to pick a fight." An implied *again* hangs between us.

"Yes, I did. I'm an Aries." Bailey rolls her eyes at herself.

I don't smile at the joke. Bailey has never shied away from the spotlight. She thrives on attention, good or bad. It's why she tries out for every school play, attends every club at least once, and even ran for student government last year. She fiercely stands up for what she believes in, and if anyone dares to disagree, she makes it their problem. I like all that about her . . . most of the time. I just wish she didn't drag me into her antics.

Bailey rambles on. "But like . . . it was fine. They got their pickles, I got mine. Life goes on. Nobody got punched or anything. So, what's the problem?"

"I just . . . didn't want them to see me like this." I gesture to my outfit.

"Like what? Like *yourself*?" Bailey's expression softens slightly. "You know none of them would be assholes about it, right? And if they were, well, *then* there would be punching."

As much as I appreciate Bailey's pledge to defend my honor, I can't help but feel anxious. She wouldn't actually resort to violence on my behalf, right? That sort of thing would bring on way more attention, which would be so much worse.

"I'd rather just . . . fly under the radar."

"Are you afraid they'll be transphobic about it? I mean, everyone was cool when Emily came out in middle school. No one deadnames her or anything."

That's true enough. Emily isn't even the only trans person at our school. There are a couple of trans boys on the soccer team, and I've never heard anyone be a jerk to them about it. They're better players than most of the cis dudes, and one of them is dating a cheerleader. I don't know how to explain to Bailey that it's not about transphobia. Or maybe it is, but it's not about the kind she's thinking of. I'm not like Emily—stunning beyond belief and wielding impressive skill with an eyeshadow palette—or like the trans boys at our school—athletic and self-assured.

I don't fit the boxes society pushes on us. I've never been good at being a girl, but at least I understood the rules. If I decide that I'm a boy, the rules will shift. And what if I'm just as bad at being a boy? I'm not even sure I *am* a boy; I just know I'm not a girl.

All of that feels like way too much to explain, so instead, I change the subject. "It was weird they thought I was your boyfriend."

"Okay, but that was kind of cool, right? They clocked you as a boy!" Bailey smiles encouragingly and holds out the spare pickle. "Also, we'd make a cute couple."

A shiver runs through me. "What?" She can't mean it. She *can't.*

Bailey tilts her head to the side as if in thought. "I mean, yeah, why not? It could be cool to start the school year with a boyfriend."

It never once occurred to me to worry about this. For all our years of friendship, Bailey has never indicated having a crush on me. Has she? I mentally run through our whole friendship—from meeting in ballet class when we were seven, to unceremoniously quitting ballet when we were eight, to every sleepover, every fight, every joke, and every shared bag of fruit snacks since then.

Bailey's the most important person in the world to me. Her friendship runs its roots directly into my heart. But what if it isn't actually friendship? What if it's something else? That would change everything. It would *ruin* everything.

My face feels hot, my breath comes short, and my hands shake uncontrollably. I tuck them between my knees, willing myself to calm down. It doesn't work. Like . . . at all. I feel like a rabbit staring down a wolf.

Bailey carries on, unperturbed. "And, I mean, you're my best friend. It's like a total no-brainer. I already love you platonically, so why not romantically too?"

"You *know* I don't want that sort of thing," I try to explain.

"I mean, with boys, yeah. I remember the whole Ethan thing.

You were really freaked out." Bailey scrunches her brow in puzzlement. "But I thought that was about him being a boy or whatever."

So had I. Ethan was nice. I thought so, anyway. He'd linger in the hall by my locker to chat about anime, give me origami flowers, save me a seat at lunch. I didn't realize what was going on until he went full flash mob by the bike racks to ask me to the dance. I don't think I even gave him an answer. I just ran away, and we never spoke again. Shortly after, I cut off my hair and started wearing my dad's sweatshirts and flannels to school.

"It was about the whole thing," I start, not sure how to explain the depth of my revulsion at being viewed romantically. "It was about being, I don't know, *desired.*" I shudder. That was when it clicked for me. A boy looked at me and saw a future, and all I saw when I looked at him was a cage. Everything I've done since then has been in service of becoming invisible. If they can't see me, they can't want me, and that's all that matters. I think suddenly of Lady Gwendolyn and her dueling knights, for some reason. "It was like he thought that was the whole point of my existence, to play some role in his romantic theatrics. Like I'm some kind of accessory or something. I don't want anyone to think of me like that ever again."

"Okay, well, you're obviously not an accessory. You're the whole damn fit." Bailey cracks a grin I can't return.

"This isn't a joke," I say.

"I know." Bailey's smile falters, her voice tapering as her shoulders slump.

Neither of us speaks for a moment. With us, quiet is usually a sign of comfort. We don't need to fill every second with words.

Sometimes it's enough just to be together. But this isn't the same. This is a hostile silence, waiting to be broken so it can have an excuse to lash out.

"Do you know why I picked the name Archer?" I ask eventually.

"Something to do with Robin Hood?" Bailey grunts. "Anti-capitalist king shit or whatever?"

"It was because of Artemis."

"Okay, but she's a *girl*, right?"

"Goddess of the hunt." I shrug. "But she's also an unofficial symbol of like . . . not marrying guys."

"So . . . lesbians?"

"Among other things." I avert my gaze.

"Okay, but I'm not a guy, Archer. I'm not Ethan. I'm your friend."

"Artemis's hunters gave up all romantic entanglements too. They rejected the idea that romance was central, that it was the most important—"

"Okay, but you know they say the best romances start as friendships." Bailey breezes right past what I'm saying, clearly not listening. "That could be us!"

"Stop it!" I shout much louder than I need to. "You're not hearing me. I said no."

"Wow, okay. Let a girl down easy." Bailey winces.

Anger flickers to life inside me. "Stop acting like I'm the one who's being unreasonable. *You* sprang this on *me*." And totally steamrolled over my attempt to come out too.

"Seriously? You're rejecting me, and somehow that's *my* fault?" Bailey shoots to her feet. "This is bullshit." And with that, she storms off.

I'm halfway around the faire by the time my brain catches up to my body. There's a stitch in my side, and I'm really regretting the last turkey leg. Vendors line the path here, selling trinkets like clockwork pendants, fresh flower crowns, and historically inaccurate candles in various colors and shapes. I spot a tote bag that says *Living in the Snark Ages* and snort. I turn to point it out to Bailey, but then I remember she's not with me.

My breath catches in my chest and moisture pricks my eyes, but before I can even summon the presence of mind to try to stop myself from crying, the crowd from the joust enclosure roars, scaring my tears away.

I meander down the road toward the sound of clashing steel and nickering horses. There's a fence between me and the spectacle, but I can hear an announcer's voice, repeating the same dramatics from before. Two knights, one noble lady. A love triangle for the ages.

I don't linger to watch. I know how this goes.

Instead, I examine the booths in front of the joust arena as they prepare for the onslaught of potential customers once the show ends. One is a kilt peddler, another is a face painter, and at the edge of the row is a roped-off area with practice dummies made of straw and a bucket full of wooden swords.

A man in a loose, flowing shirt and floppy hat frolics down the path. "Come one, come all! Learn the ways of the joust! Become a squire of the faire!"

The crowd parts around him, and people look on with curiosity at the fighting ring. An eager group of teenagers around my age tumbles into the enclosure where a woman in chain mail and leather gloves hands out the swords. My heart sinks as I recognize them—it's Francesca and the Noahs from before. None of them are looking at me now, but that could change at any moment. I want to turn away and slink into the shadows, but I can't make myself move.

"Seriously?" Francesca says, leaning on the ropes.

"What? It's historical enrichment!" one of the Noahs calls back.

Francesca sighs. "So was the traditional dance lesson, but you said that was stupid."

"Well, I might've been into all the prancing around if it had included more swords." He swishes his wooden blade around inexpertly. "Plus, how will I ever earn my lady's hand if I don't first beat Noah to a pulp?"

My stomach clenches, nausea rising inside me.

"Do you bite your thumb at me, sir?" cries the other Noah, adopting a cringe-worthy British accent.

"She shall be mine and mine alone!" The first swings his wooden sword in wide arcs.

"Nay, I think not! Fair Francesca deserves better!"

"You besmirch my good name!"

"We literally have the same name, dumbass," other Noah says dryly, then clears his throat as if remembering the essence of the bit. "And thou art nasty!"

"Not as nasty as thou! I shall make you bleed!"

"En garde!"

The two clash their blades together in sloppy chopping motions, eager grins on both their faces.

Francesca rolls her eyes and groans. "Come on guys, can we not?"

I feel suddenly hot with anger. Boys fighting over a girl who doesn't want to be fought over? In this economy? This is an insult to feminism or whatever. I know they're just repeating what they saw in the joust, but Francesca isn't an actor in a play. She might not be my favorite person in the world, but she doesn't deserve to be treated like this.

No one deserves to be treated like this. *I* don't deserve to be treated like this.

I'm awash with the need to run—but to where? From what? I remind myself that I'm safe, for all the good it does. No one is hunting me; no one is hurting me. So why do I feel like I'm being watched, like I'm the one being assessed for romantic suitability instead of Francesca? Instead of Lady Gwendolyn?

Bailey's face rises in my mind, her eager smile faltering when I rejected her. I know I wasn't nice about it, but how was I supposed to be? I thought I was safe with her. I thought she of all people would understand.

I look from a weary-faced Francesca to the blissfully ignorant Noahs to the woman with the bucket of swords to floppy hat guy. Surely *someone* will stop this.

Before I know it, I'm stepping forward, ducking under the rope, and grabbing a wooden sword from the bucket.

Guess that someone's going to be me.

"Hey!" I yell, slashing my sword down between the Noahs. "Cut it out."

The Noahs pause.

"What the hell?" One of the Noahs stumbles back.

The other lets his sword arm go slack. "Yeah, man. What's the deal?"

Adrenaline crackles through me, so charged that I barely register the novelty of getting called *man* in this situation. "She's not an object," I grunt.

"Huh?" The Noah on my right makes a face, leaning in like he didn't hear me.

"She's not an object," I repeat, gaining steam with every word. "She's not some trophy you get to win by waving a sword around. She has, like . . . feelings, you know."

"We know that," says the other Noah, looking offended.

"Do you, though?" Francesca scoffs.

I turn my wooden sword on the other Noah. "Have you even bothered asking her what she wants? Maybe she doesn't like either of you, did you think of that? Maybe she just wants to be your friend and have that mean something, but all you care about is whether or not she'll date you."

The way they silently blink at me with their mouths open is answer enough.

I barrel on. "She's more than a prize. She's more than an accessory. She's not just some romantic conquest or a checkbox. Stop acting like that's all that matters. She's a *person.*"

I taste my tears before I notice I'm crying. Salty rivers run down my cheeks as I gulp lungfuls of air like I've just run a marathon. Red-hot embarrassment floods my body as I realize I'm not actually defending Francesca; I'm defending myself. And this speech isn't for the Noahs; it's for Bailey, wherever she is. I try to hold the sword steady in my hand, but my whole body shakes.

"Dude," one of the Noahs says—I've lost track of which one, my vision blurred with tears. "We're just messing around."

"Yeah, it's really not that serious," says the other.

"Okay, but . . . he's right," Francesca's voice joins in. "I'm not really into either of you. Plus, I'm sort of already dating Amanda."

"What?!" the Noahs say in unison.

"Why didn't you tell us? You made us look like total idiots!" one of them continues.

"Nah, you did that to yourselves." The blur that looks like Francesca shrugs, then turns my way. "Hey—thanks for defending my honor, I guess. Are you okay?" She takes a step toward me. "Do you need to sit down or something?"

"I'm fine," I mutter, despite the obvious evidence to the contrary. I wipe my nose on my sleeve, knocking my cavalier hat askew in the process.

"Wait a second. I know you," one of the Noahs says.

"Yeah, aren't you—"

"Archer?"

I whip around to see Bailey standing there. She looks me over, in all my sweaty, tear-stained glory, and her brow furrows in concern. How long has she been standing there? By the look on her face—wide eyes and a concerned frown—long enough.

"I've been looking all over for you—I came back to the tables, but you were gone."

Behind me, the Noahs start making loud kissy sounds.

"Oh my god, shut up!" Bailey yells. She brushes past me, shoving her finger into one of the Noahs' chests. "Would some self-awareness kill you?"

The other Noah raises his hands in surrender. "Hey, we didn't start it."

Bailey bristles. I can practically see the steam coming out of her ears. "Yeah, you kinda did."

"Hey, you, uh . . . Archer?" the Noah being stared down by Bailey calls over to me. "Come get your girlfriend out of my face."

The elation I feel at the use of my new name—the first time anyone but Bailey's said it—is immediately drowned out by revulsion at the assumption that we're dating. I want nothing more than to escape my own skin in this moment. I want to be anywhere but right here, facing down the Noahs, Francesca, and even Bailey who all seem to think my value is in who I date or if I date or that I am in some way, shape, or form a dateable human.

"Fuck all the way off," Bailey says, a hard edge to her voice. "We're not together, okay? And we're not going to be."

"Ohhhhhh burn!" One of the Noahs laughs.

"Re-ject-ed!" the other chants.

"It's not like that!" Bailey stomps her foot. "Archer is my friend. Archer is my *best* friend. We're each other's person, but, like . . . it doesn't have to be romantic for it to matter. Stop making it weird. Just . . . leave us alone!"

"With pleasure." Francesca steps between them, grabbing each Noah by the hand and dragging them off into the crowd.

I sink down onto a hay bale as the energy crash hits my body. My legs feel wobbly, and my head feels heavy. I put my face in my hands, but I don't have any tears left. I just want to nap for a hundred years—maybe forever if it's one of those magical slumbers that can only be broken by true love's kiss.

Bailey sits down beside me, her weight shifting the hay bale slightly. We sit there in silence for a few minutes. There's so much to say, but also . . . there's nothing. We said it all to the Noahs instead of to each other, but it's out there now.

"You dropped this," Bailey says eventually, holding out my hat.

I duck my head so she can set it just right. Her fingers brush the outside of my ear, and she pulls her hand back, expression faltering like she isn't sure anymore what's okay and what's not. But physical intimacy was never my boundary. Why should it be now?

I lean in, letting my head fall onto her shoulder. "Thanks," I mutter.

"Hey, Archer?" Bailey puts her arms around me, holding me close. "I'm really sorry."

I sigh deeper into her embrace, shaking my head against her shoulder. "Yeah, me too. We're cool."

"No, I need to get this out." Bailey pushes me back so she can look me in the eyes. "Archer, I sincerely apologize. What I did was wrong and selfish. Can you find it in your heart to forgive me . . . for eating both pickles?"

A laugh breaks from my chest, surprising even me. "I think we're gonna be fine."

"Are you sure? I know this is a deep betrayal."

"Just buy me another one, and we'll call it good." I wipe my eyes and hold out my hand.

She takes it. "Deal."

THOMAS MARLEY'S FAKE BRIDE

IAN M. CARLISLE

To the reader of my tale, know that it is more advice than a warning. Advice on how the use of magic can cause great trouble, even if you should live to put your story to paper as I, Thomas Marley, have.

The year was 1669. I had a reputation as a, well, *libertine* youth in my community, a small city named Farthing. It was not unfounded, admittedly; as a child, I never had an avoidance toward ladies as some of my peers did, but come adolescence, I was more than eager to see what the now-very-attractive local lassies looked like without their dresses and bodices. Some of them were even willing to show me, and then go a bit further. Suffice to say, I spent some nights in a barn with the owner's daughter, or in the bedroom of someone else. They enjoyed my company, and I enjoyed theirs, so I saw no issue with it.

The same could not be said of my parents. That summer, shortly after I turned eighteen, they took me to the sitting room of our house to speak with me frankly.

"Thomas," Father said. "This libertine life of yours must come to an end."

I tried to feign ignorance. "What libertine life?"

"Don't lie, Thomas. You're rather bad at it."

"Having such a reputation is simply unbecoming of someone of your stature," Mother added. "We are a highborn people, and we must maintain a high character to match."

I said nothing else. I was smart enough to know not to argue with my parents when they were unhappy; otherwise, they'd only get angrier.

"It's a miracle you've not fathered any bastards," Mother remarked, before smiling. "But we do have a solution to your . . . *reputation*. Marriage."

"W-what?" I asked. "To whom? I'm not really courting anyone." *Not in the traditional sense, nor only one,* I thought as my head and heart suddenly felt as though they were on fire.

"We can find someone, if need be," Father assured. "Despite the nature of your reputation, it has made you quite popular with the women of Farthing; though why that is I can't fathom, since it sounds like you're hardly a loyal lover. Still, it should be no trouble. Unless you can find a suitable bride-to-be on your own?"

"I . . . perhaps with a little time?" I stuttered. It was the first thing that came to mind that *didn't* leave me at my parents' whims.

"Well, if you do, don't hesitate to tell us!" Mother said, her voice eager and chipper. "Thank you for being understanding of this, Thomas. Don't forget, though, we can ask around for any potential brides ourselves if you wish it."

"Right, thank you," I said, holding back a sigh to hide my displeasure as I left the room, though I did hear my parents continue as I left.

"You think he'll find his perfect bride on his own?" Father asked.

"I hope so," Mother answered. "Better he marries someone he loves than someone who's convenient. Why do you think I married you?"

Only after reaching my room and closing the door did I let out that sigh. I flopped onto my bed like a dead fish and lay there all night, my mind flooded with thoughts about how to approach my parents' mandate. *Marriage,* they said; a bond of romantic love to last until death, or so I'd been told by everything I'd ever read. It would indeed do away with that reputation my parents so hated—presumably. At the very least, it would turn sleeping with other women into the crime of adultery. This despite the fact that every lord and king I'd ever heard of had his mistresses, and he never suffered for it.

It's good to be the king.

For my part, however, it was the "romantic love" aspect of marriage that kept me awake that night, staring at my ceiling as my thoughts precluded slumber.

For I had never felt that romantic love and had come to believe I never would. I could say I loved my partners without hesitation, but my love for them wasn't *romantic.*

I couldn't say my partners felt the same. Most would talk of how "romantic" they viewed our liaisons, some even suggesting we should be bound together by marriage and love forever, not noticing my confusion and sometimes discomfort at the notion. They also never seemed to quite understand when I tried to explain my lack of romantic feelings toward them. There was no shortage of young women in the village who would marry me, but none that I would marry in return.

Why none of the young women I knew ignited romance in me, I never could figure out, only that they didn't; and if romance must be present for a good marriage, then I could never marry.

I got nowhere contemplating my bedroom ceiling, so I decided to do what any befuddled person should: seek friendly advice. The following afternoon, I mounted one of the family's horses, Barley, and rode to a small house on the southern end of Farthing: a pretty little thing of sturdy masonry walls and a wooden roof, with flowers planted around it that always seemed to be in bloom. After dismounting and tethering Barley, I knocked on the door. It opened on its own.

Any other soul might have recoiled in fear. I simply shook my head and entered. "You'll scare the wrong person by doing that one day, Meg," I said, the door closing behind me, again seemingly of its own will.

"I knew it was you, so I had nothing to fear," came Meg's voice from the kitchen. "You have a very distinctive knock I've come to recognize."

"I guess I've visited you enough by now, you would be able to tell," I said with a chuckle as I entered the kitchen.

Meg was sitting at her table, dressed in a sandy-brown blouse and white apron, while books and cups floated around her. She'd occasionally wave her hand, and a cup would pour into a large bowl resting on the table, or a book would float before her so she could read it.

"Have I come at a bad time?" I asked.

"Only if you're wishing to have our weekly visit now instead of this evening," Meg answered, not looking up from her work. "I have a treatment for acne to finish."

"Your own?"

She paused to turn and stare at me, her face unblemished save for a furrowed brow. "Do I look as though I need it?"

"When have you ever?" I replied.

Her vibrant green eyes widened, and she blushed like a smitten heiress, quickly turning from me and looking back at the open tome floating before her. "For someone with no romance in his heart, you certainly have a talent for saying romantic things."

That gave me pause. "I wonder if that's why every other girl in town thinks I'm the most romantic man around?"

"I'd certainly believe it," Meg agreed. "Curse you and that silver tongue of yours."

I smiled. "You shan't be cursing it later tonight."

She chuckled. "Are you just here to tease me, or is there something more serious?"

I lost all sense of fun and sighed. "It's something more serious, I'm afraid."

She nodded, still maintaining her floating books and cups. "Well, out with it."

"My mother and father want me to marry."

The floating objects lurched. For a moment, I worried they would hit the ground. But Meg caught them with ease, and gently floated them to rest on the table. "Marriage? *You?*"

"It's their idea, not mine." It felt nice to say that, though I didn't need to.

"Clearly." Any other girl I knew would have gotten on one knee and proposed to me right there, but Meg simply rose from her seat to walk over and take my hand. "Come, perhaps we *should* have our weekly visit a little earlier."

Meg took me to the sitting room and lightly pushed me down onto her only sofa. She summoned a pair of tankards from the kitchen that seemed to fill themselves with warm tea as I told her of my conversation with my parents the previous afternoon and of what they expected of me.

She *tsk*ed. "I did tell you to make a better effort to hide your dalliances. *I* can keep a secret, but those farm girls and merchant's daughters and *especially* the apprentice seamstresses? They spread words like rats spread plague."

"Mock my mistakes later, Meg," I said, not in the mood to be chastised. "I need a solution to this little marriage problem."

"Maybe you're overthinking it. Just marry some woman and have mistresses. The king does it, along with every other lord in the country."

I sighed. "Inability to avoid charges of adultery notwithstanding, what if the woman I marry wants a *married* life? One based on a romance and love that I could never truly give? I will *not* live so dishonestly. My parents may begrudge my libertine reputation, but never have I lied to a woman about what I wanted."

"Then why do they keep falling in love with you?" Meg asked.

I shrugged. "They see romance where I see none?"

Meg didn't seem so convinced. "And telling the wife about your lack of romantic feelings isn't an option, I suppose?"

"By hell itself, *no.* I've seen the loveless marriages of our neighbors, how cold and detached they become, how jealous they are of my parents. I wouldn't wish that on anyone, and I certainly wouldn't want to cause it myself."

Meg smiled and nodded, leaning over to wrap an arm around me. "I suppose I can understand that."

I leaned into her embrace. "Have I ever mentioned how much I appreciate you understanding me like this?"

She chuckled. "You don't need to. I can see it in your eyes."

"Now who's sounding romantic?"

"You still do it better. I think it's a sign you read too many chivalric epics."

"You say that like it's a bad thing."

"Time will tell if it is, but right now your knightly sense of honor is getting in the way of solving the problem."

I sighed and leaned back on the sofa, bringing my hand over my face. "I don't suppose you could cast a spell on my parents to make them give up this whole idea?"

Meg snorted and said, "Not without possibly harming or killing them, or myself, if I did something wrong. Magic manipulation of the human mind is . . . *incredibly* difficult, to say the least." She sounded like she would gladly try otherwise. "What if your wife passed shortly after you married, and you proclaimed you'd never take another?"

I scowled at her. "You are *not* murdering a woman I marry."

"It doesn't have to be a *real* woman." With a lift of her finger, she brought a large book before us and hovered it in the air to be read. "With my magical talents, many of them much safer than mind manipulation, I can put a creation in place of a real bride, and then she can 'perish,' as it were, shortly after your marriage."

I tried to read what was written in the book, but most of the symbols were incomprehensible to my eyes. I suppose one would have to be a person of magic to understand them. Meg's suggestion was perfectly clear, however.

"I like the sound of it," I said.

"Wonderful!" Meg was perhaps a bit *too* eager for this plan given the melodic sound of her voice, but I was glad for the help. "I can do something more than acne cures and pregnancy prevention potions for once! And by the way, Thomas, you still owe me for that last one."

"I thought they were free when it's with you?"

"The one *before* that."

I felt a jolt in my heart as I remembered. "I . . . didn't bring any money with me."

She giggled. "Worry not, you can get it after we choose a method of faking your bride."

"Right then, what about a simple illusion?" I offered, looking at a picture in her grimoire that depicted a magician casting such a thing.

She shook her head. "That one's a bit *too* simple. An illusion only tricks the mind, so she would show no physical presence. No reflection in a mirror, no eating any food, no getting wet in the rain. The trick would be noticed immediately."

I hummed in thought as Meg turned the pages, stopping occasionally to glance at the magics within. Most of them she shook her head at. "What about this one?" I pointed at an image of a magician summoning a human-like figure from a circular pattern on the floor. "Conjuration. Why not simply summon a temporary bride for me?"

Meg raised her brow. "Do you really want to marry a demon or something similar?"

I winced. "Never mind."

"I thought not. Besides, if you do, they don't take 'temporary' as an option."

I groaned. "I don't suppose it's possible to simply construct a fake bride, is it?"

Meg paused in her page turning and began rubbing her chin with her finger. "Actually, you might have something with that."

"Wait, you *can* do that?"

"You've heard of homunculi, yes?"

"I . . . haven't." The word sounded familiar, but I could not place it.

"They're constructs of clay and mud. Most magicians make them small and goblin-like to save material, and since they don't expect them to do more than household chores. But the most robust of them are nearly indistinguishable from a human."

"I like it!" I cheered at the idea. "How do we make one?"

Meg sighed. "That's the problem, I'm afraid. I remember what ingredients I need, broadly speaking, but I *don't* remember the procedure."

"It's not in this book?" I asked.

"Not this one," she said, floating the tome back to its place on a shelf. "Building a homunculus is such a field of study in and of itself that whole books on the subject alone have been authored. I *had* one, but it's been stolen."

I rose from my seat and proclaimed, "By who? I'll visit the thief and get that book back myself. I'll fight them for it if I have to! No one steals from one of my friends!"

Meg smirked, and somehow, I felt as though I'd spoken too soon. "Well, since you're volunteering, it was stolen by Harrison Whately. He probably still has it in his house."

"Loner Harrison?" I asked, surprised. "That obnoxious old fart who lives in that creepy manor north of town?"

"The same," Meg grumbled in disgust.

"How'd you manage to lose something to the likes of him?"

"He's a fellow person of magic, albeit a rather mediocre one.

He visited one day and grabbed it off the shelf when I was distracted."

"Why?"

"With him? It's anyone's guess. He's the sort of man who thinks knowing one unique thing about the world makes him its most special and unfettered resident." She looked up at me with big pleading eyes and a pouting lip. "It would be very helpful if you would go and get that book back for me."

"Do I get to know why you can't retrieve it yourself?"

"Well, if we want to do this quickly, someone needs to gather the ingredients for the homunculus. Do you know what they are?"

I sighed. "No, I suppose I don't. I'll get the book tomorrow afternoon, if you don't mind. What's its title?"

"Thank you very much, Thomas. It's titled *A Revelation on Homunculi,* and I'll make it easy to find." Meg then gave me a hungry smile. "But you're still going to need some rest, so perhaps you should go to bed early today. Which means we have something else to do early."

I stayed the night at Meg's. She insisted on it so she could make sure I got plenty of rest after . . . *exhausting* me and giving me a hearty dinner before putting me to bed in her guest room. She claimed it had the best bed. However, "plenty of rest" apparently meant "let him sleep until midafternoon," so it wasn't until evening that I set off.

Before I left, she gave me two things. First, a small compass she said would help me find the book in question. The second was a sword in case I needed to stay true to my word and duel Whately for it. It had perhaps the shiniest, most polished blade I'd ever seen, like it was forged from silver instead of steel, to the point where I was mildly hopeful I wouldn't have to stain it with Whately's blood. Not that I wouldn't hesitate to do so if he tried to harm me first; it's why my parents had me learn the sword to begin with. Defense. Still, the idea of a fight had soured overnight, and I was hoping to steal the book back from Whately without one.

Harrison Whately wasn't a man I was personally acquainted with, but all of Farthing knew about him, albeit as a solitary old man with a foul attitude who almost never left his home, leaving that to any servants he hired, and then often fired on some angry whim of his; hence the name "Loner Harrison." Him being a person of magic like Meg made the solitude more understandable (Meg preferred it herself) but not his distasteful demeanor.

I rode to the outskirts of Farthing where Whately's residence stood. It was a larger house than I was expecting, especially for a single resident. It looked like a small manor, wide and with two floors and possibly an attic. I tethered Barley at the end of the front path and walked the rest of the way. Once at the door, I knocked.

But there was no answer, so I knocked again. "Whately?" I called.

This time the door did open, but on the other side was a servant woman. She wore a black dress and white apron, and her skin seemed especially smooth and shiny, almost like fine clay or porcelain. "Master Whately is asleep at present," she said, her voice oddly monotonous. "May I be of service?"

"I'm . . . looking for a book," I said after recovering from her odd appearance and speech. "Does Mr. Whately have a reading room?"

"More than that. Master Whately has his own personal library with a few hundred across his shelves. You believe Master Whately has the book you seek?"

"Someone told me he did." I figured it wise to omit *who* specifically.

"For what reason do you seek this book?"

I had to scramble for an answer that wouldn't paint me as ill-intentioned. "Curiosity."

"Curiosity?" the servant woman questioned while I was mentally kicking myself and thinking of *another* answer.

"Yes. I want to see if the book in question is real or not; I didn't think it was until somebody told me so, and they said Mr. Whately had a copy. I simply want to see it for myself."

"What is the title of this book?"

"*A Revelation on Homunculi.*" No need to lie about that.

She nodded. "Master Whately does indeed possess a copy in his mystic book collection. I will gladly show you to his library so you may see it."

The servant woman led me inside and down a central hallway, which every room on the first floor seemed to branch from; I was *more* than content to remain behind her. She moved with an unnatural smoothness as she walked. It was a bit unsettling to watch and only made me more suspicious of her. To say nothing of the couple dozen other servants lining the hallway walls, most of them women and all of them as still as statues, not even *blinking*. I could swear they weren't even breathing. The servant leading me stopped at one door and gestured toward it. "This is Master Whately's library. He was utilizing the book recently, so it should not be too obscured. Nevertheless, take your time, but do treat the book with care."

"Thank you," I said, trying to keep the unease out of my voice.

She had not been exaggerating when she called this room a library. Each wall was covered by a bookshelf, or several, that reached to the ceiling—a ceiling at least half a meter above my head. I despaired at having to search the entire library for one book, even if it was one of a kind. Nevertheless, I took out the compass Meg had given me to help find the book. It seemed to be behaving like any old compass, its needle pointing one direction only.

But when I happened to glance at the window to see the sun setting, I noticed the compass wasn't pointing north; quite the opposite. I followed where it was pointing to a small table with a pile of books resting on it. The servant had said Harrison had been reading recently. All I had to do was read the spines, and there it was, *A Revelation on Homunculi* sandwiched between a few other tomes. I was giddy with my good fortune that Loner Harrison had left the book on a table, rather than a shelf.

Perhaps he never expected anyone to come looking for it, I thought to myself as I strode toward the library's exit, making sure there weren't any servants waiting outside. There not being any in sight, I crossed through the doorway.

But then I felt something *change.*

It was as if the very air became colder and yet also heavier. I felt my sense of alertness and dread rise suddenly, along with an urge to look over my shoulder. I could have sworn that the hallway to the front door was suddenly longer than it had been. All of this made one thing clear: I had to get out of Whately's manor as fast as possible.

But before I could even start running, I was blocked by a figure that had somehow appeared in front of me where there was none before. It was the servant woman who'd answered the door; but I suddenly felt there was something *wrong* with her, more so than before even if I could not note what it was. Even her unnaturally smooth skin wasn't worrying me as much as this *other* feeling I could not place.

"You have taken something from Master Whately's library," she said, her voice still stoic and monotonous, but somehow tinged with malice. "Without the Master's permission. You said you came only to confirm the book's existence."

"Well, I lied. And it's not his," I said. "He stole it."

"It is the *Master's* book now, so says he. You *must* return it."

"I *am* returning it. Returning it to its rightful owner."

"You will not leave without returning that book." The servant started coming closer, moving her arms as if she were preparing to lunge at me.

I put my hand on my sword and drew it out slightly to show it off. "Do *not* come closer," I warned. "I don't want to harm you."

"I must see the Master's possessions returned."

Then she really *did* lunge. I leapt to the side to evade and fully drew my sword, pointing it at her. The servant seemed to not notice or not care because she turned around and lunged at me again, impaling herself on my blade before I could duck away from her. As she froze from the wound, I noticed something that made my blood run cold.

She wasn't bleeding; instead, her wound seemed to be *burning*, and the "flesh" around it seemed to be boiling as it melted into thick liquid like mud.

The servant finally recoiled off my sword and let out an inhuman scream like a mad chorus of crowing roosters and screeching barn owls, grabbing at the stab wound that continued to sizzle and spark embers like a dying fire while her skin bubbled and melted.

I wasted no time in running for the front door, my sword still drawn, and the book firmly in my other hand. As I went, other servants lining the walls, men and women alike, came awake and moved to block or grab at me. I swiped at one to my right, leaving a slash across her chest that burned like the stab wound. Another leapt at me and impaled himself as the first servant had, garnering a similar wound for his efforts. After a third servant fell to a slash across her neck, the others backed away, apparently wary now of the sword I carried. All I needed to do was swing or point it in their direction, and they kept their distance.

I ran. The front door was almost in reach when a figure fell from the ceiling to block me one more time. This person, with his wrinkled face, sunken eyes, unkempt beard, and most tellingly, angry expression, was actually human.

"Mr. Whately, I presume?" I said.

"You have something that belongs to *me*!" he barked. "It's mine. Give it to me."

"It's not yours, thief!" I shot back, leveling my sword at him. "I've already cut down enough of your servants—don't make me do the same to you."

"It's mine *now*!" Whately roared as he drew a sword of his own and jabbed it at me, forcing me back toward his horde of servants.

"You think you can best me in a duel?" I sneered as I whacked his blade away with my own. "I've been learning the sword since I was only six years old. Now stand aside."

"Ha! En garde, fool!" Whately just laughed me off. "Anything you can do, I can do better! I'm a person of magic." He swung his sword again, clumsily, and was easily parried.

"Yes, a mediocre one from what I've been told," I taunted.

"I'll show you mediocre!" Whately snarled, as he kept lunging at me with all the grace of a drunkard, missing or being easily parried.

"For a person of magic, I'm not seeing much of it," I noted.

"I'm not wasting my prodigious mystic talents on a lowly thief," Whately huffed.

Still, he kept striking at me poorly, not yet giving up the fight.

"Give it up, Whately!" I barked, getting frustrated as I parried another swing. "You can't beat me. I'm taking the book back."

"Lies! I'm Harrison Whately. I *can't* lose!" he screamed with another lunge.

This time he did manage to nick me on the arm through my sleeve. It was only a flesh wound, but it still stung and seeped some blood onto my nice clean coat.

I may have lost my temper then. "Have it *your* way, you talentless *gascon*!"

A simple slash of my sword knocked his from his grip before I ran through his stomach.

Unlike his servants, Whately did bleed, his shirt gaining a dark stain. I pushed him off the sword, and he fell to the floor, clutching his stomach and mumbling strange words. I heard the thundering footfalls of his servants coming our direction, and I nearly broke the door down, bashing through it. I ran down the path to Barley and cut his tether as I quickly mounted his back.

"Allons-y!" I cried, kicking Barley to run as fast as he could from that cursed manor.

It was night by then, but Barley knew his way back to Farthing by instinct, and so we were there in a matter of minutes. I did direct him toward the guard station on the edge of town first, as I had to do something to clear my conscience.

"Guards! Guards!" I cried.

One of them, a sergeant in a scarlet uniform, answered me. "What's wrong?" he asked.

"Old Man Harrison is injured!" I said. "His servants are tending to him, but someone should check to make certain he's recovering."

The sergeant motioned for his fellow to join him. "How's he injured?"

"An accident," I said, quickly thinking of an excuse. "He . . . stabbed himself while polishing his display suits of armor."

The sergeant raised his brow. "He has those?"

"Yes," I said hastily. "Now if you'll excuse me, I must be off."

I rode back to Meg's house, confident all would be well, or at least hoping it would be.

Meg put me into the best bed as soon as I got to her house, and I fell asleep almost as soon as the blankets were over me. Perhaps they were enchanted? Regardless, I awoke to the smell of tea and French toast resting next to my bed, but also a very strange musty smell coming from elsewhere in the house, like a combination of fine spices, dead grass, and manure. I ate quickly and emerged from the bedroom to find the source of the other smell. In the sitting room, Meg was hovering *A Revelation on Homunculi* and several jars around her while a cauldron of bubbling liquid sat in the center of the room.

"What perfect timing," she said. "Your bride will be ready shortly."

"Will she smell as bad as the mixture you're making her with?" I asked.

"No. Quite the opposite; she'll have no odor at all. Not at first, anyway."

I sat back and let her finish. She poured some more herbs and liquids into the mixture before sending her jars back to their cupboards. She read from her book one more time and then waved her hand over the mixture while speaking strange words. The bubbling liquid rose from the cauldron and shaped itself into the form of a human.

Thus, there stood in the cauldron the form of a naked woman with skin as smooth as porcelain and a sheen to match, though with natural black hair. I had to admit, she was truly beautiful, like Venus being born from sea-foam.

"You've outdone yourself, Meg," I said, my voice filled with wonder.

"I do have a talent for these things, do I not?" she cheeked. "What shall you name her?"

I hadn't thought of that. "Eve?"

Meg scowled. "Eve? That's unimaginative."

"Well, she shouldn't have any old name. Do *you* have a better idea?"

"Genesis?"

I raised my brow. "You just said 'Eve' was unimaginative, and then you suggest *that*?"

We ended up bickering over her name for an hour; the homunculus simply stood there like a statue, unconcerned. Finally, I said the simplest name I could think of.

"Molly?" I asked.

"Molly," Meg agreed.

"Alright." I turned to her. "Come out of the cauldron then, Molly."

The homunculus obeyed and stepped out and did nothing else.

"Molly, how do you feel?"

"I am fine."

I shuddered. It was the same emotionless voice from Whately's servants. "I don't think she'll play the part of fiancée very well, Meg."

"I will be your fiancée if you wish," Molly said, as monotonous as her first words.

Meg winced and nodded. "I . . . have a solution to this," she said. "That spell to change your parents' minds you asked about earlier—I can use it to control her."

"Didn't you say that was dangerous?"

Meg shook her head. "Since she doesn't have a truly *human* brain and mind, it's not the same. Neither she nor I will be in any danger from it. Hold on."

Meg sat on the sofa and began speaking more magic words as she closed her eyes. When she opened them again, they were filled with swirling colors, like flowing paints mixing together. I heard movement behind me and turned to see Molly stumbling around.

"This will take some getting used to," she said in a voice similar to Meg's, if a bit deeper. "But it should still fool your parents enough for our purposes."

"We'll need to get her—or you, some clothes," I said.

After a trip to Meg's closet, we found a simple dress Meg had been gifted as a payment that happened to fit Molly's form. She wore it as we rode through Farthing back to my abode, Molly riding sidesaddle right behind me. When we arrived, we entered without knocking.

"Mother! Father!" I called, trying to sound excited. "I'm home! And I've met someone!"

There was a clattering of feet on the floor as my parents rushed to greet us in the foyer. They hastily threw their arms around me first, ignoring Molly.

"Oh, Thomas!" Mother cried. "We've been worried sick these last two nights!"

"Where have you been?" Father asked.

"With her, actually." I pointed to my guest. "Her name is Molly."

"Molly . . ." Father prompted.

"Sheldon. Molly Sheldon," Molly said, before visibly wincing at her answer.

It took all my willpower to not put a hand to my face as Mother asked, "Sheldon? I thought the Sheldon you know was named *Megan*, Thomas?"

"Molly's her cousin," I said, trying to sound convincing in my lie. "She's visiting, and we sort of fell hard and fast. I'd say I swept her off her feet, but she did as much to me as well."

"Oh, how romantic!" Mother swooned, not noticing me roll my eyes.

"You wish to marry?" Father asked.

"Yes," I said, making a show of looking at Molly with dreamy eyes. "We *know* we're each other's destiny, despite the short time together."

"Indeed," Molly agreed. "There's no other man for me but Thomas."

"Then let's not waste time!" Mother cheered. "The backyard is all ready! I'll go get the priest. Dear, you get us some witnesses. And Thomas, you and Molly must practice your vows. We'll have everything ready in an hour!"

"Wait, what?" Molly and I said together.

Mother and Father certainly had not been wasting any time on their end. Molly and I were quickly rushed out to the backyard and onto a hastily erected altar surrounded by cheap wooden stools, while Mother and Father ran off to collect the others. Instead of practicing our vows, I looked into Molly's eyes, keen to ask Meg a question.

"So . . . what's the plan after we're married?"

She looked at me, confused. "I thought you had one?"

"I . . . don't. Not really."

"Well, we probably shouldn't stay in your parents' house. I can't control Molly all the time, and they'll notice when she's behaving more like, well, *herself*."

"I'll have to move out then, at least until Molly's 'death.'" But I only had to think about that idea for a few moments to find a problem. "I don't know where I'll move to, though."

"You can move in with me. I've still got the spare room, and no one else is using it."

I chuckled. "I suppose that is the easiest answer. Though, at that point, I might as well be marrying you directly, Meg."

She chuckled as well. "Marriage being too romantic for you is why we're doing this." She paused to think. "Then again, I suppose if *I* were to marry anyone it would be you."

"Why is that?"

"Well, I don't think I want a traditional marriage either."

"You don't feel romance?"

"I don't know about that. I just don't have the time, or the desire, to commit to a traditional marriage. I quite like being able to fend for myself. And when it comes to wanting companionship and pleasure for a night, well, that's where you come in."

She gave me a bright smile that would have made a more romantic man's heart skip a beat or three. I just smiled back. "You're my best friend, Meg."

"In schemes and pleasure," she added.

Right as she said that, Mother and Father returned with a few of the townsfolk and a befuddled-looking priest. His Bewilderedness was shoved before us by Mother before she, Father, and the rest of the witnesses sat on the stools. Once he recovered from his—I assume—kidnapping, the priest read his lines before saying, "If there is anyone here who believes this couple should not be bound in holy matrimony, speak now or forever hold your peace."

There was silence as my parents watched with glee, the townsfolk with annoyance.

"In that case," the priest started again.

"I object!" two voices said near the back.

Everyone looked to where the shouts had come from. It was the two guards I had sent to Whately's. They were standing there, very still, almost like his servants.

"For what reason do you gentlemen object?" the priest asked.

The guards said nothing as they walked up, eerily stepping in time with each other. When they reached my parents, they grabbed them by their collars and held their swords to their necks. My parents and the other guests shrieked in horror, and I reached for my own blade, which Meg had let me keep.

"What are you doing?!" I cried. "Unhand my parents!"

"I have a deal to make with you, Thomas Marley, you thief," the guards said, their voices not their own, but still recognizable; especially when I realized their eyes were clouded in swirling colors like Meg's.

"What do you want, Whately?"

"You know what I want," he said through the guards' mouths. "I want my book back."

"It's *my* book, you talentless fraud!" Meg-in-Molly shouted.

"It's the last magic book I need for my collection, Sheldon," Whately said. "And I *will* have it *now*."

We both growled in frustration as Whately grinned on his stolen faces.

"Thomas! What's going on?!" Mother cried. "What are these guards talking about?"

I could only stare down at Whately's puppets as my mind frantically tried to think of something, *anything*, to do.

"I have an idea," Meg whispered to me. "But I'll have to release my control of Molly and give up the ruse. What do you think?"

I looked between the homunculus standing by my side and my parents with swords at their throats. It wasn't even a question. "Whatever you have in mind, I'll do it."

Molly nodded, then turned to the puppeted guards. "Allow Thomas time to get it, and you'll get your book, Whately."

The guards nodded. "Very well, be hasty now."

I needed no second bidding. I rode Barley with all speed to Meg's house where she was already waiting outside with the book. She quickly hopped on with me, and we sped back to our waiting enemy. "I hope you know what you're doing," I said, as we dashed through town.

"I do," she replied. "And we're very fortunate that Whately doesn't. He's using the same mind manipulation spell on the guards as I was on Molly."

"I kind of figured."

"Well, he's doing a bad job of it, and *that* will be his undoing."

We rode into the backyard where Whately's puppets were still waiting. Dismounting Barley, we both walked toward them as they lifted my parents from their seats to approach us.

"Thomas must hand over the book," Whately demanded. "For he's who stole it."

"As you wish," Meg said, handing the book to me.

"You toss the book, and I'll toss your dear parents."

I scowled but nodded. "On three, then," I growled. "One."

"Two," Whately said.

"Three!"

The guards shoved Mother and Father forward, while I tossed the book into the air. Behind me, Meg suddenly belted out, "Begone!" in a singing voice.

The guards stopped in their dive to catch the book, screaming in Whately's voice until it suddenly faded away. They fell to their hands and knees, breathing heavily and looking around in confusion.

"What happened?" the sergeant asked.

"Mind manipulation magic," Meg answered as she floated her book back into her hand.

"Mind . . ." the junior guard started. "That ungrateful old bastard! We go to make sure he's well, and this is how we're repaid?!" They both left in a huff, swearing prison for Whately.

I breathed a sigh of relief and sat down on the grass, thanking the Fates that it was over.

And then Mother reminded me it was not. "Thomas Marley," she said, pointing at Molly, who was still standing motionless on the altar. "Who is that 'girl,' *really*?"

It was not a fun explanation, and Mother and Father were *very* angry.

"I cannot believe you, Thomas!" Father bellowed. "A fake bride?!"

"Well, you never said I had to marry a *human* woman," I said.

"This isn't funny, Thomas!" Mother added.

"So Thomas doesn't want to marry," Meg chimed in from where she'd sat down on a stool. "What does it matter?"

"His *reputation,* you scarlet woman!" Mother growled. "I can't have a libertine as a son! It isn't proper for highborn people."

"The king is the highest born of them all, and he has enough mistresses for an army."

"That's no excuse for Thomas," Father intoned.

Meg threw her hands up in the air. "Alright, you want him married? Well, here then." She grabbed me by the hand and pulled me to the altar where, somehow, the priest had remained. "Marry us now, sir," Meg ordered.

"I . . . alright then, um . . ." the priest stammered. "Thomas, do you?"

"I . . . Meg? What are you doing?"

"Marrying you, you beautiful fool."

"But don't you want to be married to someone who will . . . ?"

"Give me the 'married life'? I told you, I don't really want that now. I might not ever. And since you don't, either, it sounds like the only people we could marry are each other, no?"

"I . . ." She was right. If neither of us wanted to live the married life, then being married would be purely to appease other people. We could continue on as we always had, her with her focus on magic, and me with my many intimate friends.

Though, for this, Meg was truly my best friend.

"Well, Mr. Marley? Do you?" the priest asked again.

"I do."

"Meg Sheldon, do you?"

"Absolutely."

"Then by the power vested in me by the city of Farthing and by Almighty God, our Father who art in Heaven, I declare you husband and wife. You may kiss the bride."

I did, and she kissed me back, quite vigorously. Molly clapped, but we were more delighted at how disgusted my parents looked at it.

"That's no kiss of romance," Mother groaned.

"What are you going to do with . . . her?" Father asked, pointing at Molly, who had taken a seat on a stool. She rose from it and nodded.

There was only one answer I could think of. "Come along, Molly. Let's go home."

With the wedding, such as it was, over, we headed back to Meg's house. We figured it would be best to spend our "honeymoon" there. I walked, leading Barley while Meg and Molly were his riders. My marriage may have lacked in romance, but that was no excuse to not be a gentleman.

We saw the two guards as we went through Farthing proper. They were carrying away the unmoving body of Harrison Whately.

"What happened to him?" I asked.

"Backlash from using a mind manipulation spell on two people at once, and then having it suddenly severed," Meg said. "The human mind isn't made to handle it, so it perishes instead."

"Did he know that could happen?" I asked.

"As Meg said, he was a very mediocre magician," Molly provided.

"Well, thankfully, I'm now married to a brilliant one," I said.

"Once more, the most romantic words come from the least romantic person in Farthing," Meg remarked with a smirk, as we made it to her house. I helped Molly off of Barley first.

"Shall I prepare your bedroom?" she asked.

"Thank you, Molly," Meg said. "But that isn't necessary. Why don't you relax? It's been a busy first day of existence for you."

"As you wish, Meg," Molly said as she entered the house.

"Will she be like that . . . *forever*?" I asked as I helped Meg off of Barley. "That stoic speech and mindless devotion she has reminds me too much of Whately's servants."

"I've heard whispers of how to set a homunculus free of its creator, but nothing on making them feel their own thoughts or emotions," Meg said. "Still, I'll gladly look into both."

"It should be easy for so brilliant a magician. When will you start?"

She cupped my chin in her hands. "After we have our honeymoon."

I chuckled. "Mother and Father will never approve of this."

"Their son is a married man, as they wanted. If they don't like it, that's their problem."

She pulled me into another kiss as vigorous as the one from our wedding.

Like Mother said, no kiss of romance. But it *was* the kiss we wanted.

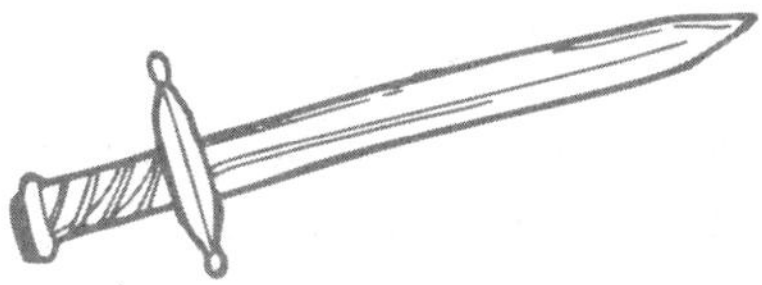

SWORDMAIDEN

KALYN JOSEPHSON

The forge was sweltering, the air viscous with the scent of ash and molten metal. With each press of the bellows, the furnace exhaled a new breath, burning bright like the maw of a dragon. The furnace stretched nearly twenty paces across the back wall of the forge—meant to give easy access to a line of smiths working simultaneously—and was usually tended by the younger girls not yet charged with the Forging.

But today, there was only Miradet.

She placed her sword into the flames, the force of them singeing her skin as she waited for the metal to heat. When it glowed a vivid, unvarnished white, she drew it from the furnace and set it upon her anvil. She was quick with her inscription, etching the intricate character for "strength" into the shining face of the blade with her carving needle.

Then she picked up her hammer, driving the spell into the sword with each strike, the same way she had every day for the last four years. Heat, scribe, strike. Heat, scribe, strike. She knew the rhythm more intimately than her own heartbeat, and she gave herself to it so thoroughly, to the heat of the forge and the crafting of her sword, that she almost didn't hear Davina.

She looked up to find the other girl hovering in the open doorway, already wrapped in a Bastillian Day dress of pure white. Her long golden hair, usually bound in a braid to keep it safe from the fire, flowed in loose curls about her strong shoulders. She wore her sword in a sheath across her back, its rose-gold hilt rising over her shoulder like a Scorover's tail.

"I said, your father is calling for you," Davina repeated with growing disdain. Not only for the threat the forge posed to the dress she had been waiting years to wear, but for Miradet, whose every action seeded Davina's hatred of her deeper. To have been sent on an errand to fetch her had likely rankled her pride, but one did not tell the Head Swordsman no.

"It's two hours yet to the ceremony," Miradet replied. "I will be there."

Davina looked as though she wanted to argue, but then her full lips twisted, locking the words inside, and she turned on her sandaled heels. But Davina didn't need words to make her point. That Miradet was still here, crafting her sword on the day she was meant to give it away instead of preparing for the Bastillian itself, was a slight to all Swordmaidens.

Davina would already be telling the others, touting Miradet's actions as further proof that she thought herself above them.

For while they primped and preened in preparation for the Bastillian, where they would exchange their swords for a hand in marriage, she was in the forge, dedicating herself to a blade that could not love her back.

It was an insult to their way of life, to tradition, and her father would surely berate her for it when he heard. But like the others, he misunderstood. Miradet did not resent tradition the way they believed; she venerated it. To be a Swordmaiden was to bring life to the village, to offer it protection from the monsters of the wood.

But where the others were prepared to gift their blades to the husbands who would command them, Miradet had no interest in partnership, in sharing her life or her sword with another. She did not want to part with her blade.

She wanted to wield it herself.

It was a secret she harbored in her breast like an ember of the furnace, tending its glow with each swing of her hammer even as she recognized its hopelessness.

For a Swordmaiden could never wield her own sword.

Once, their order had roamed the land in its defense, the craft of Forging practiced in every village from the forest to the sea. But then a maiden had sought power beyond her station. She slew the Goddess Iythalene of the wood, who in turn cursed the order with her dying breath: With every cut, their blades would beget a new monster.

In time, the art of Forging was shunned, and then lost, harbored now only by their village, where it was carefully controlled. For a Swordmaiden's blade could still be wielded—so long as it was by another's hand. And so Bastillian Day was born, its purpose twofold: to find each blade a wielder, and each maiden a partner, for theirs was a power passed down through generations.

Miradet sealed the spell into the sword with a final blow before quenching it in a basin of water. The sudden cooling would harden the blade, a part of the Forging cycle alongside tempering, in which the smith sought a balance of strength and flexibility, a challenge made even greater for a Swordmaiden, whose weapon was no normal blade.

She had Forged hers from Cloudmetal, a rare ore that produced a blade of pale turquoise run through with veins of gold, a substance stronger than any steel and twice as light. Between it and the countless spells Miradet had hammered into the blade, the years of sweat and toil and dedication, she didn't need the Bastillian to tell her the worth of her sword.

She had crafted something worthy of the gods, and now she had to give it away.

With the time before the ceremony dwindling, she went on to bind the tang in a simple leather hilt before sharpening the blade with polishing stones until the edge sung when drawn through the air. The sword was easily a two-hander in size but wieldable by one due to the lightness of the Cloudmetal, and as she spun with it through the open forge, pacing through steps she should not know, she felt complete. As if the sword were only another piece of her body—and to part from it would be to sever a limb.

Then do not, came a distant thought that hardly felt like her own.

Something moved at the corner of her eye, and she lowered the sword at once, an excuse already on her tongue. But it was only

Smudge the cat, sliding from the flames of the furnace with the grace of liquid metal. His white fur was gray with the ash that was his namesake, but he was otherwise unharmed, if a little toasty to the touch when Miradet bent down to scratch behind his ear.

Many of the townspeople feared him, thinking him some remnant of the Goddess Iythalene, but Miradet had found him a fast friend, something she was in short supply of. Besides, the goddess had been dead a hundred years. There was nothing left to fear of her but a memory and the monsters that roamed the wood.

"You'll have to come visit me after today," she told him. "I'll have no reason to come to the forge once I'm Swordsworn."

Smudge peered up at her with impossibly bright green eyes, knocked his head against her hand, and then trotted outside. She longed for a little of his ease at life, his freedom—but she just as swiftly quashed the feeling. She was a Swordmaiden, one of the select few capable of crafting the enchanted blades that kept their village safe.

Miradet took one final look about the forge, at the stations her fellow Swordmaidens had labored upon for years, at the furnace with its comforting heat and the tools she'd left scattered at her table, and sheathed her blade. Then she followed Smudge out into the daylight.

Woodmir was not a small village, but it was compactly designed, its cobblestone streets weaving in and out of one another in a winding maze that would leave any visitor disoriented. It led to the impression of constant bustle, the sounds from two streets away echoing and coalescing as if beside your ear, so that even as Miradet walked alone toward the Bastillian square, she felt surrounded.

Smudge trotted beside her, Miradet fancying him an escort to her execution. For each step toward the square felt heavier than the last until, by the time she emerged into its wide expanse, she had stopped walking altogether, her sword clutched in white-knuckled hands.

The square teemed with people, reverberating with shouts and laughter like the hiss and pop of the furnace's fire. Revelers clutched skewers of meat and vegetables, plates of fried cheese, and dough powdered in sugar as they rushed to join the growing crowds before the swordplay demonstrations. Others milled about in the center, taking in this year's presentation of swords, which would soon include her own.

There was a rhythm to it all, a heartbeat, that Miradet had never attuned to, which made her feel like a stranger peering through warped glass, unable to parse what she saw beyond. She had always been withdrawn, but the people of the town mistook her reticence as heartlessness, something her opinion of the Bastillian only furthered. As if love could only exist in romance, and not in the space between the strike of a hammer and the blade it shaped.

The Swordmaidens lingered alongside stands displaying their blades, answering questions about their crafting techniques and peering coyly at the boys who observed them. They were all clad in fine dresses, their hair combed and styled, with delicate strings of jewelry about their wrists and necks that shone bright as their smiles. Many of them would never have worn jewelry before, or a dress so fine. When you spent every day in the heat and soot of the forge, such things were an extravagance.

"Miradet." Her father spoke her name like a command, and she turned reflexively toward him. He, too, was dressed in his finest: an emerald tunic trimmed in gold and a thick brocade of a cloak, pinned to his shoulder by a Cloudmetal leaf that marked him as Head Swordsman. At his hip rested the blade her mother had crafted as a Swordmaiden before their union, the hilt carved from the rare horn of a Skalvax.

Her father's dark eyes swept over her disheveled state, taking in the soot stains on her clothes and the disarray of her braid, and he made to block her from view of the square. "What do you mean by showing up here in this state, Mira? Your mother would be ashamed of you."

She didn't know what her mother would think of her, for she had died beneath the claws of the Shalomar not long after Miradet's fifth birthday. A monster of legend, the creature was the only one of its kind and had roamed the wood for as far back as anyone could remember, impervious to even the strongest of Forged blades.

And Miradet's mother had tried to kill it.

Which was why whatever her mother would think of her, she did not believe it was the same as her father. She had seen the craftmanship of her mother's sword; no Swordmaiden made such a thing simply to find a husband. There was a reason her father was Head Swordsman, and it hung at his hip.

"I wanted to present my sword," she told him.

"You should have washed and dressed first," he chastised. "Have you been at the forge all morning?"

Her words crisped to ash in her mouth. She didn't know how to explain to him how important perfecting the blade was to her.

At seventeen, the magic that enabled her to craft would soon leave her, and so she had stolen every moment she could in the forge, knowing that when the sword was finished, everything would change.

There had been a time when their power was not so fleeting, when they could craft sword after sword in a lifelong calling. But with the death of the goddess at a maiden's hands, that power had waned, and it became rarer each year, making each Swordmaiden's role all the more important.

"Father," she said softly. "Must I give it away?"

His brow darkened. "We've spoken of this, Mira. That sword doesn't belong to you; it belongs to the village."

"I know, it's only—" Only what? That she thought herself above their traditions just as Davina claimed? She wasn't the only one who didn't want this. Many of the girls looked forward to it, but some among them had no interest in boys at all. The village had no qualms with that—unless you were a Swordmaiden. Then tradition came first, for it was tradition that kept them safe from the wood.

After all, one did not tell the Head Swordsman no.

Miradet proffered the blade before she could talk herself out of it. Her father took it, and she retreated the way she'd come, refusing even a glance back. She hadn't parted from the sword for four years. Even now, she swore it called to her, and she feared that if she took so much as a step after it, she would rip it from his hands.

Back home, she cleaned the soot and grime from her skin and washed her hair, the color slowly returning to its usual yellow. She bound it back into its braid and sought the dress she had chosen for the occasion. Like those of the other maidens, it was an unaltered white, the waist bound by a cord of gold. It flowed in solid silk from corset to ankles, shrouded by a sheer layer that reached up to the hollow of her throat and billowed about her arms.

She felt like an imposter.

It was not the dress, which was beautiful and fit her well, but the cleanliness of her pale skin, the absence of her Forging leathers and the blade that should have been at her side. But this was what it meant to be a Swordmaiden of Woodmir. At thirteen, every girl born to a Swordmaiden was tested for the magic to Forge, and the select few who possessed it took up the tools of a smith, crafting the blade she would one day gift for her hand in marriage.

As the daughter of the Head Swordsman, who was the keeper of their town's traditions and the greatest warrior among them, Miradet had worn these expectations like a noose about her neck from the day she turned thirteen. She would Forge a sword her family could be proud of, and then begin a family of her own.

The trouble was, she didn't *want* that kind of family.

Miradet enjoyed being alone. She found solace in silence, strength in self-reliance, and the thought of having to share herself with another made her heart ache. She wanted nothing more than to take up her own sword in defense of the village and all those beyond it, but if her father knew how she truly felt, if the village knew, they would only see it as yet another sign of her strangeness. Another rejection of the tradition that had built Woodmir, that kept it safe.

So Miradet donned her dress and went to meet her future husband.

The streets had swelled with people in the short time Miradet had been gone, everyone drawn by the lure of festival sweets and games and something more ephemeral. There was an allure to Bastillian Day that called to people, like a song on the air. For many, it was the closest they would get to the thrill of Forging, to magic. For others it was the chance to change their future, and their family's future, through a good match.

For Miradet, it felt like a lament.

"Come now, Mira, can you not muster a smile today of all days?" came a voice in her ear. She refused to acknowledge it, not wanting to encourage him, but today Nox would not be dissuaded. He swung around before her, the fringe of his honey-brown curls brushing his forehead, his smile the tilt of a blade beneath her chin. He was handsome, she couldn't deny him that, his black tunic and trousers framing a lean build. It was not the physical thought of him that turned her away, but something deeper.

"I like your dress," he told her, walking backward with the confidence of the capable swordsman he was. His father was second to none in the village save for Miradet's own, and he'd been in training since he was a child, something Miradet had always envied. But that was all of Nox Avernos that she desired, despite the entire town's expectation that she swear herself to him.

Nox drew to a halt, forcing her to do the same. The crowd ebbed and flowed about them, preventing her from stepping around him as he leaned in close and whispered, "Keep my sword warm for me." Then he was off into the rippling crowd, his laughter a discordant note in her ear.

Miradet was still until she felt the press of a warm, furry body against her leg. Even through the folds of her dress, Smudge's heat permeated, the rumble of his purr as calming as the lavender she tucked beneath her pillow. She crouched down to scratch under his chin. "Be very happy you are a cat, Smudge. No one expects anything more from you than what you are."

Would Nox even listen if she told him she had no concern for romance? She was certain he had no true interest in her, as they had so little in common outside of swordplay, but he had made it clear over the course of the last year that his only focus was obtaining her sword. While most suitors would be satisfied with any blade so long as it won them the hand of a woman of her station, Nox had his father's shadow to escape, and only the best blade would do.

For like so many fools before him, he had sworn to slay the Shalomar.

Smudge bopped her hand with his head, then turned about. She straightened and, with the cat as her guide, entered the square.

Like the others, her sword had been set upright upon a gilded display, bearing the length of its azure blade to the glow of the festival lights. Already a crowd of men had gathered before it, Nox at the center, all waiting for the explanation of how she had crafted it. For most, it was an opportunity to highlight the uniqueness of their swords, or the skill with which they Forged them, but it was mere ceremony for the Head Swordsman's daughter.

Most of these men would petition for her hand if she offered them a stick.

She took up her station beside the display, a strange relief swelling in her breast to be so near the blade again, as though it had been waiting for her. Around her, several of the other girls had drawn decent crowds as well. Many of them had Forged beautiful swords, Davina chief among them, but others had made theirs as simple and as straightforward as they could, content with offers from boys who sought them not for their station, but for themselves.

They would have used common metals, like steel and blackiron, and fused it with the basic magic of the River North or the bark of a Heartwood tree. How many had opted for adding powdered stone to the ore for strength, the simplest and safest of modifiers? Their blades' powers would be modest, increased strength, quicker speed, and yet some part of Miradet longed for that, the ease of walking a path so many had walked before you.

She would not know what magic her blade was capable of until someone wielded it, until she chose a husband and they were Swordsworn.

"Mira," urged her father, and she snapped back to the press of expectant eyes before her. By tradition, the offers of marriage couldn't begin until she had given the customary address, and some not so small part of her wondered what would happen if she only stood there in silence. Her father would be disappointed. She knew well the look of it on his face, though she'd grown no better at bearing it. The village would talk, but they always talked, their voices a constant wind at her back.

But what would become of her sword?

The thought of that blade gathering dust, shunned as unworthy, was what finally parted her lips. "My name is Miradet Sorensen, and I hereby present my sword for your consideration." The words were rote, a speech she had practiced a thousand times. "Its core is formed of Cloudmetal, taken from the depths of the wood."

At this, a murmur of appreciation spread through the gathering, Nox's dark eyes turning covetous. Whether or not they had come for the advancement of station that a match with her would provide, to have a blade formed of Cloudmetal was an opportunity all on its own. There was only one other in the village, and it hung at her father's hip.

"For its magic, I used the antler of a Godstag." The hum of conversation rose at this, for a Godstag was one of the few creatures of the forest that had not succumbed to the monsters within after the goddess's death. They rarely strayed near the village, and to have found the corpse of one not poisoned by the monsters' darkness was remarkable in and of itself. But Miradet had been willing to travel deeper into the wood than any other, and her sword showed it.

The ore of every sword was Forged of three items, and she had only shared two: the metal with which she formed the blade, and the magic that she had bound the spells to. The third and final ingredient was the modifier, the item that gave the blade its nature. It was where the smith had the greatest freedom, for anything could modify a sword.

Most chose a type of stone for strength; the boys who came to Bastillian Day were looking for blades of power. Others picked gemstones for durability, or pine needles for the sharpness of the edge. Davina had used the claw of a Calraptor, so that her blade might sunder the flesh of its enemies.

But Miradet had chosen something else.

She met Nox's hungry gaze in the center of the crowd as she said, "For its modifier, I used a leaf of the Mothertree."

Several among the crowd gasped, a few drawing back. Even Nox seemed uncertain, casting an imploring glance at her father, who had swung his heavy frame before Miradet to block her from the crowd.

"Did you misspeak?" he asked, though it was not a question at all.

"I did not." She had sought something supple, something malleable, with which to modify her blade, and there was only one substance that would do. The leaves of the Mothertree were impervious to the elements, unbreakable and evergreen, yet flexible and soft. But the Mothertree was more than a tree; it was the temple of Iythalene, of the goddess whose magic had given birth to the monsters of the wood.

"What were you thinking, Mira?" her father said.

"I did what was best for the sword," she replied. "The goddess is gone, Father. We have nothing to fear from her any longer, and the leaf was what the blade demanded." She didn't know how else to explain it, the feeling that had told her how to craft her sword. It was as innate as the pulse of her heart or the draw of her breath, the same feeling that made her certain that in their short time apart, the blade had longed for her, too.

"You foolish girl." Her father's voice was iron. "Who will want you now?"

Some small selfish part of her thrummed with elation at those words, though the greater part churned with guilt. She'd had no desire to embarrass her father, nor to ruin the ceremony. More than anything, she wished she could be the daughter he asked of her. She knew that he was only looking out for her, for the village, and that their traditions were there to protect them, but she did not *want* those traditions, as hard as she had tried.

She did not want this, and perhaps the sword had sensed that.

"Father, I—" The apology died on her lips, for that was when the first howl sounded.

It was low and rasping, a pained keening that haunted the nightmares of the village. Miradet had only ever heard it once before, on the night her mother died.

The call of the Shalomar.

For a moment, all was still, as though in prayer that they had collectively imagined the sound. Then came the second call, closer than the first, and a steady panic coursed through the square.

"Return to your homes," boomed her father's voice. "Take cover! Swordsmen, to me!"

The square fell apart into chaos, villagers fleeing in all directions as the swordsmen fought their way to her father's side. They drew their blades, metals of silver and gold and blackiron glinting in the light of the full moon as the ground began to shudder and buckle.

Miradet seized his arm. "Please don't, Father. No one can fight it!"

"Get inside, Mira!" He shook off her hold, face resolute.

Miradet retreated a step as a shape detached itself from the darkness, emerging fully into the torchlight of the square. It had the vague structure of an animal, a body like a mountain with four limbs and a head, but it had a neck too long and coiled to be natural and more eyes than teeth. Its hide was the unbroken hue of pitch, the edges undulating like scraps of cloth.

Her father called orders to the others, maneuvering them into formations and dispersing them about the perimeter, but Miradet knew as surely as they did that there was no point. The Shalomar rarely ventured into towns, but those it had visited had been left devastated in its wake.

Did you come for me? she wondered to the shifting mass. Had she brought this down upon them with her use of the Mothertree?

The Shalomar let out a third and final call, and then it descended upon the swordsmen. They swept aside its blows with swords enchanted for strength, slashed at it with blades edged in fire and ice, but no matter the magic they wielded, the monster did not falter. The first swordsman fell beneath its claws, the second breaking between its jaws. And then the Shalomar stood before her father.

He drew the Cloudmetal blade her mother had Forged, the blood of his kinsmen gathering at his feet, and charged.

Miradet had seen her father fight before. There was not a man in the village who could best him, and he had felled his fair share of monsters. But for all his swiftness and strength, no man's blade could pierce the Shalomar's flesh. It had him on the ground in moments, its claws pressing into his chest.

Miradet didn't stop to think; she grabbed her sword, ripping it from its sheath, and ran toward the monster.

With each step, something changed. Her body grew lighter, faster. Strength descended through her muscles like a tonic, her fingers dexterous on the hilt. The monster's many eyes watched her come with the air of one who had been waiting a very, very long time.

Yes, whispered a voice in her head. *Yes!*

The monster didn't dodge as she swung; why would it, when no blade had managed to cut it before? Yet as the edge of her sword carved across its chest, its impervious hide split, spilling black, brackish blood and filling the air with the scent of salt. The monster reared onto its hind legs with a cry, and Miradet swooped down to drag her father to safety. He was alive, groaning from the pain of his wounds, but alive.

"Mira?" he asked groggily. "Your sword—how?"

"Rest, Father," she said softly. "I will handle this."

The other swordsmen had retreated well before she struck, but seeing that her blade could pierce the Shalomar's flesh, more than one reached out to her for it. She ignored them, plunging back into the fray to the sound of a foreign laughter in her head.

Destroy it, trilled the voice, and this time she knew it for the sword's. *Destroy them all!*

Something had sprouted from the monster's wound, a pinprick of green in the mass of black, but she didn't stop to inspect it. She danced between its swipes, drawing her sword across its legs and claws, its shoulders and chest. The sword guided her, as she guided it, and she realized in that moment that she could not part from it any more than her own heart.

She was it, and it was she, and she loved them both.

With a final, swift lunge, she drove the point of the blade deep into the monster's chest to the sword's cry of delight. The Shalomar's roar rattled the trees, the square, the very earth, and in that moment as she and it were connected through the sword, Miradet saw something. Or perhaps she heard it, or already knew it, but it was there inside her head, sprouting like a seed.

When a Swordmaiden wielded a Forged blade, anything they cut begot a new monster. But the creature before her was not just any monster—she was the original. The last of the Goddess Iythalene, whose own body had been twisted by the curse the moment she cast it, her mind and purpose lost to the creature's dark magic.

The curse she had meant to be a gift.

All her life, Miradet had been told that Swordmaidens had brought the monsters down upon them. That they were responsible for the death, the destruction, and could not be trusted with the swords they created. It was why the Bastillian existed, why they gave their blades to partners who could wield them in their place.

All because a maiden had sought power beyond her station and killed a goddess.

"But we didn't kill you, did we?" she asked of the beast before her.

The Shalomar—*Iythalene*—was barely breathing. She slumped to her monstrous knees, bending over the blade in her heart. Words were lost to her, stolen along with her natural form, but when Miradet had forged her sword of the Mothertree, she had opened herself to the goddess's magic, and in return, it gave her the truth.

The memory struck her like the quench of cold water, the magic piercing her very being. Images formed in her mind as if from a half-remembered dream, until all Miradet could see was a young woman wrapped in white. Her red hair was bound into a crown upon her head, her freckled skin streaked with sweat as she fled into the wood's embrace.

There, she found the Mothertree, its massive trunk hollowed out to form Iythalene's temple. Miradet felt the woman's relief when the goddess offered her shelter, felt her own wonder and astoundment at seeing the goddess in the flesh. Her face was round and full, her hair dark and long and interspersed with many braids and beads of Cloudmetal, and she listened with true concern as the woman explained how she'd fled the man she was to marry.

That he pursued her even now.

Iythalene promised her protection, but the man had crept in as they spoke. Thinking his future wife held captive, he slew the goddess with the blade the woman had Forged. With her dying breath, Iythalene uttered a curse meant to strip the maiden's sword of its power, to make her useless to the man who wanted only her magic, but she was weak and dying, and the curse unspooled from her. It spread to every maiden, to every sword, corrupting their power.

She had roamed the wood ever since, seeking a death she could not find.

"I understand," Miradet said softly and pulled the blade free to its satisfied sigh.

Iythalene collapsed onto her side, her many wounds sprouting suddenly with stalks of green. They grew from her body in vines and flowers, and from her chest came the beginnings of a tree, its roots burrowing into the ground and its trunk rising tall. It stretched yearning branches to the sky, leaves of impossible silver catching the moonlight and throwing it back, illuminating the square.

And her father's horrified face.

The other swordsmen had started to creep closer, the fear in their eyes darkening their faces, but it couldn't hide the envy underneath. They wanted her sword, which thrummed in her hand like a well-tuned instrument, humming a song only she could hear. It was pleased with itself, with the blood slickening its length.

Then something darted before her, letting out a roar so terrible that for an instant, she thought the Shalomar had revived. Even the men cowered back, their swords brandished before them, and for an instant, Miradet saw the shape of a great cat, its fur rippling like the flames of the furnace fire, its eyes the deep burning orange-white of hot steel. And then there was only Smudge, fur raised, fangs bared, daring the men to come any closer.

"A familiar of the goddess," muttered one of the men, as another helped her father to his feet. He leaned heavily on the swordsman who supported him, her mother's blade still clasped in his other hand.

"Mira," he rasped. "What have you done?"

The urge to defend herself rose, but this time, Mira swallowed it back. Some part of her knew they wouldn't believe her, that no matter how many truths she shared, they would still shun her. So it was not them she spoke to, but the faces that had begun to gather at the edge of the square, to the maidens whose swords lay scattered across the earth.

To Davina, she said, "The curse is broken. Your sword is yours now, if you want it."

Then she picked up her sheath and turned on her heel, Smudge trotting beside her, and let the streets of Woodmir swallow her.

The first rays of dawn broke over the wood as Miradet entered it, her sword slung across her back and Smudge at her side. She had packed light, taking only what she could carry. It was a two-day trip through monster-infested woods to the nearest village, but she was not afraid. Not anymore.

Oh, must we go? crooned the blade. *There were so many there who wanted to fight us.*

To steal you, she replied. *To take you from me.*

The sword giggled, an almost childlike sound. *They would come to regret it.*

But they would try, and that was all that mattered. As long as she remained in Woodmir, she would never be safe, her sword a prize to be won in the villagers' eyes. Besides, now that the curse was broken, she was free. Swordmaidens could wield their own blades, and all around her were towns plagued by monsters without a sword to defend them.

We go to the next town, she told the sword. *And then the one after that, until the title of Swordmaiden is no longer spoken in a hushed whisper.*

The sword seemed to delight in that, its pleasure rippling through her. *Oh, yes, yes. Then we will have many new foes to fight.*

Yes, Miradet agreed. *And we will be the greatest among them.*

The sword chuckled. *We will be a god.*

At that, Smudge's eyes glowed brighter.

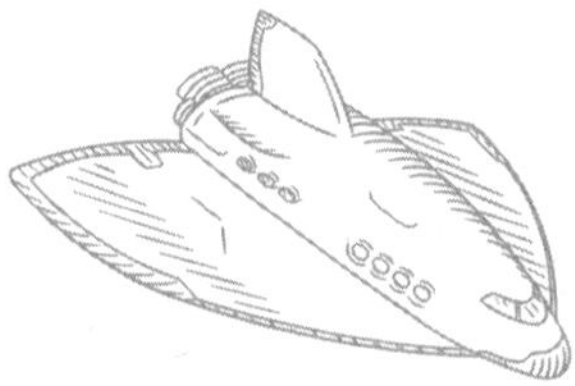

FLYING SOLO

CLAUDIE ARSENEAULT

47 Hours Before Puppet Contact

When Narcisse stepped inside the meeting room and found the nine Visors arranged around the sleek black arc of a table in full regalia, he knew he was in trouble. Everyone else in his year had received their confirmation hearing by now—a final formality before they were allowed to fly into battle against the Puppets—and the longer his turn took to come, the deeper the rumors swelled. Narcisse had told himself they were saving the best for last, that they couldn't afford to reject a pilot of his caliber.

When nine dark-red visors turned toward him, their glossy surfaces catching the bleak light, his unshakable confidence cracked.

Then he noticed the slim circlet placed at the center of the table, a beautiful silver band with matching wrist bracelets, and his heart sank into his heels. The Pairing Simulator. He had to resist the urge to run. He was not a child, and he was tired of being treated like one.

"Young Narcisse," said the rightmost Visor, and the foreboding hiss of the voice modulator reminded him of an airlock opening into space, heralding his doom. "You've never worn one of those, have you?"

Narcisse gritted his teeth. Ever since he had been forced into that first Paired training flight, he had done everything he could to avoid a repeat experience. The sense of another sharing his mind had made him nauseous—a full-body revulsion that had almost made them crash into the trainees on his left. Narcisse had slammed the control to disengage Pairing and liberated his Wing from his teammate, and as his ship righted itself, the side wing becoming a top fin once more, the awful sensation of shock crawling over his skin had subsided.

He never wanted to Pair again, but Wings were two halves of a spacecraft that clamped together and enhanced each other. Precision, fluidity, stability: They all increased when two Wings connected. Narcisse didn't *need* the enhancements, though. He flew his solo Wing better than every single Pair from his cohort.

Unfortunately, their Wings were designed to function better when Paired in more crucial ways. Pairing heightened the intensity of the fin's sharp edge—the ripper—and let it cut through the Puppets' seams faster, and it enhanced the filtration systems essential to survive the release of toxins whenever a squad opened a Puppet.

Before the Pairs, pilots lasted four or five encounters before they could no longer fly, and the toxins left them disabled for life.

Now they could launch on almost fifty battles before they needed to cede their Wing to a younger pilot, and the long-term effects were minor. Most went on to fly Needles, the ships capable of creating subspace pockets through which the Great Quilt could escape the Puppets. The generation ship, pieced together from countless vessels ages ago, had been traveling space like this for centuries.

But Needles required Pairing too. Everything designed to fly out to space and protect the Great Quilt needed a Pair. A weight pressed down on Narcisse's shoulders as he contemplated the presence of the Pairing Simulator at his confirmation hearing, like his crumbling future had a gravity of its own.

"No, Visors," Narcisse said.

"Why not?"

The question came from the second Visor on the left, their voice softer through the modulator, inquisitive. For an instant, Narcisse considered explaining again how sick the Pairing made him feel, but roiling bitterness extinguished the thought. Everyone had dismissed him before. They said he exaggerated, that he would get used to it, that he only needed to find the right partner—and wasn't that what the Simulator was for? It would Pair Narcisse with every single person in its database until it narrowed options down to a few of the best matches. Torture, as far as he was concerned—and pointless.

"I fly better solo," he said.

"Unsurprising, since you refuse to practice as a Pair," one of the Visors pointed out.

At least he was ready for this one. "Records of my training will show that Pairing always hinders my performance, whether in space or in simulation."

He articulated each word as calmly as he could, burying his fear under layers of practiced cool. The last thing he wanted was for the Visors' Council to treat him like a—

"Child," the central Visor said, and Narcisse cringed. "Without a Pair, you will die. We lose enough of our brightest youth in battle against the Puppets; we will not make it a certainty."

"Either you Pair, or you stop flying," another added with a gesture toward the Simulator that was far too casual for the condemnation they had just enacted.

Narcisse stared at the band waiting triumphantly in the middle of the table's arc, its metal reflecting the pale ambient light. The kaleidoscope of invasive links terrified him, and a cold sweat trickled down his nape at the very thought of wearing it. He did not understand why his cohort peers had all been so eager to shove the cursed thing on their heads—not until he'd caught two of them taking bets on who would be the lucky pilot to Pair with him. Narcisse might fly better solo, but his skills were so far ahead of everyone else's, they all hoped to benefit from proximity. They didn't care that he hated every second of the Pairing.

The Visors didn't either. They were ready to throw away their best pilot because he couldn't stand to Pair.

Narcisse stared at the Simulator, his heart so far up his throat, he expected to be sick. He felt hot, and cold, and like black tendrils were extending at the edge of his vision, darkening it until there was nothing left but him and the silver band.

He wanted to fly.

But he wanted to fly solo.

"I can't," he said, but the words emerged garbled, survival instincts trying to pull them back before they could make it through the hatch.

The central Visor's head tilted up, and even with the red-tinted glass masking most of their expression, Narcisse *felt* the raised brow. Condescension radiated off all nine of them, and it hardened his resolve.

"I will not Pair," he said again. "I know what I want—I know what's best for me. Please, let me fly solo!"

"Arrogant, selfish child. Thousands of pilots have flown before you, and all have Paired. It is how the Wings are designed; it is what the Great Quilt needs to survive. You refuse to bond with even one other person? How is your squadron to trust you? Bah!" They swept their arm through the air before slapping their palm down on the table. "You're grounded."

The eight other Visors nodded, some with force, others with hesitation.

Grounded.

Narcisse's ears rang from the finality of it, but before he could shake himself out of the torpor, the comm badges of all nine Visors beeped in a chorus of alarms. Their bodies tensed, and as a few reached for the badges, the central one gestured toward the door for Narcisse.

"Your hearing is over," they said.

And it would be his last. Grounded. The word echoed in his mind. Narcisse swallowed hard and forced himself to turn heel. He had reached the door when the Visors patched their call through, and it slid closed behind him as a terrified voice reported:

"Visors, we have three approaching Puppets. Contact in forty-seven hours."

32 Hours Before Puppet Contact

Narcisse hadn't slept all night.

No alarms had sounded yet, but his squad's quarter was buzzing with rumors. They had all been called to an early, impromptu, mandatory training session—no doubt to tell them their first real battle against the Puppets was coming. Except they wouldn't face one, as was typical, or two, which had almost destroyed the Great Quilt four decades ago, but *three* of them.

Impossible odds, even with all hands on deck. No wonder everyone in the squadron had received the call.

Everyone but Narcisse.

When the others' wrists had beeped and buzzed, his had remained silent. Grounded, despite such dire odds.

Narcisse had thought it had gone unnoticed, but as the newly minted pilots streamed out of the dorms, one stayed behind.

Echo was a tall and thick girl, different from him in almost every way: muscular where he was thin, brown-skinned where he was paler than the stars, a poor pilot where he excelled. Okay. That wasn't fair. She wasn't *poor;* she was only ordinary, an average flyer in every respect, and she seemed content to stay that way, which irritated him more than the lack of skill itself. Even now, on her way to the hangar for their ultimate training session, she'd chosen her engineer frock over the form-fitting pilot suit.

She stared at him, silent—normal for Echo. Her verbal communications were limited to the occasional repeated words, but she spoke the Great Quilt's sign language faster than anyone else.

<You're still in bed.>

"How perceptive." He half-signed his answer as he voiced it, too lethargic for more. He should've dressed and gone to the training sims, at least, but what would be the point? They had grounded him.

<They won't let you fly solo, then.>

Bitter anger flared through Narcisse. Since the day Echo's Pairing simulation had put Narcisse high on her list of matches, she'd dogged him. She constantly offered help with his Wing, started idle conversations about her latest audio drama obsession, or stared at him from across the hangar and sighed. She had never commented on his insistence to fly solo, but he knew what she wanted. Over the years, Narcisse had refused every invitation, thwarted as many attempts to get them teamed up during training as possible, and hid away in the training simulators more often than not. It had never stopped her entirely, and she had a knack for finding him when he wanted to remain hidden, but at least she'd never formally requested for them to Pair.

She was probably pretty smug about it now.

<Everyone in our cohort has a Pair partner,> she said. <They're calling an old pilot in for me.>

And there it was. Everyone else expected the two of them to be a match. His mother had gone as far as saying he needed to get over himself, that Echo was a perfectly acceptable Pair, and it couldn't be *that* bad if pilots had done it for generations. But how would she know? No one needed to Pair to work in hydroponics.

Narcisse grabbed the edge of his blanket and rolled over, turning his back to her. If he couldn't see her hands, he couldn't see her mockery either. After a few seconds, she sighed and shuffled away.

Off to fly. Off to fight the Puppets.

Narcisse brought his legs to his chest as his throat tightened, and the world pressed down on him.

24 Hours Before Puppet Contact

The Great Quilt's alarms blared.

Everywhere through the massive generation ship, broadcasts would provide citizens with the estimated time of contact and advise everyone to be secured for warp before then. The daily routines would be disrupted for the following two days as the Great Quilt shut down in preparation.

The Puppets' presence distorted time and space into malleable strings, which the Needles knit into a new pocket for the Great Quilt to escape through. Whenever a pursuer got too close, the Quilt sent out two fleets: an attack squadron of Wings to meet the Puppets head-on, keep them busy, and wound them as much as possible; and a squadron of Needles for their escape route. Narcisse had seen images of the old Puppets—generations ago, when they hadn't resewn themselves into amorphous abominations—and he'd always thought the vaguely human shape made them more terrifying. Contact happened every few years and was a cause for nerves, but the Great Quilt always escaped the Puppets.

This wasn't a routine contact, though. Three Puppets. The alarm wouldn't say, to avoid a panic.

Narcisse didn't have the sense to be afraid. It was hard to feel anything but numbed injustice and the lead in his muscles.

The last time they'd had Puppet contact, five years ago, Narcisse and his cohort had been young recruits, children still, and they had helped pilots get ready. He had known, then, that this was what he would dedicate his entire life to.

Over the last few years, he had spent more hours in flight—real or simulated—than he had sleeping. Nothing compared to the pounding of his heart as he slipped between Puppet tentacles, the pivoting world as he spun the Wing, the familiar, slick control spheres under his palms. Everything moving at speed, his instincts attuned to every parcel of information, his reflex honed to perfection. When Narcisse flew, the rest of the world faded. There was nothing but him and his Wing.

He was the best the Great Quilt had to offer, but they would rather risk facing three giant monsters than let him fly solo.

He should have been out there; he had prepared for this his entire life. Without flying, Narcisse didn't know what to do with himself.

If this was the Visors' final decision, perhaps it was just as well for him to die when the Puppet tentacles crushed them all.

7 Hours Before Puppet Contact

Hunger eventually drove Narcisse out of his wallowing. The cafeteria only had to-go paste left, its kitchens closed for the warp, but he shoved the entire tube down his gullet and felt himself revive. *Always put fuel in the tank*, the instructor used to say.

The fuel only ignited his anger.

Nine anonymous adults had decided his fate. They'd tossed him out the airlock like unrecyclable debris because he refused to break himself to fit into their mold. But the Great Quilt couldn't spare him. Everyone said they hadn't seen a pilot like him for decades! And he was supposed to stay grounded while all the other Wings took flight? Absolutely not. Whether the Visors wanted him to or not, Narcisse would fly with the rest of his squadron.

Could he take down one of the three by himself? Even for him, doing the job of a dozen Paired Wings was a tall order. But would any less prove that he was at his best when solo? A good performance wouldn't make the Visors care. He needed to make himself invaluable, to protect the ship where it would have otherwise been destroyed—and if that also made him sick, then so be it. So did flying Paired, and so did staying grounded.

Determination settled in the pit of his stomach alongside his meal, and before setting off, Narcisse slipped into his pilot suit—a second skin for him, more comfortable and familiar than anything else he'd ever worn. He stalked through the empty corridor leading to the Wing hangar. His Wing wouldn't be scheduled for launch, but if he could release the magnetic clamps, he could fly out of the hangar between two others, no problem. He would be out of there and speeding toward the Puppets before anyone could tell him otherwise.

The low klaxon of the alarm echoed through the hangar as he slipped in, muted for this last night before the Puppets' arrival.

In five hours, this place would be swarming with pilots hopping into their Wings, giving their controls one final check before they flew out of the hangar for battle. With his entire class now qualified, every single Wing would be flying out.

His included, if all went according to plan.

Narcisse slid past a stack of large fuel crates, eager to set eyes on the sleek form of his Wing. Instead, he found Echo crawling into the bowels of his spacecraft, its side panels wide open. Fear and fury sparked inside of him, burning his circuits until he could only stare at her as she worked. Why was she here? In his Wing? It wasn't even supposed to fly again!

A sizzle and a curse drew him out of his daze.

"What—hey, get out of my Wing!"

Echo startled and crawled back out. Strands of brown hair escaped from her tie every which way, giving her a wild look as she leaned on the ship with a grin and launched into rapid signing.

<And here you are. You're so predictable, Narcisse. I knew you wouldn't let them ground you. They should have too. It's a wonder there's not a whole guard squad waiting here to arrest you.>

Narcisse's hands clenched. Secrecy and surprise were the only weapons he had left, and she could ruin it all. Would ruin it all. And she'd come here to gloat?

"Call them, then," he spat, the high pitch of his voice echoing in the otherwise silent hangar. He hated how scared he sounded.

Echo rolled her eyes. <How is *this* a better plan than telling the Visors that you'll Pair with me?> She tapped her chest with emphasis, anger sharpening each of her movements.

"I don't want to Pair with you," he stated.

<Yeah, don't worry, I got that message loud and clear years ago.>

They stood fifty feet apart from each other, glaring across the hangar's expanse. Narcisse wished Echo would simply disappear, that he didn't have to deal with her right now. He only wanted to hop into his Wing and fly. That was all he was good for, and all he had ever asked for. At a loss for words to convince her, he tilted his chin up and strode with utmost confidence toward his Wing. Perhaps if he acted as if she wasn't there, she'd make herself scarce.

Echo's shoulders drooped as he passed her. <I don't understand.>

He barely caught the signs at the edge of his vision and was considering pretending he hadn't when she tapped his arm, forcing his attention.

<Stop being so prideful. You don't need to prove to anyone you're the best. We all know; we've always known. You're going to kill yourself over it.>

"Of course you think this is about pride."

He made to turn away from her, but she grabbed his shoulder with one hand and signed a furious <What *else*?> with the other.

Narcisse's head swam with frustration. What was the point of saying it out loud? His trainers had promised he'd get used to the Pairing, his parents had told him to drop the tantrums and become an adult, and the Visors had said he had no choice but to Pair if he wanted to fly. No one believed him. They all thought he was being ridiculous.

"I don't want to be Paired," he said through gritted teeth.

<You could at least tell me what I did.>

Narcisse stared at the frustrated crease of her brow, confusion spreading through him. This wasn't about her. "Aren't you here to stop me? You were literally tampering with my Wing."

<Not *that,*> she signed with a frustrated huff. <In general. I could never figure out why you hated me.>

"I don't." Well, right now he did, a little. She *was* in his way. "Except when you're ruining my day, like now. If you're going to tell the Visors what I mean to do, just get it over with."

<I came to help.>

"Help," he repeated, freezing with his hand over the command to open his Wing.

"Help," she echoed, a rare sound from her. She tapped the open panels. <I was "tampering" with your filtration system. I knew you'd try to fly solo, so I figured I'd fix it to work better unpaired.>

"That's . . . possible?"

Her face fell, doubts encroaching on her prideful smile. <Well, it's never been tested, but I think it is. I've been studying the schematics.>

The rush of emotions slamming through Narcisse left him stunned, unable to parse fully between the surprise, the gratefulness, the doubts. "No one ever offered that," he said, his tone so sharp it could have sliced a Puppet's stitch.

<Well, I am. I can undo it, if you want to go kill yourself faster.>

As soon as her hand moved toward the wrench at her belt, he grabbed it. "No, no!"

She snatched her wrist out of his grasp and stepped back. <Then I think *thank you* is what you meant to say.>

"Is there anything else you can do? I want to destroy one of those Puppets by myself, but it'll be a challenge even for me."

Echo scowled. <You can't take down a whole Puppet on your own. The toxins . . . > Her hand fell slowly as she trailed off. <My modification isn't a miracle. It's a tweak, an upgrade. Without the Pairing—>

"I don't want to Pair. Not today, and not ever!"

<I can't believe you'd rather poison yourself than work with someone else.>

Deep disappointment marked her movements, and every one of them felt like a stitch tightening in his stomach. In the stillness of the hangar, he stared at the first person who had ever tried to make solo flight possible for him, and he let burgeoning hope pierce through years of dismissal.

"I would rather poison myself than be *Paired.* That's not the same. The process of linking—of having another's mind melded into mine—it makes me sick. It feels a thousand times worse than the toxins. Like something is crawling on my skin and through my heart. How am I supposed to fly in those conditions? Why would anyone endure that every day?"

Echo stared at him, and more than once her hands moved to sign, only to drop down again, her thoughts incomplete. He reined back the temptation to go on. He'd said too much, way too much, and when had that ever turned out well for him? The others already sneered behind his back, called him cold and arrogant when they thought he couldn't hear, but they at least talked to him and praised his skills. If they understood how he loathed the Pairing—how unfit for it he was—they might never accept him again, even in pretense.

Narcisse *liked* being around people. He wanted to fly alone, not *be* alone, but some days it felt impossible to have both.

<I didn't know it was that bad,> Echo said eventually.

She . . . believed him? A hot flash of hope dizzied him, and he leaned against his Wing for support. Echo hadn't questioned or dismissed him at all. Relief washed through him, leaving him empty, and he squeezed his eyes shut as he struggled with it. Echo set a hand on his shoulder, bringing him back.

<I don't want to Pair with you if you don't want it.>

Narcisse's ears buzzed from her words. *Everyone* wanted to Pair with him, Echo most of all. He had woven that truth through his entire life and acted accordingly, making himself inaccessible. But she didn't sound like she was lying, and if she believed him, shouldn't he offer her the same, at least?

"All those invitations . . ."

<Pairing is supposed to work off compatible personalities. I thought we might make good friends.> She shrugged as if her words hadn't sewn a pocket to a whole new universe, and then she squeezed his shoulder. <Don't die out there, Narcisse. I can't fix an entire Wing overnight, but with more time to study and tests, we might find other ways to make a single Wing better. No matter what the Visors think, generations of Pairing doesn't mean it's the only way to survive.>

"They won't let you try." His throat was dry, his voice a raw whisper. "They wouldn't listen to me."

<You came here to prove them wrong,> she pointed out, <so hop on. I'll get this fixed up and tamper with your magnetic clamps. I'm set to be number twelve out of the gate, and I'll leave room for you to slip out when I launch. Oh, and one of the three Puppets *is* lagging behind, and we've been ordered to focus fire on the first

two . . . in case you want to zoom past them and get an early start.>

Narcisse gripped her upper arm and squeezed it, his words failing him in sign and speech alike. Echo seemed to understand, and she returned the gesture with a solemn nod before crouching once more into the bowels of his Wing.

Puppet Contact

After the fifth ping from Command, Narcisse had had enough of their reprimands. Every message so far had amounted to an order to fly back and face the consequences, but from the moment he'd settled in his Wing, helmet and gas mask on, he had known this was the right decision.

"Command, this is Pilot Narcisse. I will dock once this third Puppet is taken care of. Now let me work. Over."

He shut down his comms and reveled in the silence of his Wing. It wouldn't last—once he approached the Puppet, all his sensors and alarms would beep at him, demanding attention—but for a moment, he could pretend it was only him and deep space.

Him, a full squadron, and three Puppets.

Their massive forms loomed in the distance, blotting out the stars, an elongated mass of toxic gas held by a thick, flesh-like, purplish fabric with a scattering of flat, solid "eyes" in positions that varied from one Puppet to another. Nonsensical tentacles protruded from their bodies—some were enormous arms that could crush the Great Quilt, others smaller appendages. Each one was covered in cilia-like structures meant to defend the seams.

Made from a thin, stretchable material, the seams were the Puppets' only external weakness and could be sliced by the Wing's ripper, a thin band that emitted vibrations at a perfectly calculated frequency to tear the fabric. Or something like it. Narcisse had never cared for the details. The seams glowed a sickly green through Narcisse's visor, easily distinguished from the main body. Once enough had been ripped apart, the gas pushed out and exposed the vulnerable organ inside to the Great Quilt's main weapons.

It was time.

Narcisse split from the main squadron, gliding upward as the Wings began drifting closer to one another, each finding its matching Pair to augment filtration and ripping capabilities. Echo's ship made a full spin on itself before it settled on its side, in position for Pairing, and the in-flight salute sent a burst of warmth through him. He pushed his ship through a tight loop in response, then he engaged the thrusters fully, dipping down to pass under the first two Puppets that his squad would soon be battling.

A large tentacle swept through space as he flew closer, forcing him to dive and twist—and then he was on the other side, the pair of malformed gas bags behind him and a single Puppet in front. Just the one, no big deal—never mind that any one of these things could destroy the Great Quilt.

Narcisse locked his nerves in a tiny corner of his mind. He could do this—and he would rather die trying than accept the Visors' decision. With Echo's mods to the filtration system, though, he might never have to. He was the best, and he would take down this Puppet on his own and live to tell the tale.

His confidence surging, Narcisse pushed his Wing forward.

Squadrons of Wings split the assault between decoys and rippers, some distracting the Puppets and drawing firepower while others flew in close and sliced their ripper through the seams. There would be no decoys for Narcisse, but he had no intention of submitting himself to the full brunt of the Puppet's defenses.

Every one of these monsters had different configurations, and Narcisse scanned his target's as he approached. The large tentacles formed a strange crown over it, with two toward the bottom. Despite the appealing crisscross of seams near the top, Narcisse knew the Puppet's defenses would be denser there. He tilted downward, hoping he'd have an easier time with the lengthy seam running along the bottom tentacles.

Between one second and the next, the chaos started. Cilia extended off the tentacle at his approach, releasing bursts of energy—flat waves from the small, short ones, and beams from the elongated ones. His consoles beeped with a dozen alerts, but Narcisse had long since mastered the art of filtering out the superfluous. He focused on the beams, tilting and spinning his slim ship to avoid direct hits, and rode the waves at the proper angle, gritting his teeth as they shook the Wings with their force, but never slowing down. The Wing sped along the massive tentacle, weaving and dodging as best as it could and allowing the shields to tank the rest as he brought himself over the seam.

Up close, the bump of stretchy material rose over the surface, a hill he'd need to cut through. If he flew in too quick, its resistance would tear his ripper apart—and with it, the entire ship's balance. Slowing down turned him into an easy target, however, and there was only so much his shields could take, especially as an unpaired craft. But this was what he had trained to do every day, the very technique he had perfected. He accelerated until he'd almost smashed the Wing into the seam, then slammed the brakes, activated the ripper's vibration, and tilted it into the tissue.

The cockpit rattled with the strain coursing through the ship's hull, and his shields screamed with every new hit, the lights inside flickering. Narcisse held steady, slicing the fabric until the shields had almost completely discharged. He slid himself out, banked away, and pushed his thrusters to the max, zooming out from the thick of the danger.

In a squad, Paired Wings cycled in and out relentlessly, each half taking turns to slice through with their ripper. It was fast and deadly, and they could open several seams at a good pace, unraveling the front of the Puppet. Narcisse needed time for his shields to recharge between every pass, and he expected to take as long cutting one or two stitches as a squad needed to split the length of an entire seam.

It didn't matter. One or two was enough, and Narcisse knew when to bide his time and when to risk it all.

He cycled back and forth, and with each pass, the stitch unravelled farther—but so did his shields. Every time he darted away from the stitch to recover, they restored less of the power. If he dove in like this, they'd crumble the next time he sustained fire. He shut down secondary sensors, lowered the automatic flight dampeners, and removed a dozen superfluous elements of the interface overlays, redirecting every sliver of power to the shields before looping. Part of him itched to wait longer before diving in, but one of the Puppet's long tentacles was wrapping around, eager to come help squash this bug harassing its lower sphere. Once it was within range to add its own surface cilia to the assault, no amount of shield power would save Narcisse. Whatever he had now would have to do.

He plunged in again, zipping through waves of force and focused beams, his line as direct toward the stitch as he could make it while dodging. One last time, he shut down thrusters and reversed impulse, slowing the Wing into a steady course, slipping the vibrating ripper through the seam's fabric. The emergency light flickered as his shields blared, and he whispered a soft "Come on, we've got this" to his poor Wing. On his console, the estimated distance left to cut plummeted, and his heart swelled as the number went from three digits to two, then hit a big zero.

The resistance on his ripper vanished, and he burst forward.

Narcisse pulled up and away as a puff of yellow-green smoke spewed out of the opened hole, clinging to his spacecraft and slipping inside. Echo's ship-wide filter caught most of it, and the extra gas mask over his mouth caught the rest—for now. Narcisse tried to enjoy the last few clean breaths he would get as he brought his Wing into a tight turn, bringing himself perfectly perpendicular to the small hole he had just created.

A single broken stitch leaking toxic smoke, a tiny opening into the giant Puppet. Barely enough for a solo Wing to fly through.

Not even Paired filters could sustain the full brunt of the Puppet's inside gas for long. Narcisse prayed Echo was an even better tinkerer than she knew, and then he pushed his ship's thrusters to full power for one final plunge.

In but a second, he crossed the threshold of the sliced seam.

The world shifted from open space, grotesque purple skin-flesh, and flashing energy beams to an endless cloud of yellow-green.

Every alarm blared as Narcisse flew within the Puppet, bringing his Wing in an upward curve toward the heart of the sphere. His overlay was nothing but static, forcing him to shut it down and rely on proximity sensors and the Wing's thin viewport to gauge his position. Toxins filtered into the Wing and through his mask, and an itching, burning sensation grew at the back of his throat with every new breath. Narcisse shut down his shields entirely, redirecting the power to thrusters and filtration before pushing his engine even further.

Flying through the cloud of toxic gas felt both faster and slower than anything else he'd ever done. Particles slid from the viewport at incredible speed, vanishing instantly, yet nothing else seemed to change. He had lost track of the outside skin and flew toward the theoretical organs only on instinct, hoping his little Wing could carry him fast enough to beat the growing burn in his lungs and the cramp of his muscles. Despite the filters' best efforts, the toxins ravaged his body. Pain flared through it with every breath. He could barely focus on the piloting.

Then suddenly it was there: the heart—a juicy, bulbous sack of thin, translucid skin.

Vulnerable.

Light-headed, his own heartbeat a distant sensation through the haze of pain, Narcisse swooped close to the organ, ignited the ripper once again, and plunged it in with a quick spin.

The tear reverberated through the Wing's hull, a shock wave

of groaning plates immediately followed by a blaring heat alarm. Narcisse stared at it, then at the red all over the Wing's fin, on the console's schematics. He blinked. That was bad. Had he lost the tip of his Wing to whatever had been in there? Was it splashing? He needed to focus, but his lungs were on fire, and his mind had slowed to a crawl. He was slipping, his body shutting down from the toxins. He had to get out, had to find the open seam.

Narcisse flew away from the heart, blinking hard to chase the slinking darkness at the edges of his vision. Strange currents pushed at his craft, the gas shifting in waves that he did his best to ride. The visor's interface flickered in and out, and when he tried to turn the seam highlight back on, it beeped an error at him.

So much for that, he thought, before a powerful cough wracked him from head to toe, and the world blurred as consciousness slipped away, escaping through the seams of his mind.

Narcisse blinked, unsure how long he'd lost consciousness. Seconds, maybe? Any longer, and he might not have come back.

The fleshy inside of the Puppet's skin loomed over him. It rippled in erratic movements, creating the unstable waves through the gas. Was it . . . thrashing? Grim satisfaction spread through Narcisse. Even if this made escape harder, the seams constantly shifting, he at least had proof he had stabbed the monster where it hurt.

He pushed his Wing downward until he crashed into the wobbling skin, flying alongside it, hoping to find an escape route. The burn in his lungs had spread to his skin, too, and his coughs had taken on a wet, dangerous sound.

Idly, he wondered if he would have even reached the central organ without Echo's filters.

A current slammed into the side of his Wing, spinning it. Narcisse clenched the controls, struggling to right himself and bring the Wing in line with the current. The hull groaned and creaked, and there was a low scraping that sent a shudder down his spine. What could be doing that? Was the toxin corroding pieces? No one had flown inside the clouds long enough to properly examine its impact on the Wings. The thoughts occupied his mind, a perfect escape from the swelling pain and certainty of death closing in. Narcisse let them carry him, just as the strange current carried his Wing.

Then he was in outer space again, green toxins dissipating as they escaped, the transition out as sudden as his entrance into the Puppet.

Five Paired Wings flew into formation around him, their shields protecting him from the brutal return of the cilia assault. Several stitches had been torn apart, creating the opening through which he'd emerged. Narcisse pulled what little strength he had left to turn both shields and comms back online, and sent a wide broadcast.

"Command, this is Pilot Narcisse." Every word hurt, and his voice was a raspy croak. He needed to keep it short. "Heart pierced. Medical . . . needed. Echo . . ."

Narcisse never finished his sentence, as if airing his condition had been enough to worsen it. With a final, horrendous cough, his body gave in, and he lost consciousness.

FLYING SOLO

Three Weeks After Puppet Contact

Inhale.

Exhale.

Narcisse lay in his hospital bed, propped up into a sitting position, the world around reduced to the tiny bubble of himself, his burning lungs, and every painful breath.

Inhale.

Exhale.

He had spent the last few weeks drifting in and out of consciousness, kept alive through an oxygen mask and constant monitoring, but the doctors had judged him stable enough to breathe on his own now. At first, he wasn't sure he agreed, but he had survived his first day.

Inhale. Exhale. It hurt, but it was growing more and more natural.

Echo slipped into his room, still in her engineer frock, her ear pods no doubt playing one of her audio dramas. She'd been in and out a lot, sitting by his bedside either lost in her current episode or sketching in a large notebook. The only time he'd been awake enough to follow a conversation, she had scolded him.

<I didn't bolster your filter so that you could dive inside the Puppet on a suicide mission.>

He'd offered a weak thumbs-up, and she had huffed and stormed off.

Judging by her smile when she noticed him, Narcisse had been forgiven now. Or she was in a better mood.

<You're awake!>

"Tell me," he said, and the words burned his raw throat.

Narcisse squeezed his eyes shut and signed the rest, forcing his weak muscles to go through the motions. <No one will mention the Visors in front of me. All they talk about is my health.>

<You almost died,> she pointed out, before settling in the chair by his side.

Maybe they thought it wouldn't matter whether the Visors might allow him to fly solo, because none of them believed he'd recover enough to pilot a Wing again.

<The Visors are still reviewing your case,> she said. <I showed them my modifications to the filters and have been brainstorming other ideas.> She tapped the top of her notebook, then added, <As I don't have an official Pair partner, they *have* allowed me to stop flying and focus on this. I had to convince them it'd benefit Paired Wings, too, but now I'm collaborating with the chief engineer.>

She grew more animated as she went on, her signs speeding up until he struggled to follow. Narcisse gestured for her to slow down.

<They won't admit it,> she added, <but they were very impressed with you. Everyone was.>

Narcisse squeezed his eyes shut, letting pride and relief wash through him. If it worked—if the Visors let him fly solo—all this pain would be worth it. It didn't matter how long he needed to recover, or how hard the process would be.

And he owed it to Echo, who had ignored years of rudeness to help him.

"Echo," he whispered, before signing as emphatically as he could, <Thank you.>

A ferocious grin spread across her face. <Three weeks late, but I'll forgive you, given the circumstances. Now get some rest because I'm going to need a pilot for all the test runs I intend to put my Solo Wing through.>

<Don't worry,> he signed. <I'll fly again.>

PAPER REBELLIONS

RUKMAN RAGAS

When stories died, they became dragons.

"The achingly perfect person I am won't survive the breaking you are," the fierce flamed dragon told me. His soul used to be a romance novel. He was gentle red in the palm of my hand, scales of weathered pages and bones of titled spines.

I laughed and kissed him on the nose, tasting blood from the paper cut. "You will do more than survive. In fact, you will thrive and keep your story so safe that no knight will wrest it from you."

Taking a step back, he spread his majestic red wings, made of pages and spines that I had stitched together, and flapped twice. He caught a grappling current, floating up with his little wings straining.

"Until we meet again, Iniyan of the stormy peaks. May you keep swimming against the current, and my heart, though it may belong to many, will always be yours first," he bellowed, his voice fading as he took to the sky.

Pulling down the brim of my hat, I watched him anxiously as he flew away from the desolate wasteland around my tower. It was his last flight out of my high tower, and if I had done my job correctly, I would never see my romance dragon again. He would travel wide and far, carrying a hundred banned love stories with all their salaciousness and uncensored boldness. He would go to anyone who wished for a love story, and I, with all my love and half-broken heart, would never wish for romantic love.

"Dramatic little rogues, aren't they?" a voice laced with envy murmured behind me, and I turned to face Lark.

The best way to describe Larkspur the librarian would be an accounting ledger come to life: The buttons on her perfectly ironed shirt were always done up, her hair was tamed into a neat braid over her shoulder, and her horn-rimmed glasses shone like polished medallions. She usually stood with a welcoming smile and a shrewd confidence, teeth bright against her olive skin. For the year that we'd worked together, at least half a dozen dragons and sprites had departed my tower to carry tales all over the world.

But there was a seriousness to her now. Her lips were pursed, almost angry, and her eyes were as sharp as swords. Beside her was Trang, junior librarian, and a striking contrast; wildflower tattoos spilled down her arms onto her hands, and a haphazard scarf was thrown over her shoulders. Something was wrong.

Lark saw my expression. Her jaw flexed. "That will be the last romance dragon to fly out of New Storks for a while," she said.

My skin prickled with trepidation. "What?"

The librarians brought me the books the Brigade wanted gone, and I animated them, making sure they could fly far back to the grand archive, or take stories to people who wanted them. Animation was a fickle art; more books failed to find wings than those that did. Without a constant supply of books from the librarians, there was not a lot I could do.

Trang looked at Lark with alarm. In that moment, I deeply related to the junior librarian, even though I knew little of her beyond her association with Lark.

"Don't tell me we are capitulating?" Trang scoffed.

"There are ways to fight back, Trang," Lark said slowly, as if she were measuring out the words. "Sometimes you have to make concessions."

Trang rushed to her feet. "Give them an inch and they'll take a mile," she snarled.

"Remember the consortium's guiding principles, Trang," Lark said sharply. "We preserve; we don't fight."

They were librarians, but more importantly, my handlers. Archivists, especially those belonging to the animator consortium, were an endangered species these days.

"What does this new development mean for me?" I asked, and their attention snapped toward me.

Lark took a breath, then delicately explained that the Knights Brigade was slowly expanding its influence.

"You must leave New Storks immediately, Iniyan. The city just had its election, and starting tomorrow, the new mayor will enact some new rules about what records I can keep and what the shops can sell. This may be my last shipment for a while."

"I wanted to go north anyway," I said, trying to keep my voice level to not betray the disappointment. From the way Trang winced, I didn't succeed. "I've spent long enough in the tower, and it doesn't make sense to be a sitting duck when they come."

She gave me a relieved smile. "I'll let you know when it's safe to come back. Rules and times pass, but books persist."

"You could come with me," I said, trying to disguise the keen edge of desperation. "We could visit the Londonium ruins, even cross the sea to listen to the storykeepers in the Copper Isles."

There was a stillness to her that I had only seen once before, at her mother's funeral a year ago. She'd leaned against my shoulder as I held her upright. We were both sixteen, and we'd had no one else but ourselves and our chosen vocations. The pyres hungrily tasted her mother's bones, and she had sworn away her name and past.

Since then, our lives had aligned together, our shared paths pushing us into one neat space. She was my best friend and more. Hers was a heart burning, full of passion, an almost-sickness consumed in the infectious flames of romance. And mine was cursed not to burn, though I had always thought we had hit the right balance between us. But all at once, there was a shift, as if an error had come in the books, weighing one side against the other.

"I can't," she said, her voice thick—and for a moment, I saw what I had missed entirely the first time; the way her shoulders hunched inward.

I reached for her, but she stepped back, leaving me clutching empty air.

"Iniyan," she said simply, not even looking at me. She didn't say we should end things, or that my half-broken heart wasn't enough for her. But she didn't need to.

I felt like the wind had left my sails. Heartbreak was a terrible incision, even for hearts like mine (I had always wondered if my heart would ever break, and here was the vicious confirmation, the almost physical rending).

I was only able to say, "Oh."

"It's just not enough, Iniyan," she said. I wondered whether she meant the travels or me, wondered if she had traced the shape of my being and found it wanting.

"Oh, have your lovers' spat in some forgotten corner after I'm gone," Trang hissed. "There are more important things at stake here, Lark. If you send Iniyan away, we are giving up the fight against the incoming regime."

"Part of fighting is knowing when to choose your battles," Lark replied carefully, but I saw through her measured words and could feel her growing annoyance. "I can talk to the mayor, but for that, we must first choose when to fight."

"This is not what I signed up for, Lark."

"Sometimes we have to do difficult things," said Lark. "There are still vulnerable people in the city who need the libraries and our work, and if it means I must do this to serve them when the Brigade comes, then I will do it. This decision is not up for debate, junior librarian Trang."

Trang pulled out a crumpled poster from her pockets. It was garishly painted, calling for the banning of certain titles, and she thrust it at Lark. "Even if it means abandoning them?"

Lark closed her eyes, hiding the sheen of tears. "We have to pick the battles we can win."

"Suit yourself," Trang snapped. But as she turned away, one title on the Church's list caught my eye. My breath hitched as Lark rushed to fill the angry silence left in Trang's wake.

"I've sent word to the consortium, and they should be setting you up in another town. I'll send someone to do the packing. Travel safe."

"I will," I said, hoping she didn't hear the lie. I was not leaving New Storks, not with what I had seen on the page; among the range of books the Church and its Knights Brigade wanted gone, there was also *The Haunting, Uncommon* emblazoned in the center of the flyer.

I didn't doubt the consortium would set me up in another city-state; after the Breaking, old magic went extinct, and even new magic like mine was a rarity. My animator powers would be welcome in another city, one where the consortium faced less pushback than New Storks.

The Church of Everlasting and its Knights Brigade claimed the loss of our magic was a punishment from above, for people loving who they did, for living as they were, without fear of the Creator. But where old magic fled, new magic appeared; with enough intention, braiding, and just a little bit of soul, one could will things to be. Books into dragons, research papers into nighttime wisps, and records into butterflies that flitted and carried their tales toward some great library or to people who needed them, depending on the faction asked. And for a boy without hope, standing at the precipice of the world, a book could be what made the difference in slanting the fall one way or the other. And I would do anything to not see *The Haunting, Uncommon* banned.

RUKMAN RAGAS

The gates of New Storks reared up ahead of me, daunting and ominous. The Church's influence could be seen everywhere; there were rumors that the Museum of Remembrance was under investigation, and the Fourtrees Inn, owned by my aunts, was supposed to have closed temporarily. There was a consignment of knights posted at the gates, one of whom was examining my papers with undue attention. Gooseflesh prickled across my neck as I stood in the rain, waiting for him to finish the inspection.

"Visiting for the mayor's inauguration?" the knight asked, looking me up and down, eyes narrowed with suspicion.

"Y-yes," I said, trying to tamp down the nerves.

In the last few days, I had called upon multiple favors to avoid the series of reassignment letters sent my way—they couldn't claim I was disobeying if I never got them—all for a chance to save *The Haunting, Uncommon*. But none of it would matter if I wasn't allowed into the city to meet its author, Benjamin Flores.

The Haunting, Uncommon by Benjamin Flores told the tale of a runaway trans boy who found refuge in a haunted manor under the care of an elderly musician, and every night, a ghost visited him to teach him to play the keys. It was released to moderate reception, until the Knights Brigade caught wind of its suggestion of a world beyond their preaching—and began their campaign to ban it. The book was not particularly unique in its struggles, but it was one in which I sought my peace several times, for there was such empathy in the pages that even if it didn't mirror me exactly, it found my heart.

The nervous smile I had plastered on began to slip. The guard stared at the paper, then at my face, then at the paper again. "Eh, does anyone in the consignment know how to read Maraic?" he called, before giving up.

"No funny business, boy," he said threateningly. "The Knights Brigade might be new to the city, but we are determined to bring it back to the Everlasting Light."

I nodded vigorously even as blood rushed to my ears.

Past the gate, my unlikely ally waited.

"I wasn't sure you'd come," Trang said by way of greeting. She'd watched my exchange with the knights with a sardonic smile.

"Were you able to locate Benjamin Flores?"

"You always looked so straightlaced and stuck-up," she continued, ignoring my question. "Color me surprised when Lark's sweetheart himself contacted me, not just to disobey her explicit order, but to arrange an illicit animation."

"Lark is not my sweetheart"—not anymore—"and it is not an illicit animation if I get permission from the author," I said sharply, ignoring the fresh pang of heartbreak the words unleashed, even though I entirely despised "sweetheart" as an endearment. "Section 23A of the Archivist Codes for Animat—"

"Save that for when she finds you." Trang waved her hand.

The archivist consortium was divided in these matters, with some believing in preserving knowledge (if asked "For whom?" the old fellows would stick up their ancient brows and say "The future") and others in disseminating it. As an archivist of old novels, I was not held in great regard among either faction, and that was exactly how I liked it. But people still engaged in small rebellions; letters thrown to the wind, banned books smuggled out to a travelling archivist who had the training to animate them.

"Suppose I help you. What do I get out of it?" Trang asked.

"You save a book?" I said incredulously. "Isn't that what you were fighting Lark for?"

She smiled, a wicked flash of teeth. "That's where we differ, young archivist," she said, as if her chicken-boned self was hundreds of years older than me. "I look beyond saving books. I want to make sure that the books find those who need them. If I help you with this, will you animate some other books?"

I stared at Trang, my mouth lifting in a surprised smile. "If you ask nicely," I said, "I just might."

Trang's smile sharpened. "I promise I will remember to say please. Now follow me."

Meeting Benjamin, or *Benji*, as he corrected me, was still an experience I would never forget. He was a gentle man, all bones and soft speech, and he let us into his house as soon as he saw Trang.

"They think it's a badge of honor," Benji said, his reedy voice rising slowly above the din of pattering rain. "That the book being banned is somehow a sign of it being elevated."

Benji, in his exile, had settled into his new city, but his room was filled with paraphernalia from his home. He sat with unrestrained energy.

"They are always so quick to say that, aren't they?" I said, in between sips of the tea Benji had served us, trying to disguise the jittery tremor in my hands. People had such strange perceptions of banned books, possibly limited to the five famous ones they saw in their stores.

"It is an insult." Benji's voice, so carefully controlled, slipped. "They labeled it—labeled me and my life—as obscene. The banning of *The Haunting*, it was not surprising, but it still shocked me. To have evidence of all that hate, and now I hear they even shuttered the press that printed it."

I moved closer, taking his hand in mine. It was papery and liver-spotted. His will, however strong it had been before, wasn't enough to hold onto this world for much longer.

"*The Haunting* will find people who need it," I said, my voice catching just a little bit. "I promise."

He nodded, and just like that, I caught a wisp of his soul, feather-soft and tea-warm, covertly between my fingers.

After Benji drifted off to an uneasy sleep, Trang walked me out. The mayor was enforcing nighttime patrols. Dim gas lamps lit the empty streets, and suddenly the chill caught up to me, winding itself around my limbs and misting my breath. Meeting Benji had left me both excited at the prospect of archiving *The Haunting* as a dragon and exhausted at the state of the world.

"You have everything you need?" she asked.

"Perhaps," I answered. "It is not an exact science, you know. But I have a whisper of his soul, and only time will tell if I can coax *The Haunting* to be a dragon." Well, time, needles, and a lot of luck, but I didn't want to lower Trang's opinion of me any more. And doubt had already crept in; even if all went well, and I could archive *The Haunting*, *Uncommon*, it was one book out of the dozens challenged in New Storks, let alone the hundreds banned across the city-states. What could I and my paltry magic do against the world?

"I don't particularly like people of your profession, archivist. Your order is more concerned with building some old library and preserving things than helping people," said Trang.

"I suppose that's why you are a librarian," I said lightly.

"A rogue librarian," she corrected with a smile. "I'm surprised you asked to meet at all, considering how spineless the consortium is."

I swallowed, trying to hide my discomfort. Technically, making unapproved dragons out of recently banned books didn't violate the consortium's rules, but it did toe the line a little too close for comfort. Archivists had been banished from the consortium for less. A vision flashed before my eyes: being dragged before the council, forced to watch my license burn, and banished to eke out a living among the forgotten. I shuddered at the thought. But *The Haunting, Uncommon* was a book I'd risk it for.

The city hadn't changed in the last few days, but there was an undercurrent of worry. The Memorial Museum of the Great Migration had yellow tape on the front. Anxiety crept through the streets with a slow but steady burn. New Storks, the city I had known, had changed—and not for the better.

She inclined her head. "But I suppose your lot can't be all that bad since you're here. Does Lark know you're taking your time leaving town? Or do you need somewhere to stay?"

"Don't worry about me. I'll figure something out," I dithered. Lark couldn't know I was in New Storks. She'd uncover my intended subterfuge with just one incisive look. I couldn't go to my aunts either; their inn had been closed recently, and they had to enough to worry about without adding my troubles to the mix.

But the junior librarian shook her head.

"C'mon then," Trang said. "I can't let you freeze to death. You have to keep a secret, though. We're heading to the Library of the Banned."

The Library of the Banned was unlike any other library I'd visited; it did not rise up lonesome against the city's skyscape or attach itself like a symbiote to a college or school. It was located past the streets with paving stones, past the city hall where the mayor had held conferences on the importance of making sure that the children did not see certain people existing, and down a quaint little avenue lined with four new saplings.

"Fourtrees?" I exclaimed. Trang narrowed her eyes at me, suddenly suspicious, but the door cracked open before she could say anything.

"Iniyan," Geetha gasped, before whisking me into a hug with a familiar strength. She was like a cloud, welcoming and soft, and thankfully, that had not changed along with New Storks.

"Auntie," I greeted her, still surprised that the center of the operation was my aunts' place. "I'm glad you are doing well."

"As well as I can in these times," she said. "But I'm glad to see you back here."

"I suppose you had no intention of telling me you came back to the city."

I spun in surprise.

Lark, with the might of cardigans and buttoned shirts, stared me down from the house's foyer. She was still, the air between us reverberating with all the hurt we'd sidestepped.

"I meant to," I stammered. It was a lie and she knew it.

"What are you doing here?" Trang intervened. Lark's gaze shifted from me to land on Trang.

"I was here to get my copies of *The Haunting*. Despite the mayor's missteps, my library still needs them."

Trang scoffed. "I'm sure you can find a nice shadowed corner to hide them when your mayor visits."

"At least I didn't abandon my duty," Lark snapped back. "There are rules and good reasons why we obey them. Without the consortium and the mistresses of libraries, we could lose centuries of knowledge."

"If those rules mean picking whose stories are worthy of being kept on the shelves, you can keep your consortium to yourself."

"Children." Geetha's voice was gentle but firm. "There are bigger things to fight than ourselves."

She turned to me sternly. "You are staying for dinner." Then she looked at the girls staring daggers at each other. "In fact, you all are staying for dinner. Mariana, my darling wife, needs help setting the table upstairs. Nothing good comes of fighting on an empty stomach."

She steered us upstairs, past the stacks and towers of banned books that now decorated her floor, to Mariana. Tall and stately, Mariana greeted us with a smile, and without a word, she put the girls to work setting the dining table. I followed Geetha back into the kitchen, grateful to have a moment alone with her.

"When did you get into the business of libraries?" I asked Geetha as I helped her serve stew. I was surprised by it and more than a little hurt that they hadn't told me—but I hadn't been the dutiful nephew, either, with how I'd avoided telling them about my underhanded schemes.

"Well, I didn't particularly plan to get into libraries. But I saw what the city was moving toward with the Everlasting missionaries and the mayor's connections to the Knights Brigade. I was so angry, I wanted to fight back." She laughed. "I'm still angry, but I'm doing something. We're doing something. We've gathered so many books they want gone, Iniyan, and I'm delighted to have you back here."

"I'm surprised you've recruited Lark, though." I waved back at the table where a sullen Lark and Trang were helping my other aunt set the table. Lark was a stickler for rules, and for her to join in the extrajudicial fight against censorship meant things here had gotten much worse than I thought.

"She has her own way of fighting back," Geetha said. "That girl hates breaking rules, but her heart is in the right place. And the good thing about taking action is that you don't have to agree with everyone on everything, Iniyan.

"We fight on every level," she continued, gesturing at the floor below. "Lark brings us the books the mayor asks to be removed, Mari is a member of the association of parents who go up against the challengers weekly, Trang supports people who're affected by the bans, and I gather the contraband goods here, hoping my archivist nephew visits and is willing to animate them. All of us might not see eye to eye on every way we fight back, but the important thing is we are here."

"Of course I'm willing, Geetha. The consortium would not take offense"—I hoped—"if I animated a few books. We'll send some copies to their grand archives too."

She smiled.

"And I'm assuming things have not worked out well with Lark either?"

I sighed. Aunt G was one of the few people I'd told about my particular disposition—a heart that didn't want for romance.

"I couldn't love her the way she wanted me to," I said. "And our relationship never really recovered." I laughed, and every ugly thought I'd suppressed fell out of me. "I feel like I care too much about these friendships when no one else seems to, like these relationships are way stations before they reach their final destination. But I've always treated each and every one of them as destinations. Maybe it's my heart that's broken, Aunt G."

She set down the bowl in her hand and turned to me.

"Come here," she said.

She placed her ear against my chest, listening.

"There," she said, after a bit. "There's nothing broken there. You could do with some regular exercise, though."

I grinned, despite myself.

"But really, Iniyan, there's nothing right or wrong about the way we love people. Some people will say what your aunt and I have is wrong, against the Everlasting or whatever their creed is. But there is no hierarchy to love, nothing that proves one form is worthier than another."

She pulled me into an embrace. I laid my head against her shoulder. Aunt Geetha gave the best hugs, solid and reassuring.

"I don't make false promises of vague futures like 'you'll find someone,' child, but look around you now," she whispered. "You are beloved. I'm sure it doesn't feel enough, especially when you only see us and our love so infrequently. And it is hard to hold your heart in your hand for every friendship, only for it to be trampled. But in all my years, I've seen so many different bonds flare to life, with all kinds of love. And you have to believe me and keep putting your heart out there, keep being vulnerable, because there are people who'll love you with the same ferocity you love them, even if it is not the same kind."

We stayed like that for a moment before Mari called us. We carried the food back to the table. Dinner was a reserved but joyful affair. My aunts were great hosts, and they even managed to get a laugh out of the girls, and just for a moment, it was as if the outside world fell away.

After dinner, Lark gathered her books, thanked my aunts, and marched toward the door. Before she left though, she looked at me, and I could read the warning in her posture.

"Remember, Iniyan, we preserve; we don't fight." *Don't do anything stupid*, she meant.

I nodded. I wasn't sure if what I was about to do was stupid, but I knew it to be right.

The dragon was difficult. Benji, who had become impatient to see the dragon after my fourth trip to his house, commandeered a wheelchair and came back to Fourtrees with me every day. Geetha and Mariana were delighted to have him there, and he sat in the corner, watching me work and offering unsolicited commentary ("Shouldn't the cover be sage-green over sable? The illustration needs to be an inch higher. Would that binding even survive the breeze, let alone the spring storms, boy?").

Imbuing will was difficult business that might take a minute or a day, depending on many things including my skill, the will, and the spell that would wake the dragon. Usually, the book would take form quickly, either as a sprite or a wisp or a dragon. But *The Haunting* refused to become a dragon that would be able to escape the constraints of New Storks. Though other books had refused to become dragons in my hands, they were waiting for the right archivist to tease out their desire. But I couldn't afford to wait for another, not when Benji had so little time. My nails were bitten to the skin, and though I was careful to hide my frustrations from Benji, I could tell he was starting to lose hope.

The time I had before the Knights Brigade began their persecution was limited. Their people were at library board meetings, and from Lark's dispirited reports, they had been successful in challenging many books—specifically, *The Haunting, Uncommon,* not just in New Storks but in several hundred libraries across the city-states.

Mostly, Benji slept. We all knew he didn't have long. I desperately wanted to get his little dragon done, animated, and flying free. Whatever came next, even if my singular magic couldn't protect everyone I loved, small rebellions and small magics must be worth something.

I sat by his bed, watching his chest rise and fall, twirling the bit of his will I had caught. Maybe the reason his dragon refused to come alive was because I was asking it to flee. What if I asked his wisp of soul to fight?

Just then, Trang opened the door, her face white as a sheet.

"The Knights discovered the Library of the Banned. They are coming with a warrant to arrest Benji."

The copy of *The Haunting, Uncommon* on my lap levitated, before it promptly burst into pieces. *Do not scream,* I told myself again and again, even as the clamor outside demanded my attention.

The siege of the library started with protestors and priests of the Everlasting. They stood by the street, holding up signs about the obscenity of Benji's book in particular, and how children should be protected from it. The congregation outside had slowly swelled in number until it was impossible to tune out their calls. Their incessant chanting accompanied almost every moment of our lives inside the library.

There was a knock on the backdoor, followed by Trang sneaking in to find a gloomy convocation.

"What is this, a funeral?" she exclaimed.

Lark shot her a reproachful look, though without much of an effect.

"Might as well be with how they are baying for our blood out there," Geetha said. "I have to say, I'm surprised to see some familiar faces who are protesting the existence of that poor man's book."

"Those are a few loud sparrows," Lark promised, but there was less certainty to her now. "They will be gone soon."

Somehow, I doubted that.

The next day, the crowd had almost doubled. The Knights Brigade, which had slowly started trickling in, now formed a barrier with their shields and armor. I was busy working small spells on the books Geetha wanted out of the library in case the worst were to happen, imbuing papers and tomes with temporary magic, just enough to get them out.

Lark cast a disapproving gaze on me, but the consortium's likes and dislikes could go to hell. My aunts' collection was priceless, and we could not afford to wait for the consortium to approve every little thing, or all I animated would be ash.

Despite our refusal, the Knights started demanding a forced evacuation of the premises. The mayor, a charismatic man with blond hair and a winning smile, came to entreat with the protestors, and suggested that maybe, the books were corrupting the children, and illegal book animators should be caught.

And soon, the Knights were armed with nets and bows to shoot down the paper wisps and book dragons that escaped the library's chimney.

"How are you planning on legally fighting back now?" Trang said.

"A lot of good that you both have done," Lark replied, before turning to me. "You should have stayed away, Iniyan." Her words were half pleading and half accusatory. As if this was my fault.

But the hurt choked me; I had not the words or strength to defend myself.

"You don't own him, Lark," Trang interrupted. "And don't talk to him like that, not after what you did."

"After what I did?" Lark barked out a laugh—cold and hurt. "I was the one left unsure if he had ever loved me. If he felt for me as much as I felt for him. Don't you dare judge me, Trang. All I tried to do was what was best for both of us."

"You assumed it," I burst out. "You assumed that because I don't care for you romantically, I didn't care for you at all. You assumed I don't have a heart because it is not like yours."

"Children." There was a note of warning in Geetha's voice, even as Mariana laid a hand on her wife's shoulder.

Lark looked stricken, and the world became blurry as a film of tears lined my eyes. My heart thundered, and I could hear its every labored beat. I was supposed to have the right words for Lark, not the wrong ones that made her cry. I should have made a dragon that could actually fly. There were no words to comfort Lark, no dragon for Benji, and nothing at all for me.

A sudden warmth filled my hand. I looked over. Trang held my hand in hers, fingers threaded through mine. She felt solid, even though the world felt so lonely and dark.

"You have a habit of making singular decisions in supposedly dual partnerships," Trang said to Lark.

Lark made her way to us, now hunched and small. She was crying, I was crying, and even Trang had a misty look in her eyes. "I'm sorry," she whispered. "I was afraid, and hurt, and I acted too quickly to think. I'm sorry for that."

I nodded, not trusting myself to speak.

"I suppose I should say sorry as well," Trang said. "For going off on you. I don't apologize for being right, though."

We all laughed at that, and my aunts came around to give us all a group hug.

"We will get through this," Geetha promised. There was uncertainty in her tone, as if she was not sure of the truth.

Benji read to us that night, his voice calming and quiet as he painted the vivid picture of escape and discovery. I thumbed through my copy of *The Haunting*. Immense shame ran through me when I realized that even if I animated *The Haunting* now, the crowd outside would catch the book dragon and imprison it, maybe even throw it to the flames.

Benji tousled my hair. "You tried your best, kid. Maybe this is the end for *The Haunting*, but I'm sure there will be some copies that survive. I've had a good life, and while I've regretted many things, *The Haunting, Uncommon* is not one of them. And meeting you, in these final days, has been an unexpected delight for this old man. Death is not the end; they threaten our books and paper dragons, but when I go, I will rise above the ceilings, above the cities, and above their hate. I will watch over you."

Had I tried my best, though? The consortium was clear on what it would do to archivists who used their power to fight. They would drag me in front of the council, disgrace me, and throw me out, without an affiliation or access to a system. But the image of him rising above stayed with me. So what if the consortium threw me out? What if I dared to do it anyway?

I knelt, almost a genuflection, meeting Benji's watery eyes.

"Benji," I whispered, "how would you like to be a dragon?"

The next part of the story, well, there were a dozen different versions if you asked around for it. Some said the dragon descended from above and spewed flames at the knights. Or that it ate a couple of them for dinner and used their armor as toothpicks. My personal favorite was that the dragon was actually a troupe of interpretative dancers hired by the opposing city-state to trick the Knights Brigade. If you asked me, though, I'd tell you this: The grand library of New Storks suddenly rose up, unfurling itself from coils of books, like an old man stretching his limbs after a very long time. The library dragon lifted itself up, unsteadily at first but limber as it got used to its new body, and roared at the Knights Brigade, who had broken ranks in face of the library coming literally alive. I would tell you that it had winked at the city, and that we had tears in our eyes as we held his other body.

He chased them across the city, rallying people through the boroughs. The Knights, now joined by the Everlasting's missionaries, tried their best to outrun the nascent dragon of books. The people, emboldened by the display, rallied behind the librarians and joined in on chasing the Knights.

That was the end of the Knights' presence in New Storks, and soon after, the people elected a new mayor, as the dragon had threatened to eat the one they had. Benji was ecstatic to be his beloved book's spirit, and when he passed, it was peaceful. While I had no idea where Benji's spirit and soul went, his iron will and that of *The Haunting* was very much alive in the book dragon, who—true to his spirit—spent most of his time sleeping.

The consortium kicked me out soon after, but the fight went on. We still had book challenges to face. I animated as many papers as I could, not in the service of some grand archive, but to make sure that the books reached the people who needed them. Together, we all swore that we'd keep the fight going at every level, for every person who was censored, erased, and banned.

We buried Benji on the hill overlooking the city. And when I went to visit him, weeks after the taking back of the city, Trang was sitting by the plot, legs contorted into some impossible shape, with a book in hand.

"Didn't fancy seeing you here," she said.

"I missed him," I said, forlornly looking at his grave. I missed his steady presence, reedy voice, the smell of powder and lavender, and even his crotchety comments on bindings and paper selections. You never notice just how much space someone takes up in your life until they are gone.

She patted the grass beside her as we watched the sun set over New Storks. I collapsed ungainly onto it. After weeks of working together, we'd graduated to an understanding silence. Neither of us were much good with words, but we were good at sitting alone together.

"It's not over, is it?" she said. There was such sorrow in her words, and I wished I had another answer.

"Nope. The consortium will probably pull out of the city, the Knights may regroup and return, and a thousand other things could go wrong."

"True. But a thousand other things could go right."

"Suddenly the optimist," I quipped. "The work never ends. There are always books to save."

"Work never ends." She got up, dusted off the dirt, and looked at me, before handing me the book in her hand. "But I'm glad to be doing it with you."

DO YOU SEE ME?

ISA FIEL

Breathing in the night air, Yoli could almost forget she was supposed to die tonight.

She plucked the guitar strings as she perched on the porch's weathered futon. Every few notes, she shifted her fingers so that the song would be just a half-step off. As the tightening of her chest grew unbearable, she nearly tore the strings strumming to a new key, ignoring the phone she'd turned off and tossed beside her. No matter—Amá's messages were burned into her memory.

>hija cántale mejor por favor

>i prefer you alive even if you are unhappy than dead to make a point

Yoli stopped at the end of the musical phrase, staring at the hazy sun dipping behind the horizon. It was quiet here, different than the sounds of small-town traffic and nosy neighbors back home. Just the wind whispering through branches, birds chirping, and the cozy creaking of wood from the cabin. The perfect place for an escape.

Yoli sighed. Her friends had whispered excitedly to her to wait outside while they prepped whatever it was they'd brought, and she'd taken the respite to practice, letting the music wash over her like a cool waterfall. At least, that was the goal.

A haunting call, beyond her view of the darkening forest, echoed. Too heavy and mournful to belong to a bird. Her blood chilled at the sound.

"Why aren't you wearing your splint?"

Yoli whirled around as Kiana slipped out onto the porch, looking pointedly at the guitar in Yoli's hands. Her partner had already traded her day clothes for silk polka-dot pajama pants and her favorite Stitch crop, curls tucked beneath her pink-and-orange bonnet. She'd tossed Yoli's green flannel over her shoulders like a blanket.

The tightness in Yoli's chest loosened enough for her to give an amused huff through her nose. "Aren't we supposed to live on the edge?" Kiana frowned, and Yoli immediately knew what she was thinking. *Your wrist never healed right,* the doctors had told her. *You need rest, or the tendonitis will only get worse if you keep playing.* The thing was, Yoli couldn't bring herself to care about it tonight.

They stared at each other before Kiana sighed. "You haven't told them yet, have you?"

Yoli looked away. "I'm not going to. Not yet. After."

"After?" Kiana asked incredulously as she sat down next to her. "Yoli, that accident wasn't a coincidence; mule deer don't just—"

Yoli resisted touching her bruised cheekbone, stealing a glance at Kiana's matching one from when they'd collided in the car. "Maybe it was rutting."

"In summer?"

"What do you want me to tell them?" she responded. "'Thanks for coming to celebrate my eighteenth. Don't worry about the family curse trying to kill me; you should be fine?'"

Kiana was quiet for a moment. "Your mom survived . . ."

"But at what cost?" Yoli grabbed Kiana's hand because she couldn't let her bitter words do all the talking. "She sang to it to stay alive, but she's not happy. Not really, not anymore." And Yoli couldn't do that to Kiana, who had plans and dreams for the future with her. Not when Yoli's life had become dead weight the moment she was born.

"I don't care," said Kiana, as if reading her mind. She reached out and laid a hand on Yoli's cheek, fingertips brushing the earrings Kiana had gifted her that morning, her thumb running over the bruise under Yoli's eye. "Stop worrying about holding me back—I saw that look—and think about what's best for you."

"I am," Yoli huffed. She gestured to the forest around them: to the cabin where Raúl and Leah were setting up, then back at Kiana. "I'm being as selfish as I can with all of you tonight."

Never mind the deer incident. Never mind the salt Yoli had feverishly thrown around the cabin when they'd gotten there. Never mind the candles lit inside or the chains slithering around her chest. She was here, in the middle of nowhere, with the people she cared about most in the world. There was no way the curse would travel this far to find her tonight.

Just one more night. That's all she needed.

Kiana pursed her lips, and Yoli leaned over to kiss her, an attempt to offer comfort, when a screech tore through the air: shrill and guttural at the same time. Kiana startled, while Yoli stiffened. The screech faded into something that resembled sobbing, but the shock of it reverberated in her bones.

Kiana swore under her breath, and her fingers curled around Yoli's arm. "Yoli, I don't know what you're planning, but please don't tell me that you're going to face that thing alone."

That shook her out of it.

"I'll be fine, Ki." Yoli started packing her guitar into its leather case. "My birthday's almost over, and the curse hasn't got me yet. It won't attack with all of you here." Shouldn't, at least. Family curse and all. She ought to have said something else, something to draw Kiana's mind away from this conversation, no matter how awkward, but the words stuck in her throat.

"They still deserve to know," Kiana whispered. "You know they care about you just as much as I do. I don't know why you're so adamant about keeping this to yourself and not letting any of us help—"

"Because it's my burden, Ki." Yoli swallowed down the lump in her throat. "My curse, my responsibility." Her chance to prove that living and being happy weren't mutually exclusive. "If something goes wrong, I don't want you guys getting hurt trying to help."

"And what if you die?" Kiana studied Yoli with a watery gaze.

Maldita sea, Yoli couldn't meet her eyes. "I'll tell them," she said. "I promise, just . . . not now." Not when the faint sobbing had tapered off to a too-familiar song, and the chill had spread to her limbs and her now-throbbing wrist.

"Okay," Kiana said tonelessly. "Okay." Yoli's insides curled, wanting to take it all back, but Kiana stood up, adjusting the flannel on her shoulders. "The others are waiting. Let's go inside, yeah?"

The sun dipped behind the trees. The wind grew stronger. The tightness encircled Yoli's lungs as she relented and grabbed Kiana's outstretched hand, jostling the guitar strap onto her shoulder. Kiana's words tumbled around in her mind as they went inside.

And what if you die?

Amá had told her about the curse when she was fifteen and screaming at the world. Trophies and awards thrown into the trash, throat hoarse from crying, Yoli had snuck over to Kiana's place and spent three days there until Kiana's mother finally convinced her to go back home and "make up with your ma, Yolanda."

Yoli had no idea what finally made her snap—a reminder for an upcoming college exam, another thoughtless comment about her lack of love life, another pamphlet for early admissions, her damn wrist flaring up *again*—

In the end, it didn't matter. Years of sleepless nights, overflowing schedules, and bone-crushing pressure . . . all explained by her mother as they had sat in their tiny living room: "Yolanda, you have three years left."

She remembered the taste of apple gone sour on her tongue.

"Our family is cursed," Amá had continued, sitting on the couch across from her, unable to meet her eyes. "When a woman turns eighteen, tu cuántos-tatarabuela visits them with a choice: sing to her or be taken into the river to drown." She'd hummed the notes to a very familiar tune. *Mi do mi mi so fa . . .*

Yoli had been skeptical. "We're haunted by La Llorona?" Amá had only winced.

"Every culture has their version of her; this one is our family's burden to bear. I faced her when I turned eighteen. So will you."

Yoli had shaken her head. Amá was not a liar, but this . . . "I don't get it, what does this have to do with anything? The perfect grades and recitals you had me do? Why do we—I mean, how does she—" Thoughts buzzed around angrily, too many to put into words, and Yoli had latched onto the simplest one. "What's the catch for singing?" Because there was always a catch.

"The price of living." Her mother finally glanced at her—and for the first time in years, Yoli had seen her as someone else beyond *mamá.* Were her eyes always so empty? "You sing, but she takes your chances for happiness away. You may live, but you will have misfortune the rest of your life. That's why I've been so hard on you, mija—for you to succeed while you're still young and able. Lo siento, if that hurt you, but your time is almost up. And you must prepare to meet her too."

Something had twisted inside Yoli then—the anger, the frustration, fading away for a moment. Tendrils of dread tugged at her heart when Amá put a hand on her knee.

"What did . . . " The question had cloyed in Yoli's throat. "What did you . . . ?"

What future did you lose that allowed me to exist?

Her mother's smile hadn't reached her eyes. "Misfortune or death. That is what awaits us."

Well, Yoli very much did not plan on either happening. As her eighteenth birthday grew near, she'd booked a last-minute cabin as far from Las Cruces as she could find. Her friends were all but happy to drop their nonexistent summer plans to spend the weekend together as another one of them entered the joys of adulthood. But Yoli would make sure that tonight would pass by as idyllic as possible. She had prepared. *I might not be able to fight the curse off,* she thought as she and Kiana entered the hallway connecting the kitchen to the living room. *But I can sure as hell run from it.* Wait out the deadline until midnight passed, and the curse would never bother her again.

She just didn't want to spend the night alone.

Raúl poked his head out from the kitchen, wearing an apron over his sleepwear, Kiana's hair clips haphazardly pulling back his thick, dark hair. He greeted them with a squint. "Glad to see the lovebirds are ready to join us."

"Not lovebirds," Yoli and Kiana responded in unison, and Leah cackled from the living room.

Raúl scrunched his nose. "Whatever you say. I need hands, people! My food isn't going to walk to the table by itself. Not you, Yoli," he said, as she'd fallen into step behind Kiana. "Go shoo to the table while we finish setting up, prima."

"Rude," Yoli responded, but she couldn't fight off the smile that climbed to her face. While she had known Kiana for years and only recently committed to their atypical relationship, Raúl was another important piece that slid into the cogs of her life. They were each other's firsts in many ways, where Raúl had learned he actually hated being romantically involved with anyone, and Yoli had learned that romance stirred nothing but a yawning hole, as people she'd known left her for another. At least, until Kiana had grabbed her hand and told her that she herself wasn't good at loving, "But would you want to try to stay with me forever?"

"Living room's all set." Leah popped her head into the hallway with a grin in her eyes. She, too, had come a long way from the awkward kid who'd slammed her lunch tray at their table and rattled off something about space in lieu of a greeting. An unconventional way of making friends, but Yoli had learned that all of them were nothing but unconventional. That said . . .

Yoli sucked in air through her teeth. "You planning on giving me a heart attack?"

Leah had the audacity to roll her eyes. "Raúl's food will," she said with a full-body shudder. "I've never seen him touch a vegetable in his life, and his favorite meal is goat cooked in its own blood. And we're *letting* him cook."

As if summoned, Raúl, apron-less, strutted out of the kitchen past the two of them into the living room as Kiana followed with a towel-wrapped pot of . . .

"Menudo?" Yoli perked up as the smell of cooked garlic and oregano passed by her.

"I need a knife!" he yelled back. "Big one from the chandelier for the cake *pleeeease*!"

Yoli ducked into the kitchen with Leah before Raúl could notice. Oh, tonight was turning out better with that promising meal.

The kitchen was a mishmash of painted wood, stone countertops, and steel utilities, as if someone had randomly designed it with their eyes closed. The used dishes were neatly piled in the sink while ingredients were strewn across the countertops, the scent of soap heavy in the air. The round, magnetic storage rack hung above the granite island.

Leah hastily grabbed the discarded spices. "You'd think he'd be better at cleaning up after himself while he's cooking. Does he want someone to trip and die?"

Yoli choked on a strangled laugh. "It's literally just a few bottles," she said, reaching for one of the knives. "You make it sound as if he's out to get—"

And just like that, every knife hanging on the rack *dropped.*

Leah's string of swears blended with the metallic clanging of steel colliding with granite, as knives bounced onto the ground by their socked feet. "*Aish,* what sort of freak stores their knives in the middle of the room face down? Yoli, you good?"

Yoli stood there, frozen, with her arm extended, glancing as nipped arm hair fluttered onto the counter. She swallowed hard.

And what if you died? Kiana had said.

Yoli's hands shook. Aware that Leah was suddenly at her side, she grabbed the first knife her fingers touched and forced a sheepish smile.

"I'm good. Freak accident, right?"

Leah narrowed her eyes, but Yoli hurried past her, clutching the knife in her hand.

The curse couldn't have found her so soon. Surely escaping home the day of her birthday would have hindered it? Did she not put out enough salt? Enough candles? If it really was here, reaching through all that protection, why wasn't it luring her out?

Leah had been too close.

Yoli ignored the look Raúl and Kiana shared when she made it to the living room and wordlessly handed him the knife. Kiana offered her the splint from their shared room, and Yoli automatically strapped it on. Raúl repeated Leah's question, asking if Yoli was okay, but Leah, who'd come in after Yoli, explained to them what had happened.

"I just put them away," she said, and Yoli felt a twinge at having left her to do that, "but when I tell you that was *weird* . . ."

Yoli gave an imperceptible shake of her head when Kiana raised her eyebrows at her. *Not now.* With a clap, Yoli plopped down at the floor table. "I have no idea what's going on," she lied, "but I say we eat cake first, then enjoy absolutely everything else I told you guys not to do for me."

The segue worked. Raúl grinned across from her and began lighting the cake candles; Leah, on her right, started picking out bowls and utensils from the stack; and Kiana's worry smoothed out as she took a seat to Yoli's left and *wow*, the menudo smelled like home and the chatter all but made her forget everything for just a moment.

Then the electric lights flickered before going out.

Startled shouts rang out as the cabin fell into darkness. Something about a fuse or generator, but any words were stifled by the sudden gale outside. The windows and doors were closed, but it didn't seem to make a difference. Aged wood creaked loudly through the walls, making the quaint feel of the cabin begin to take on the musty, wet trappings of a coffin. Branches scratched at the panes like nails on asphalt. Yoli remembered one time her cousin had carved out a replica of a death whistle. That paled in comparison to what they heard now.

Leah spoke. "I swear this is how horror movies start."

Yoli blinked as her eyes adjusted to the candles that were, thankfully, still flickering. Everyone's faces reflected hers, wide-eyed and startled. Kiana gripped Yoli's hand like a lifeline, and Yoli almost let everything spill out right there, but she bit her tongue. How could she now, knowingly, tell them all that there may be a tiny chance that she might have been wrong?

"So . . . food?" said Raúl, hesitantly holding the very large knife.

"Raúl, put the knife down; this is serious."

"Please, Ki, I'm literally the only one here who can cook with my eyes closed."

"He's got a point," Leah said.

"Ghost stories!" Yoli interrupted before they all got going. The inkling of a plan was forming, merging from the words from the porch and the wailing wind outside. She gestured to the candles around them. "It's like camping. We share stories, talk about what's out there, what keeps us up at night . . ."

Kiana's terrified expression melted as she did a double take.

Leah tapped the table with a grimace. "What better way to pass time than indulging in a time-honored tradition of tormenting each other through storytelling?"

"Glad you agree." Yoli was committed now, but her voice was still tight. "You can go first then."

Leah sputtered at being thrown under the bus, but she was never one to back down from a challenge. The storm still raged outside, but the mood had lifted with the banter and the warm bowls Raúl managed to sneak around. Everyone listened as Leah launched into a simple but disturbingly detailed story with rapt attention. Everyone except Yoli.

Instead, she listened to the howling outside, worry pooling in her gut as she picked up human-like screams within the frenetic noise. The stories were often interrupted by the storm, but everyone was so caught up in the thrill of telling stories that it led to more excuses to poke fun instead. But Yoli could only focus on the confirmation of what she knew now.

The curse had found her, tracked her down. She'd hoped, for three short years, that if she was smart enough, she could have been the exception. That she wouldn't be forced to choose between living a life of hopelessness and dying. That she could live *and* be happy—live with Kiana, pursue guitar, be the first to finish college . . .

But her third option, her way out, was gone.

Yoli blinked through watery vision. Raúl was returning a blown-out candle to the cake, and Leah was dabbing spilt soup with a stack of napkins. Kiana put her spoon back down with a look, and it was like back on the porch—Kiana urging Yoli to think about what was best for herself. But to also let them in.

And she was right, Yoli realized. They deserved to know.

"It started with a woman, long ago. Rosa Yolanda Flores," Yoli found herself saying, abandoning any prelude as she recalled the way Amá had shared the story. "From a respectable family, she married another respectable man. He gave her everything: a house, children, security. A perfect marriage. But for all the expectations their families had, something was missing. Rosa, though living that perfect life, appeared unusually cold. Somber. And despite the three children they had, the husband stayed away long hours. When he left for war, he fell in love with another woman. Younger. Bolder. When he returned, he left his wife, and Rosa and her children became destitute."

She had everything, Amá had said, baffled. *But not enough to give.*

Yoli brought her hands around her bowl, but its warmth had long dissipated. "Overcome by grief, Rosa led her children to the nearest river and drowned them, then followed through with herself. One daughter survived the attempt and managed to grow up happy despite her childhood. When she married the love of her life at eighteen, though, her mother's spirit appeared in the very clothes she'd drowned in and tried to drag her daughter into the river nearby. But the daughter had been in the middle of singing a prayer, which ended up startling the spirit so that she let go and disappeared back into the water.

"Despite the love the daughter and her husband had, their luck took a sharp turn. He was severely injured at work. She miscarried. They lost their farm. Her first daughter was killed by that same spirit and the second maimed before attempting to sing her mother's prayer. One by one, any dreams the daughter had for her life died. And so, the curse came to be, continuing as the drowned woman appeared to her descendants on their eighteenth birthdays with the choice: sing or die."

Yoli breathed in the scent of smoke as wax dripped slowly onto the cake and table. The present, pocked with the past. Her friends were silent. Would they believe her? Would they laugh it off as a scary story and ask for another? Or worse, if they did believe her, how much would they hate her for bringing them into the curse's grasp? Or hate her for bringing them to watch her die? Because if her chest collapsed on itself, and she was unable to even hum the first stanzas of the song, would she even be able to sing herself out of this mess—

Somewhere through the noise in her head, Kiana grabbed her hand. "Yoli." Her fingers found their way to Yoli's face and forced her to meet her eyes. "You're not alone, remember?"

Out of her periphery, Leah's eyes darted around with a wavering chuckle. "The story's getting a bit too immersive right now, isn't it?" Raúl couldn't hold back a snort, but Leah continued, "Not that it wasn't good, it's just . . . you're acting a bit . . ."

"Off," Raúl finished. "Which I get, because family stories are rough, if I'm picking up what you're . . ."

His voice trailed off, and Kiana's eyes followed what caught the others' attention. Yoli turned toward the creaking window, and all she saw was the hazy shadow of *something* there before—

"¡AY DE MI, ¡AY, QUE MIS FLORES CAEN!"

A flash of lightning, coupled with the rattling of every door against its hinges, and a crack of thunder swept through the cabin. There was a splintering sound of shattered glass, and suddenly a biting draft of wind tore inside, silencing the candles before anyone could blink. Everyone screamed again.

Leah fumbled trying to avoid grabbing on to Yoli's splint. "Tell me that you hired someone to jump scare us!"

"Padre Nuestro que estás en los cielos . . ." muttered Raúl under his breath.

Yoli's heart pounded so loudly, she was sure that the curse could hear it through the walls. *I can't die,* Yoli thought. *I'll sing for you, please. Just leave them alone.*

She untangled herself from Kiana and Leah, then stumbled to her feet, unable to stop herself from rambling. "I'm sorry, I'm so sorry, I was wrong and now I've dragged you all into this and it's my fault you're going to get hurt because I thought I could be the exception just this once . . ." Yoli felt around for her phone or the lighter, whichever one she found first. "I'll go—go face it and just put an end to all this."

Hands latched on to her arms before she could run. "You're going out into that?" rasped Raúl.

Leah sprung up in front of her, and yes, Yoli realized with a wince at the sudden burst of light from Leah's hand, she'd found the lighter. "What are you talking about, Yoli? It's a *storm,* for crying out loud, not a fix for proving whatever it is you're saying!" She brandished the tiny flame like a shield, keeping Yoli from taking another step forward. "I know the future is gonna be rough, but that doesn't mean you go and get yourself killed on your birthday—not on our watch!"

Another wail rang out, and Yoli turned to Kiana, pleading. "Ki, you know what I've got to do. Let me go and finish this before it comes in and I can explain the rest—"

"Kiana knows?"

"*Please.*" Yoli strained against Raúl's embrace, against Leah's words, against the flicker of unshed tears in Kiana's eyes. "I can't—I won't let it hurt you."

Thumbs were suddenly brushing away the wetness that Yoli hadn't realized was staining her cheeks. "And I don't want it to hurt you," said Kiana. Raúl's grasp loosened, but it was all Yoli could do to keep standing.

"I just want this to end," she said with a shuddering breath. "Let me finish this, please." She'd wanted her friends to understand that this was for their own good, why she tried to keep them out of the loop, to keep them from being burdened by her, but now . . .

Leah's brow furrowed. "You really need to do this?"

Yoli nodded.

Kiana slipped a hand into Yoli's. "But you aren't going on your own."

Another crash outside and, after shooting the entryway a dark look, Leah sighed. "Fine, I'll bite. Kiana's right, though. Curse or not, there's no way in hell we're letting you go out there by yourself. Not like this."

Another time, Yoli would've snarked back, but instead she sagged in relief. Leah and Kiana began coordinating the supplies they needed, and despite the warmth that fear and relief brought, a shiver ran through Yoli's body.

Yoli felt around for Raúl, finding him back by the table, rustling around for . . . something. "Raúl?" she said. "I can't ask you to come, but—"

The kitchen knife glinted in Raúl's hands and there was a hard-set look in his eyes coupled with a crooked grin. "Of course

I'm coming," he said. "Friends don't let friends run off into danger by themselves. *Honestly*, Yoli."

They stumbled through a hellish storm. Though the sharp wind stung their eyes and tree branches twisted around wildly, there was no rain. Yoli had experienced dry thunderstorms before, but none as deafening as this.

"Where do we go?" shouted Kiana over the wind. "I don't think waiting around for it to come is the best idea!"

None of this was, but Yoli didn't voice it. She squinted through the patches of forest lit by their flashlights. "Water," she replied. "There was a stream when we drove up—although how we'll hear it . . ."

"East!" Kiana tugged Yoli's arm and gestured to the other two with her light. "By the ravine, I remember." Kiana led the way, holding onto Yoli's hand, who clutched Leah's sleeve while Raúl followed behind, like a string of children crossing the perilous road.

"This 'curse,'" started Leah, "it's all real? Like, your family . . . they're all . . . ?"

"Yeah," Yoli admitted. "My mom, abuela, her mom . . . they all had to face it. They all chose to sing."

Leah swatted a branch aside. "And you . . . you're gonna sing to it?"

"That's the plan."

"And get all that bad luck for the rest of your life," Leah said with a *hmm*.

Yoli couldn't hide her wince. The deeper they walked into the woods, the more reality weighed down on her. For the rest of her life was far too long. But she'd still be alive; that had to mean something, right?

"This 'curse' or whatever—whoever—this is," called out Raúl, voice muffled, "it can't take us all on, right? We can just make it stop threatening you."

Kiana's shoulders shook, and Leah's chuckles were warm in Yoli's ear. "You just want an excuse to use that knife, Raúl, don't even start."

Silence.

They stopped, and Leah glanced back. "Raúl, this is where you say how persuasive you can be."

Their flashlights revealed empty space where Raúl had been seconds ago.

"He was just there . . ." Kiana said, while Leah whirled about, calling out his name as the air stole out from Yoli's lungs. The wind gave a piercing shriek. One flinch from Kiana, and Yoli knew she wasn't alone in hearing the haunting "*¡AY, AY, AY!*" echoing around them.

"Leah," hissed Yoli, but it was too late. No amount of light showed them where Leah had disappeared to as well. The sobbing grew louder, and Yoli almost dropped her flashlight trying to block it. "They're both—it should be coming for *me*, not them—"

Kiana's grip tightened. "They'll be okay," she said, but her voice trembled. "The storm's loud, so maybe they just got lost—"

Yoli tripped over a lifted root and fell from Kiana's grasp, crying out as she caught herself with her right hand. Her wrist screamed, and she gritted her teeth, waiting for the worst of it to subside. It wasn't long until she noticed the silence that crept in.

"Ki, where—" Yoli's eyes widened as she spun around but was met with empty air instead. Her eyes darted around for her fallen flashlight, for her friends, calling out their names. But there was nothing.

Yoli wanted to sob. They had come here because of her. They'd ventured into the forest for her. The people she cared about most in the world . . . gone because of her.

"¡Ay! que dolor, que penas las mias . . ."

Scrambling to her feet, Yoli caught her first sight of the curse. The darkness of the storm had deteriorated, letting moonlight filter through the leaves. There, hunched over the edge of a stream gurgling softly, was the curse. Its voice was no longer as guttural as before, but melodic. A thickly woven rebozo, dyed with what once was dark blue and cream, hung from its shoulders, casting a shadow onto the rest of its white dress. The air was tinged with the acrid scent of moss and wet earth.

The curse was crying.

When Yoli moved, the curse froze and turned slowly toward her. There were no eyes to see, but Yoli knew their gazes met.

Yoli found her voice. "My friends, where . . . ?" She faltered as the spirit tilted its head. Amá's voice pled with her, and the familiar song bubbled up in Yoli's throat, begging to be sung before the curse lashed out. But she was still shaking from losing sight of everyone. From being singled out. It just wasn't *fair*. "You're to decide my fate then. Damned if I run, damned if I stay."

Sing or die. She didn't want to die, but . . . what good was living with her future beholden to the misfortune of the curse? Where nothing she did would ever be enough?

Stop worrying about holding me back. Kiana's words from earlier spoke in her mind, and another memory, so long ago when they were so young and unsure: *You're my best friend. I want you in my life, no matter what that looks like.*

Yoli fell to her knees, dirt and leaves digging into her jeans. *I'll try, then, to live with my lot,* she thought, and started humming. *Mi do mi mi so fa . . .*

A sharp wind blew into Yoli's face, jostling her flyaways and earrings, and she blinked open her eyes with a flinch. The curse hovered over her, its billowy dress undulating as if underwater. Silvery tears stained its pallid, skull-like face. It was still crying, but the sobbing seemed to come from Yoli's surroundings instead. Strands of black hair had fallen out of the plait running down its nape. Just like Yoli's did when she let it loose.

The similarity was unsettling.

"Por qué?" whispered Yoli. The curse hadn't reached out to grab her, hadn't dragged her off to the stream in her silence. What was it waiting for? "Was it because your husband cheated on you? Or because you couldn't fathom your daughter finding something you couldn't have? Amá had me do everything to get a taste of what achievement was like before I lost that chance forever. I resented her for that. But now I realize I don't even know who she is. My own mother." Yoli could almost feel phantom touches on her shoulders, her arms, her hands as emotion welled in her throat. "And that's the real curse, isn't it? That we're so hurt by what the past has done for us that we burn our own futures out before we even see them. Because we're trapped in a cycle you started, and no one's learned how to stop it." Yoli took a deep breath. "Why do you hate your family so much that you would rather kill them than see them happy?"

A single blink, as if it was scrutinizing. It reached out a pale hand toward her.

Yoli recoiled, eyeing the stream behind the curse. As if noticing her doing so, the curse contorted and let out a wail, clawing at its face and hair, forcing Yoli to clap her hands over her ears. In a blur, the curse rushed back to the stream and all but collapsed at its bank, continuing to scream into the water.

Yoli sat there dumbly at the display. Amá's warning pushed her to continue singing, her heart yelled at her to demand her friends back, and yet . . .

And yet for someone trying to kill me, she thought, *this is a pathetic attempt.*

Yoli had no idea what pushed her to walk and sit down close to the water. Thoughts of *I'm going to die* shouted in her head, but the curse's words caught her attention.

"No . . ."

Its voice, ragged from yelling, was gritty. Yoli stilled.

"No . . ." the curse repeated, "me vean . . . llorar . . ." Its hand dipped into the water.

Yoli kept a wary glance on it as she retorted. "It's impossible to *not* hear you cry, much less see you do so. You can't chase someone to the ends of earth crying and not expect them to look—"

Wait.

The curse—maldición, llorona, abuela—let its hair fall as it resumed lamenting at its reflection. "No . . . no me vean llorar," it cried again. "No me ven, ¿por qué no me ven—?" Its weeping grew shrill as the pieces fell into place.

It wasn't a command—*Don't see me cry*. It was a plea: *They don't see me cry.*

For a single, horrifying second, Yoli could see the moonlight glinting off the water's surface and caught a glimpse of herself in the curse's reflection.

She had everything, Amá had said, *but not enough to give.*

"You were just like me," Yoli whispered, staring at the spirit of Abuela Rosa as the dark implication ran through her head. "You couldn't give him everything he wanted, could you? Not the love he expected. But how could you explain it? No one would've understood you. You had no one."

Yoli *had* people, and having them ripped from her side made her realize what that meant. How long did Kiana hold her after Yoli had crawled in through her window, angry and sobbing after her argument with Amá? How long did Leah tutor her, lighting up every time Yoli thanked her for not holding anything back? How long did Raúl put up with her crises, offering Yoli nothing but teasing support until she grew surer of herself? How long had her parents, yoked with sharing this curse, continued to love her in the only way they knew how?

And how long had it been since Yoli had seen all of that, so caught up with hefting this burden onto herself?

"You hurt them because you were hurt." Yoli tried to keep her voice steady. "You had no one to turn to because you were stuck where they put you." A perfect marriage. "And after you killed your children"—the curse moaned, but Yoli continued—"after seeing your own daughter choose something you never had the choice for, it was like the river all over again." Yoli gathered her courage and looked right at the spirit.

"Wasn't it, Rosa Yolanda?"

Rosa made a keening sound, clutching her shoulders as she cried. It was not the screams that had followed Yoli here, but a softer, painful release of emotion. Yoli shifted, those phantom hands following her as she knelt beside the spirit. However, she made no move to touch her.

"You never learned to grieve what you'd lost. How could you when that was all you'd known? You hurt others because no one stopped to listen, to understand. But you had time . . . You had time to learn." Strength returned to Yoli as she straightened up. "I'm sorry for you. You didn't deserve what happened. But you turned that pain onto us . . ." She stared at their reflections in the water. "And that, I'm not sorry for."

Rosa glanced up, looking as young as when she'd married. "¿De que me sirvió el dolor?"

"I don't know," Yoli responded, truthfully. There was a litany of explanations she could give, but it wouldn't be her truth. "I really don't know."

Rosa bowed toward the stream and wept.

Yoli gripped the fabric of her jeans. "I won't sing," she murmured. "I won't run. But I'll listen." Her hand found its way onto Rosa's shoulder. "As long as it takes, I'll listen to you."

The woods were silent, as if in anticipation. Yoli's heart

pounded, and sweat clung to her shirt and splint. There was a chance her offer would be rejected, that Rosa might change her mind and swiftly pull Yoli into the water before she could try to sing. She'd never see her friends or parents again, despite her efforts—

Rosa sang.

Her voice, melodic as a dream, sang of pain, of heartache and loneliness, of longing for a life she could never see with her eyes. As she sang, Yoli's chest loosened for what seemed like the first time in ages, shoulders sinking with released tension. As if she were back home, listening to Amá's voice in a new light after their fight, hesitantly sharing stories from a childhood Yoli had never before heard about. Her fingers moved instinctively, silently plucking each note of the familiar song on invisible strings. Rosa sang of regret and, in a broken voice, of a single wish. To be free as herself. She sang until the sunrise broke through the scraggly trees, and its rays reclaimed her body, fading until she left a final phrase lingering in the air.

"¿Qué más quieres . . . ?"

Yoli awoke to the sun shining in her face and birdsong in the branches above. Her limbs felt heavy, and she could feel knots beginning to form on her back from the uneven forest floor. She inhaled the clammy scent of moss and dried tears. As she struggled to sit up, she noticed her wrist wasn't throbbing as badly, though she knew it would be stiff for a while.

"Huh," was all she could say before she was tackled back to the ground.

"Yoli!" Kiana nearly sobbed as she latched herself around Yoli's neck. "You're back!"

"You disappeared!" Leah shouted in her ear. "I found Raúl, but then I turned around and you were gone. We didn't see anything or anyone out there—"

"I didn't really think it was a 'curse' curse," Raúl said in a harried voice, "but there was fog out of nowhere when you disappeared, and we got attacked by hail, and omigod, it was awful, but then Kiana was freaking *out*—"

And sure enough, Raúl's jacket was torn, and he was missing several hairclips, Leah's hair was tangled with sticks, and Kiana's bonnet was barely hanging on to her head. All three of them were covered in mud and scrapes, but talking enthusiastically over each other, completely disregarding how they were pinning Yoli down. Their hands grasped at her shoulders, arms, and hands, just like the phantom ones she'd felt with Rosa.

"The curse?" asked Kiana, slipping close enough that Yoli could trace the concern in her face. "Are you . . . ?"

Yoli smiled at her. "A lot happened, but . . . I'm good. It's over." And just like that, that beautiful smile smiled back.

"You know we're not letting you out of our sight for the rest of the week, right?" Leah tried to hide how frantic she sounded. "You're going to have to explain everything."

"Wait, no, food first!" Raúl, for how frazzled he was, was somehow still holding the kitchen knife. "I *refuse* to let all my hard work go to waste!"

Kiana grabbed the handle and pushed it down. "First of all, we aren't doing anything until we actually get back to the cabin in one piece!"

What must it be like, Yoli thought, smiling for the first time, *to be so cared for and seen by the people around you that you could hold your head up so high?*

And how, by God, did I miss this before?

DAUGHTER OF TIME

MADELINE DYER

Orla looked out of the window. The protesters were numerous today and, as her father had said, "so bloody loud." Each angry-faced man, woman, and child held a picket demanding *No messing with DNA* as they shouted aggressively at the LivXtra employees battling the masses to get inside the building.

Even though Orla had secretly designed several of the protesters' signs, it wasn't safe for her to go outside. That was the price she paid for being the daughter of Winston X. Feeney. Orla's face was everywhere in the media, and she couldn't even go out to do a bit of shopping without angry mobs impeding her. They wouldn't believe *she* was ArtoftheHeart in the forums, uploading her designs. They'd only see her as the daughter of the most evil man on earth.

And what her father was planning wasn't just stupid and

dangerous, but unethical too.

He used to read her Isaac Asimov's "The Ugly Little Boy" as a bedtime story; Orla had only held sadness for the Neanderthal child snatched in time and caged, whereas her father had become fixated on the *possibility*. "That story is, of course, science fiction," Winston X. Feeney had told reporters only the other day as he'd prepared for the big show. "But what we are doing is *reality*, and this will be the greatest thing science has ever achieved."

Now, as she watched the protestors and chewed her last piece of spearmint gum, Orla tried to ignore her father pacing round and round their apartment. They lived at the top of the LivXtra building, and Winston X. Feeney insisted upon no curtains, ever. Orla had gotten used to only changing in the bathroom, but she still hated the lack of privacy. She was constantly on display, and she knew there'd be paparazzi outside, trying to get shots worth thousands of pounds.

"I think this may really work," her father said, and he joined her at the living room window, stroking his graying whiskers. "The conditions are just right, and we've isolated enough DNA to build the base genome of an individual who should be able to survive in today's climate." He moved to the kitchen island, his feet clattering against the dogs' food bowls, spilling some kibble, but he didn't seem to notice as Jasper and Teddy gobbled up the mess.

He never bothered with the dogs, but Jasper and Teddy were the only company Orla consistently had.

"Of course, we've modified the lab to make it significantly colder," Winston X. Feeney continued. "We have to replicate the icy conditions of the Stone Age, but these creatures were used to roaming across vast lands."

"Then you shouldn't be abducting them." Orla chewed her gum a little more furiously as she made her way toward her father.

There was a glassy look in his eyes; he hadn't even heard her. "The lab is only so big, so Professor Searle has edited the genome to limit their desire to roam, and we believe . . ." He continued on and on.

Orla clenched her fists. Recreating the mammoth was one thing—a thing she didn't agree with—but keeping a wild animal in a lab all its life just wasn't fair. She knew what it was like to be caged, to have no one to talk to, no one to be with. She had no friends, and she could only picture her future as a lonely one. She couldn't imagine wanting a boyfriend or girlfriend either. Being with someone romantically wasn't something that had ever appealed to her. She'd just be pretending to feel something she didn't.

But she also didn't want to be alone. She craved connection, but it seemed unattainable. And so, she saw herself in this mammoth that her father was recreating. A poor specimen trapped in a life that wasn't right for it.

But at least the mammoth wouldn't be lonely, like Orla was, for her father's work wasn't just culminating in recreating one mammoth. LivXtra had also found a way to lock onto the life-imprint of a baby woolly mammoth from 45,000 years ago.

Orla didn't understand the time travel aspect or how it was even possible because she refused to engage in scientific conversations, but her father planned to bring a prehistoric mammoth to his lab, too. At first, it had been purely for comparison reasons. How else would they know if their recreated mammoth was the real thing if they had no baseline? But then LivXtra began working with other firms. It was now *commercial.*

The recreated mammoth was to be a male, and the prehistoric mammoth that LivXtra had locked onto was female. Suddenly, every billionaire in the world was willing to pay significant money to Winston X. Feeney to be the first to own a very special pet. There were already ridiculous bids coming in for the first calf to be born.

Orla breathed deeply, and her gaze fell on the portrait of her mother. Aileen Feeney had passed away eight years ago. A stroke. But Orla could still feel her mother's presence in the apartment: the orange sofa, the gluten-free recipe folders, the folklore books, the guinea pig mugs, the tapestry of elephants in Orla's bedroom.

She knew her mother would hate what her husband was doing. "You can only do this as long as it's ethical," she had said, ten years ago, when the family had bought the LivXtra building. She'd never been a scientist, preferring what she referred to as the "spiritual world" instead. "Don't get carried away, Win. You must only do good."

Orla took one last look at the protestors and moved from the window. Jasper had finished eating and was looking at her, his eyes brimming with love.

"It's okay," she whispered. "I've got a plan."

Ten minutes later, when her father stopped talking and went to conduct a meeting with someone important, Orla crouched in front of the filing cabinet in her room and used her fingerprint to unlock the bottom drawer where she kept some of her art supplies. She grabbed her spray paints and loaded them into a tote bag before heading down to the basement of the LivXtra building. She used an ID card that she'd swiped from a high-level researcher yesterday and swept inside the most important room in the complex.

The machine inside was a box about half her height, with a control panel on its side, and a connection to a tunnel that led out of the room and into the mammoths' arena. She stepped up to it and pressed a few buttons on the control panel, trying out the different combinations she'd acquired in yesterday's research, until the lid of the small black box slid back.

Ignoring the warning label that advised not to alter the genetic material within twenty-four hours of phase one, Orla pulled a can of paint from her bag and sprayed a hearty amount of redness inside. After a couple of seconds, the slides containing the genetic material at the bottom of the box began to move. At first, she thought it was the slides slipping about in the paint, but then the liquid began to fizz, and her smile grew like a blossoming flower.

With paint mixed into the genetic material, it would be useless, and she'd have stopped her father from making a very big and very unethical mistake. But Orla wasn't done. She emptied spray cans numbers two and three, and then, for good measure, she chucked in a pot of red ochre which was at the bottom of her tote bag.

Orla hummed softly as she left the room. She might be the daughter of the most evil man in the world, but that didn't mean she wouldn't do everything in her power to stop him.

"The Moon bleeds gently, offering new life, blessing it on the Clan, and protecting us from the Doom."

Nala swallowed her nerves and whispered the incantation carefully as she stoked the fire. All around her, the Clan was busy. Women flitted in and out of the twin caves, babies in their arms, toddlers at their heels. Children carried furs and rugs, while adolescents closer to Nala's age hauled mammoth bones.

"Keep going," Mama said to Nala, giving her daughter an encouraging nod and warm squeeze of the shoulder.

Evening sun had fallen so quickly, a heaviness creeping inside Nala's bones, trying to cool them, and she wanted to freeze the land and sky until her father was back from the hunt. Both her parents should be there to guide her through her first Tunaski as a shaman in her own right, but the crimson moon—a time when the vortexes of the universe were open, and the Clan was in danger of the Doom taking them all—had happened sooner than expected. Now she would have to do it without him.

Even though the hunters were far away, she could still protect them, locating their soul-presences in the ether. She would protect everyone—no one would get lost on her watch—and she'd finally become the shaman she was supposed to be.

"It's almost time," Mama said, her blue eyes watery, warm, encouraging.

As the red moon waned in the clouds, the Clan formed a loose circle around the shamanic hearth. The Clan's medicine woman stepped forward, bones in her hands: a horse's femur, a saber-toothed cat's jaw, and a cave lion's vertebra. She placed the artifacts at Nala's feet. A heavy ink fell over the sky, and Nala looked up at the lunar body. It bled in messy rings.

She breathed deeply amid the widening vibrations of the world. It was time.

She made the Tunaski drink quickly—an ancient recipe, passed down from shaman to shaman—and as final light fell, she watched and listened to the beat of Mother Earth as each of the Clan took a gulp. They did not waver once, trusting her completely.

When the wooden bowl returned to her, there was just enough of the pale concoction left in the bottom for Nala to join the rest of her people in the safe realm—a place of languid sound, illuminating and protecting, calming and reassuring, while Tunaski raged.

Nala swallowed the bitter liquid and waited for her vision to blur.

It took a few more moments before she felt the welcoming of Tunaski—the summoning of her essence into the red moon's realm. Her soul began to sing the melody of the moon, and she heard owlsong. Nala closed her eyes, felt damp grass, and—

Silence.

She startled. *This isn't supposed to happen! Where is—*

Her eyes flew open as a burning crimson light lassoed her. She screamed as it scalded her, and a falling sensation overtook her. She let out another scream, and her head snapped backward and . . .

Nala awoke on something hard, and too many sounds battered her ears. Her senses sought out the world, and she was immediately assaulted by . . . *everything.*

The ground was hard and dark gray beneath her, but it was like no stone or rock Nala knew. It was firm but its texture wasn't right, and everything smelled strange, like burning.

She stared at the huge angular *beasts* that hurtled past her. Smoke billowed out behind them, and fear clenched her throat.

She'd performed the ceremony incorrectly—she must've! Oh Gods. She'd been sucked into a dangerous vortex—and what about the rest of her people? She looked around, half expecting to see the Clan, but she could not feel their soul-presences here. Only *she* was in this realm. And what in all the Gods was this place? One of the lands of the lost where unguarded people in Tunaski ended up? Were there other realms, where the rest of her Clan could've been scattered because she'd failed them? Her throat tightened, and her eyes stung with tears. She had done the worst thing that a shaman could do.

She hadn't been ready. They shouldn't have trusted her.

Nala looked up and—*trees!*

She spotted them a hundred feet or so away, and her heart leapt at the familiarity. She ran for them, trying to escape the piercing sounds, unlike any animal's call she knew. Her bare feet touched wet but warm grass, and her body connected with the tree. But something was wrong. Huge walls towered above her on three sides, not like the cave walls she'd known all her life. They were too tall, too straight, the surfaces too flat, and all the same color.

Then Nala saw an animal lolloping across the grass toward her. Her breath hitched. It was smaller than a wolf—barely so—but it moved like one. His pelt was a deep brown, all one color rather than a gradient. And he wasn't alone. There was . . . well, Nala didn't know what the second creature was. It was scruffy, the size and color of a hare, but it had small, pointed ears and a scrunched-up, flattened face. And it yapped.

It yapped and it yapped and it yapped, and this set off the wolf-like animal—only he didn't howl or growl. He made a deep but reverberating short sound, over and over, that kind of sounded like an angry stag, while looking Nala directly in the eye.

She began to shake. She needed to get away. She needed to perform a spell or something to try and get out of here—if that was even possible for a failed shaman like her. She tried not to look either of the creatures in their eyes as she scanned the area, searching for a weapon in case these strange beings attacked. Their teeth looked so sharp.

She gulped, and suddenly, there was someone else there—a woman dressed most bizarrely in the color of hyena gums. If it wasn't for the slightly looser neck piece, or the fact Nala could see this woman's white face and hands, Nala might have thought this strange outfit was a second skin. The woman was saying something to Nala, but she didn't speak Clan, and Nala stayed shaking by her tree, watching as this woman fearlessly reached for the wolf-like animal and then the little yapping thing, attaching each to a long rope that she seemed to produce out of nowhere.

Nala could hardly breathe.

The woman spoke again, and by the way her tone went up at the end, Nala thought it was a question. But all Nala could do was shake her head, her eyes wide, her heart pounding until she felt like she was going to be sick. Because she'd finally realized what this woman was.

Oh my heart, she's a Goddess.

"Are you . . . are you a *Neanderthal*?"

The question seemed absurd, but Orla stared dubiously at the girl, and she didn't know what to think. They were in the smallest square of green on LivXtra's grounds, and any moment now, the paparazzi or protestors were going to follow Orla around here. They'd see this girl, and they'd—well, Orla didn't know what they'd do.

Orla's eyes widened as she looked at the marks on the girl's face—paint marks. It was red ochre. She recognized the ancient pigment, and she thought of how she'd chucked some into the genetic material as an afterthought. *Damn.* Had her tampering led to this?

"Come with me," she said, flicking her head around to check for cameras. She beckoned to the girl to follow, unable to do more while keeping Teddy and Jasper away.

The girl looked confused, but Orla was able to coax her inside—into a storeroom because it was the nearest place she could think of, with her heart pounding and her brain buzzing.

Under the storeroom's artificial light, this girl *did* kind of look like the various Neanderthal reconstructions Orla had seen. The girl was cowering at the back, shaking, among the cleaning supplies. An amber pendant hung around her neck, and she clutched the stone, muttering something over and over in a language that Orla couldn't understand.

Orla frowned. "Can you speak English?" Then she laughed at the absurdity of it—because of course this girl, a Neanderthal, could not.

The prehistoric girl continued muttering, refusing to look Orla in the eye, though she was now lifting her pendant up, like she was pointing it at Orla.

"Just wait here, wait a minute," Orla told the girl, knowing there was no point in speaking to her, but she did it all the same. She pulled out her phone, checking the time. *Damn.* It was late. "I need to check the lab." *I need to see if I can reverse this.*

Orla locked the girl in the storeroom and ran with her dogs through the building. She dropped Teddy and Jasper off in her apartment and grabbed the swiped ID card again, but when she got down to the basement, she found it did not work. The security had been changed for the control room, and she had no way to get to the black box. Instead, she stepped up to the viewing platform of the Stone Age Arena and gasped.

The mammoths were there. It had *worked.*

They both looked like she expected baby mammoths to look. Like elephants, but woollier. The two calves were side by side, nudging the ground with their trunks. They looked a bit anxious but relieved to have company.

Orla again thought of the Neanderthal girl, alone. How scared she must be. But maybe if she could see animals she was used to, that might help? No, what was Orla thinking! She couldn't risk bringing the girl here where her father might see her.

Orla pulled her phone out and began filming the mammoth babies.

"You better not post those on socials," a voice said behind her. "You haven't filed media release forms."

She turned to see an attendant she recognized. Her father had tried to set her up with this man on more than one occasion. Winston X. Feeney didn't want his only daughter marrying some stranger, bringing someone new into his secrets.

"Your dad's a real genius, you know," said the attendant.

No, he's a real abomination. Through gritted teeth, she smiled as sweetly as she could at the attendant, and that seemed to satisfy him. In fact, as he moved toward one of the locked doors, he glanced back at her shyly, blushing. It again reminded Orla of how *different* she felt. She'd never crushed on anyone. She'd assumed that was because she wasn't a normal teenager going to school, but then she'd never had crushes on celebrities either.

Eventually the attendant left, and Orla looked at the creatures again. Her father wasn't the only abomination, messing with time. Because Orla had made things worse. Her sabotage hadn't stopped the experiment—it had made it even bigger.

Her father would never forgive her for hiding a real Neanderthal from him, but she also knew what he would do if he found an actual prehistoric person in his building.

Eight years ago, he'd become obsessive. Orla's mother's ancestry DNA results had revealed a higher-than-expected percentage of Neanderthal DNA for a modern European woman, and he'd subjected her to endless testing and procedures that had led to her stroke. Of course, the doctors said her mother's stroke was just a coincidence. But Orla hadn't been able to forgive him then, and she still couldn't forgive him now.

She gritted her teeth and thought of how many days she'd spent with Granny back then. It had been her only safe space, a place her father would never step after his wife's death: her mother's mother's house.

Orla couldn't hide the girl in the storeroom for long.

But she knew exactly where she'd take her.

The Goddess had beckoned for Nala to follow her. First to a very strange cave that smelled like it was some sort of conjuring room, and then to another place that she supposed was like a hut.

Now, Nala was up high. Too high. She placed her hands on the pane of hard air in front of her and looked down. It was dark outside, except there were fires on very long poles—poles that didn't look like they were made from wood—and she could see a lot from here. The Goddess had taken her to a village. *Their* village. That had to be it. She could see lots of these "huts"—for she could only think of them as huts, even though she knew they were something different, each with their own hard air, lit by the suns inside them.

The Goddess had tapped on a certain part of the wall, and sunlight had flooded the room from a strange star on the ceiling, even though it was night. She'd shown her how to do it, but Nala hadn't liked having that control, that power. It wasn't right.

Though the Goddess didn't speak her language, Nala sensed the divine one's desire for tranquility. The moment after anyone was snatched by a God or Goddess was called "the calming," so she forced herself to think peaceful things. Gods and Goddesses didn't like angry people. They punished angry people. If she remained good and willing to do whatever it was that she was meant to do, the Goddess might tell her if her Clan were safe. She might tell her why she'd snatched Nala to this divine land, and she might let her go home.

The Goddess had retreated to a different room in the hut after offering Nala unusual clothes and food. She'd shown Nala how to lift a lever to get a stream of water even though there was no nearby river or spring. The Goddess had even demonstrated urinating while sitting on a strange, cold chair and after had pressed a button which whipped water round and round its bowl!

It was all too much for Nala. She held her shaman's pendant, even though it reminded her of her failure. *I lost the whole Clan in Tunaski. I did something so wrong in the ceremony that a Goddess snatched me up.*

Nala whispered for her parents. For anyone. A slow humming emerged from her throat. She knew the power of sound even if it turned out she didn't know the shamanic powers as well as she thought she did.

Through the air panes of the other huts, she saw divine ones moving about. Nala counted. Three in the one opposite. Two in the next. Five—or was it six?—in the one after. She waited for them to step outside their huts and greet each other. For them to say the nightly rites, for the communal goodnight ceremony to begin. For her to see who the Village Chief would designate to be on night watch. But none of that happened. The Gods and Goddesses didn't behave like Clan. They weren't a social people. Even when divine ones from different huts stepped outside at the same time, they didn't run to each other and hug. Across the night and into the next sunrise, there was no amassing for hunts, no groups for gathering. But then again, they probably didn't need to hunt or gather. They were divine beings!

They did show affection, sometimes. Older ones hugged young

ones. A God kissed a Goddess on the mouth. But they only interacted with the others in their hut. And they never sang, so the land never sang back. It was a realm of lost melodies.

There was one God in particular Nala noticed: a man who looked as old as the stars. He lived alone, and when he ventured out, she could tell he was lonely. He had no one. He seemed to have lost life's joy.

Nala wondered who the Goddess who'd brought her here lived with, or if she resided alone like the man, and if that meant she couldn't interact with other divine beings.

Nala couldn't imagine growing up and living in a hut with only her parents, or indeed with only a romantic partner—and she certainly couldn't imagine wanting to kiss anyone. Yet here if you had no partner or children, it seemed you *were* alone. There was no communal living. The joy of her life was in companionship, in having people around, all the time, for everything, without it being dependent on romance or mating.

Was this to be her punishment, to be trapped here for eternity because she'd failed to protect her people? She couldn't imagine anything worse. The Clan modeled their life on the ways of so many of the great animals. All the herds lived in groups—mammoths and aurochs and steppe ponies. The Clan were social creatures. Sure, some formed romantic bonds, sharing exclusive hearths, but there were many Clan who didn't—and they weren't isolated because of it. They were still in the communal caves and dancing in the ceremonies and hunting and worshipping together and resting under the night sky with everyone else. Still able to laugh and cry together, eat and play. There was always someone there. Someone to talk to, be with. You were never on your own, for huts were mere shelters and not cages.

The Gods and Goddesses were clearly not like the Clan, and it was sad. It was this sadness, this feeling of being isolated and trapped here—forever—that made Nala panic when the Goddess returned.

Today, her robes were a different fabric and a darker color. She was loud, too, speaking her strange language. She smelled too flowery. Nala didn't like that. But she had to go close to her and bow her head in a sign of respect before she spoke.

"Are my people okay? Have they been lost in Tunaski?"

But the Goddess just looked confused.

"Please help them," Nala begged. "They did nothing wrong, for this was all me. I messed up, somehow. I thought I was strong enough to . . ." Her shoulders shook. "Please, just help them. Make them safe."

But all the Goddess did was hold up a small rectangular thing and—

Nala's eyes widened as she saw the mammoths. She stared at them, two babies, and she spoke softly, murmuring the mammoths' incantation of her people. The incantation was a sign of thanks to the animals' spirits, for allowing the Clan to feast upon them whenever the hunters were successful. As a shaman, Nala's role was to give this thanks, and even though she didn't know if she was still a shaman right now, given her failure, the soft, rhythmic vibration calmed her. Immediately, she felt better, and she reached out to touch the mammoths. Was this a portal that the Goddess was holding? Did she need to climb inside it to get back? Was it as simple as that?

But her fingers touched the hard portal. She tried to pry it open, momentarily uncaring of how rude she was being, but the Goddess shook her head, pulling the portal away from her.

"Please, can I go back?" Nala asked, and her muscles slackened. Her vision blurred, and tears rolled down her face, even though she was trying to control her feelings. But life was *about* emotion. It was about art and music and expression, and bodies were supposed to brim with sensations for it was fervors that stirred the energy of Mother Earth. "I don't know what I did wrong in the ceremony, but I—"

The Goddess spoke again, but the words weren't like any language Nala had heard. There were sounds she'd never even comprehended, a song inside out. And then the Goddess put the portal away, hiding it in her robes, and Nala cried harder.

The Goddess beckoned for Nala's attention and then tapped her own chest, saying a word that sounded like "Orla," and Nala recognized that tapping. The Clan did it too. It meant *This is my name.*

"My name's Nala," Nala said, trying to smile, trying to appear grateful, trying to appease the Goddess. "Nala."

"Orla," the Goddess said again, and Nala really couldn't believe it. She had the name of a Goddess! *Orla.* And Nala sang her name in the way Goddesses' names should be sung.

The Gods and Goddesses were supposed to be aloof. That's what she'd been taught. They never wanted to talk to mere mortals. They were too superior for that, and when angry, they snatched mortals away.

But Orla seemed kind. She smiled a lot, spoke in a calming tone, and last night she'd given Nala clothing and food.

"Please tell me what I need to do to make sure my people are safe," Nala said, even though she knew the Goddess would not understand. "I can do the Tunaski ceremony. I can go outside and collect the ingredients for the drink, so the melody has the right energy." She glanced back at the hardened pane of air. She wasn't familiar with this land. Were the components she needed available? And what if Nala's suggestion had angered the divine one?

But the Goddess was still smiling at her, and Nala felt tension ease out of her shoulders as she realized how young the Goddess seemed. Weren't Goddesses supposed to be older than Mother Earth herself?

Maybe this Goddess is new. Maybe I'm the first mortal she's worked with. She must still be learning her powers. But I will help her.

The Clan would always help anyone who needed it. Nala started toward the door where the Goddess had entered, but suddenly the divine one spoke and rushed forward to stop her.

Nala froze, turning to the Goddess, her eyebrows raised in question.

The Goddess held up a finger for a moment and then went into another room. Nala started to follow, and the Goddess looked back, nodding, and this warmed Nala—they were understanding each other.

Inside this next room, there was a large flat thing that appeared to be made of wood, balancing on four wooden poles that looked a bit like very straight, short, and narrow tree trunks. The Goddess put some thin pieces of a light-colored material on the large flat thing. Then she reached for what looked like a stick, and she began to draw, and where she touched the stick to the light-colored material, marks were left behind.

Nala's breaths buzzed through her. She found herself humming on instinct. She wasn't a Drawing Maker herself, but like all Clan children, she'd dipped her fingers in ochre and left her marks on the Sacred Cave's wall. Nala watched as the Goddess made drawing after drawing, and Nala sang the song of the spirits, for one always had to sing to keep the spirits pleased when one was making drawings.

Nala's song seemed to surprise the Goddess at first, but then her shoulders relaxed, and she drew more and more, glancing at Nala with encouraging smiles. When the Goddess finally appeared to have finished making her art, she held up a drawing to Nala and said a word that was short and abrupt, angry, as she pointed at her drawing. It was the color of sunshine, a round ball with lots of wiggly yellow lines coming from it.

"A racing fire?" Nala thought of the stories Clan elders passed down, of fiery balls that bolted from a land far away, high up in the sky, and that made hissing sounds and brought fire to where they landed on Mother Earth. *Racing fires are bad,* her grandmother had said. *They bring death and destruction.*

The Goddess said the short word again, and she was nodding a lot, and this made Nala's eyes widen and her brow sweat. She'd been snatched in time to receive this warning—a racing fire was on its way! Her mind stampeded. What could she sing to stop a racing fire? Sweat dripped down her spine as she began a soothing song, one to counteract the coming evil. The Goddess smiled.

"But when is it going to be?" Nala asked, after she'd finished her song. "I have to warn my people in case my song isn't enough. I have to go back to the mortal realm." She ran to the hard air, pressing her face and hands against it, looking for the ghost of the lunar body that could save her. The moon was important to Clan life, for the moon was Mother Earth's guardian, her protector. The moon saved Mother Earth, blocking her from racing fires—but a big one was coming; that was what the Goddess had told her.

Nala looked up at the sky, and she felt this certainty in the way her blood throbbed through her body. She turned back to the Goddess. "Please tell me what to do."

But the Goddess just held up the drawing of the racing fire and said that word again—the angry one that sounded like "Zunn"—and then beckoned for Nala to sit as she began to draw more and more pictures of all the things that were to come to the Clan.

Nala nodded and nodded, and she sang the right spirit songs for each drawing, and the Goddess was smiling, and Nala found herself smiling, too. She was doing the right thing; the divine one was happy. And soon, soon the Goddess would add her own song when it was time for Nala to leave, and Nala's shamanic power would amplify and then she would get back home.

"Sorry, can I just ask you to repeat that?" Orla asked a week later, a LivXtra phone clamped to her ear. It was her weekly day to work for her father, and she could hardly believe what this pompous man was asking—some dude named Neil Elton Rodgers who had already told her five times that he was really, really important.

Next to her, Teddy and Jasper noisily ate their dinners, and she stared at the splashes of wet dog food as they appeared on the tiled floor. In the background, she had a light instrumental piece playing on repeat. It was one that Nala had seemed to particularly like when she'd played it at Granny's house, and just last night, Orla had had the weirdest dream: Nala, in a cave, wearing a headdress of raven feathers, lifting her hands above her head until power radiated from her fingertips like lightning and shook the world—and all the while, that same instrumental was playing. Now, Orla found that the soothing notes were making her want to sketch that vision of Nala instead of listening to this man.

"*How* many?" she asked.

Neil Elton Rodgers made a sound deep in his throat that transported along the phone line in remarkable detail. "One hundred breeding females and twenty breeding males, as soon as the expansion to the existing program is running. Have you written that down?"

She hadn't written anything, mainly because she'd been drawing. The papers spread over her desk were the only way she could communicate with Nala, and Orla's art made Nala sing. Orla loved it when the Neanderthal sang.

Orla had never been a fan of music before. She'd been so focused on art, viewing the two as entirely separate, but now she could see connections between these forms of expression. While she hadn't been making as much progress with teaching Nala English, they had connected through song and sketch. It had opened up an almost friendship between the two of them, and it really drilled home just how isolated Orla had been.

"Prehistoric World will be paying the absolute *premium* prices," Neil Elton Rogers continued, "and I also require the opportunity to discuss with your director a period of exclusivity. We've already corresponded via email on the dates that the new beasts will be brought here."

The new beasts? A bitter taste filled Orla's mouth, and she stared at her drawing of fire. She'd tried to use it yesterday to ask Nala if she was warm enough, but the Neanderthal had become frightened when Orla pointed at the flames. Since then, she'd been drawing everything else she could think of—fish, chickens, carrots, potatoes, water, the moon, anything that she thought the girl would already know. But drawing images like these wasn't yet helping them discuss the important things. Like how to get the girl home. And all Nala wanted to do was sing and look out of the nearest window, all the time, even though it made Orla nervous that the neighbors would realize Granny's house was occupied.

"I will of course pay top money," Neil Elton Rodgers said.

I bet you will.

Jasper barked, a short staccato that made Orla jump, for it was like a knife plunged into the soothing instrumental background.

"And I trust that this deal will be fulfilled as soon as is possible?"

As soon as was polite, Orla ended the call. Her phone rang almost immediately, and she breathed deeply. *Can I just have a moment to myself?*

It was her father, his name and image on the screen, summoning her for a rare dinner together. After Orla had returned her dogs to her apartment, she tried to wipe the charcoal off her fingers and picked at the paint stains on her clothes, but she needn't have bothered. Ten minutes later, when they sat in a private booth of LivXtra's bistro, steaming plates in front of them, her father barely looked at her.

"We've isolated the soul-stamps of hundreds more individuals. Ones of breeding age, so we can of course start with the new program right away."

"The new program?" Orla shook her head slowly. "I didn't think this was the plan."

"Breeding the mammoths was *always* the plan."

Orla's fork clattered to her plate. "But not right away." *And not with so many.*

"No point waiting until our first calves reach sexual maturity. We need to strike while the iron is hot." Winston X. Feeney's voice was clipped. "The next batch of mammoths is set for tonight."

"Tonight?"

"Midnight." He nodded. "There are worries about our genetic material degrading over time, especially due to the process, so time is of the essence."

Orla's eyes widened. "You're using the *same* material?"

Her father nodded. "We have adjusted the life-stamp locators, and we know that those exact molecules will work for individuals within the same family due to shared genetics. In fact, why don't you take a look at it all? A little extra studying wouldn't hurt. I know what your grades in biology and chemistry are like. You've got to get the best science degree you can before you become a mother, because you'll need to teach your children. It's imperative you understand."

I'm going to study art. She gritted her teeth and imagined a world where she'd live in university halls with other artists. Where she'd be around people, where no one would expect anything from her—academic or romantic or otherwise. Where she'd be happy.

But she knew that wasn't an option for her. Her father would ensure it.

As soon as her father returned to his office to prepare for the next stage, Orla left for the lab. Her father couldn't use that same genetic material—contaminated with the spray paint and the ochre pigment—again, in case it brought more Neanderthals here. He just couldn't! But security was tighter than last time. With tears in her eyes, she found she couldn't even get near the Stone Age Arena, let alone the lab containing the genetic material. She left, crestfallen.

Granny's house stood in darkness, no lights on, and Orla let herself in. She flooded the rooms with light and found Nala sitting on the bathroom floor, singing softly, with Granny's mixing bowl full of watery greenness with porridge oats and little black specks floating in it. And—

"Is that toilet cleaner?" Orla took the bowl away from Nala just as the girl seemed ready to take a big swig of it.

As usual, the Neanderthal didn't fight her. If anything, with every visit, the girl seemed more relaxed. Orla gestured for Nala to join her in Granny's sitting room. Orla sat on one side of the sofa, and Nala carefully arranged herself on the Afghan rug. Orla had seen her spend more and more time—even sleeping—on that rug.

Orla sighed. Time was creeping by, and soon her father would export the huge "batch of mammoths." *Export.* As if they were products. But maybe Nala could help stop more Neanderthals arriving, at least.

"There has to be a way we can communicate better," Orla said. "Because I *really* need your help now." She thought of the dream she'd had and froze. Nala . . . was she a shaman? "Can you stop my father bringing more of you here?"

Nala just stared at her. Frustration built in Orla's back—a slow, creeping tension that got heavier and heavier the more she tried to connect with Nala.

"Powers? Magic?" Orla reached for her sketchbook and tried to reproduce that image of Nala conducting a ritual, but her lines were too fast, sloppy, and it didn't have the same power.

Time was running out, and so Orla drew stars instead, and a wand—then she let out a dark laugh. She added lots of dots, as if those could be specks of glitter, though she should have just concentrated on drawing her dream vision.

And then—then her pen ran out.

She scribbled and scribbled with it, but it was no use. She shook out the contents of her bag, but it was all just loose sketches and pencil sharpeners and erasers and half a can of graphite fixative. Frantic, she searched Granny's house—but there were no drawing implements.

Orla turned to Granny's bookcase. There were numerous books on folklore and witchcraft—ones that had probably belonged to Orla's mother. Orla pulled out several volumes and held them toward Nala, pointing at pictures of goddesses and witches. Nala shook her head, though she took one of the books, holding it flat on her outstretched, open palm, and then began speaking in her own language.

"Yes?" Orla asked. "You understand?" She showed Nala how to open the book, flicking through pages, and then stopped at an image of a coven performing a spell. They were all connected, in a circle, and there were candles in the center. "We can get some candles too."

Nala crossed to the window, staring at the moon, which looked kind of red in color. But Orla couldn't let that distract her. Orla retrieved Granny's candles from above the fridge. She used Granny's old lighter to light four of them and set them on the middle of the living room table.

"Nala!" Orla beckoned Nala over.

Nala's eyes were wide as she turned around, and she stared rigidly at the flames for a few moments, before stepping toward Orla.

"Hold hands?" Orla held her own out to Nala, and the girl nodded, though she kept trying to look back out of the window. It was awkward, each at opposite ends of the table, stretching forward to reach the other. The candles' warmth licked Orla's face, and sweat formed on her brow. "What about your chanting? Do we do that now?" Orla tried to copy what she'd heard the girl say before, and she lifted both their hands up in imitation of the photo in the book.

But nothing was working.

How do you tell a Goddess to stop? Because that was really what Nala needed the Goddess to do, if the Tunaski ceremony was going to work. She tried to keep one eye on the red moon outside through the hardened air, but the flames the Goddess was controlling were flickering too brightly, and the Goddess was yelling and creating too much angry energy. Nala needed to tell her this—and that the opportunity for the ceremony was slipping away—but the Goddess was just getting increasingly jumpy.

Finally, Nala turned her back on her, her mind racing as she hoped the Goddess wouldn't see this as a sign of disrespect. She hunched her body by the hardened air, her gaze and focus on the red moon. She breathed deeply, trying to conjure the song in her mind, bring it alive in the way she knew some shamans could. She held her pendant up to the moon. It clanked against the hardened air.

"Yezzz, yezzz!" the Goddess cried, and Nala jumped as the divine being suddenly appeared next to her. The Goddess's voice rose in pitch and volume, and then she was grimacing a bit, showing her teeth.

Nala tried to ignore her, focusing back on the moon. The hut was smoky, and her eyes ached. Her mind spun as she tried to conjure the right sounds. She poured all her energy into it and then . . . she could hear the faint beat of it. It was here. She'd made it real.

Her breaths came in short, sharp bursts. She still needed the Tunaski drink. The Goddess had tipped away the makeshift one she'd prepared earlier. In the near darkness, Nala moved away from the hardened air. Her steps were light, and her pendant hung freely against her chest. She saw the shadowed shape of a bowl in the place where the Goddess had charmed water to appear from a narrow, stem-like contraption, and she picked up the bowl slowly. The Tunaski song was still a dull beat in her ears. But she'd made it real, and she could do this, too. She took a deep breath.

The Goddess began to speak. It was a question but that was all that Nala could tell.

Light flooded the hut suddenly, and Nala shrieked as she saw only white shapes and smoky haziness, her eyes unable to adjust quickly. "Darkness, it has to be dark!" She nearly dropped the bowl, but the Goddess moved her arm, and darkness prevailed once more.

Nala held her breath and listened for the drums, the notes of the song. Slowly, the faint sounds reemerged. She swallowed the lump in her throat, and in the soft darkness, she made her way back to where the brightly colored hide lay on the ground. She arranged herself carefully, folding herself up small, and placed the bowl in front of her.

Her magic felt good and strong, just as it should. So maybe she wasn't a bad shaman after all.

Nala whispered and whispered, and at the other end of this room in the hut, the candles bloomed with light again. So much light. When she looked up, the Goddess's face was framed by it, the divine one hovering over them, at the table.

A melodic tone rang through the hut once, twice, three times, four . . . and it kept going.

Nala held her hands over the bowl and closed her eyes. Conjuring sound and light was easy, but conjuring the drink? Her body trembled, and the pit of her stomach felt greasy. But then she heard it: the soft sound of droplets. *Plop. Plop. Plop.*

She did not open her eyes until she was sure there was enough, and the moment she allowed herself to see, the droplets stopped. But the drink was *there.*

"Now we have to drink." She looked up at the Goddess for a moment, then held the bowl to her own lips. She took a swift gulp, then offered the bowl to the Goddess. "Please take the rest."

The Goddess asked a question, and Nala assumed she was inquiring whether it was safe for her as a divine one. Everyone present had to drink for the ceremony to work, but there'd never been a Goddess present at one before. Nala nodded, cautious.

The Goddess took the bowl, but she did not drink.

"Drink! Drink, please! We're running out of time!"

And finally, the Goddess drank.

Uncertainly, Orla sat on the sofa, the strange aftertaste in her mouth. Her body hummed, and her head felt too heavy as she waited for something to happen. The echo of the clock's midnight chimes played in her mind. She was still holding Granny's lighter, gripping it hard, like it would provide reassurance. Nala was smiling at her from the Afghan rug, so Orla wondered if they had stopped it—even though whatever that drink was, she'd drank it just *after* midnight.

Her stomach churning, she grabbed her phone. The BBC was live-reporting her father's work, as was every other news platform in the world because it had worked. Two hundred mammoths.

Orla frantically scanned article after article for any mention of Neanderthals, but there were none. Yet. Could the drink have worked? She stared wearily around, half expecting a flurry of cavemen to appear in Granny's house. A glance back at her phone showed she'd opened Instagram without realizing, and muscle memory kicked in as she scrolled down automatically. A reel began playing, and a staccato drumming rhythm filled the room. Orla was about to apologize and turn it off when Nala lifted her hands and began making the same noise, deep in her throat.

The hairs on Orla's arms rose, and Orla found herself transfixed. She dropped the phone and left the sofa, inching closer to Nala, a sudden warmth washing over her. Nala's upturned face was smiling. A lightness exuded from the girl, and when Orla took Nala's hand—a movement she hadn't even anticipated—she felt something. A click inside her. A sense of awareness, not just in her body, but outside too. A sense of the *whole* world. Of thousands of things that she didn't understand. It was all so . . . vast. But it felt *right.* It felt welcoming. There was no sense of danger. Only . . . belonging.

Nala began to sing, and it was a song that was like . . . well, it didn't sound like anything a human could make. Her voice was truly angelic, and it filled everything, lifting Orla up.

Something inside Orla instructed her to match the notes, so pure and clear, as best she could. A strange energy wrapped around her as the two girls sang, facing each other. Orla felt something she'd never experienced before: a true sense of *belonging.* She squeezed Nala's hand harder, and Nala squeezed back.

A fluttering sensation filled Orla's chest, and her eyes drifted shut. But she could still *see*—that was the strange thing. All around her, there were people, their shapes emerging out of shadows and darkness. People like Nala, smiling and singing. Whole groups of them, hand in hand, their bodies dancing in front of a painted cave wall. Orla's head felt heavy—but she couldn't tell if that was her real body or this new one where she was in this cave, soaking up the communal energy of this land, these people, her gaze falling on red handprints on the wall and dots and circles and jagged lines that looked a little like hashtags.

Thank you—and the voice, Nala's voice, entered Orla's mind. It was like water soaking into a parched land—desperately needed. This was . . . *right*. It was communication fueled by a pulsing energy, and Orla didn't understand. But Nala was speaking to her.

Orla felt her body—a body that she was now certain was so far away—jolt, and yet she looked down and saw her bare feet on the stone floor.

It's okay, Nala said to her, and Orla realized that in this new place she was also hand in hand with Nala, and then Nala was running, and other girls were running with them, out of this cave and into bright sunlight where the sky sparkled. The air hummed with life and meaning, and Orla felt joy—pure, unbridled joy—floating around her like a soft cushion. She leaned back, feeling this world support her.

An unfamiliar energy seeped into her bones, into her mind, but it was good. Everyone was smiling, and Orla was not alone. For the first time in her life, there was an attainable future that she wanted: a future with other people, where she could make art and sing and be happy and not worry about getting married or getting a degree.

Warmth bloomed in Orla's heart. *This is what I've been waiting for.*

You like it? Nala asked, and then other girls and women were saying things to her, too, but it was Nala's voice that blossomed the strongest. *You can join us, if you like.*

Orla blinked, and something clicked in her mind. Her father's face loomed over her, a darkness in his eyes as he yanked her by the arm into a laboratory, as he forced her into graduation robes, as the attendant appeared by her side, and her father wrapped a piece of rope around Orla's hand and the attendant's. "Give me a grandson," Winston X. Feeney instructed Orla, and she blinked again, and there was a ring on her finger, and it was so tight, squeezing and squeezing.

"No!" Orla cried, and the moment she said it, the images of her father, the attendant, the wedding ring, all melted away.

We live as we want, Nala said to her. *You've warned us of so much, and I can sense this sadness and fear in you, for you do not want to live as divine ones do, but you're with us now, and we'll offer you a life with us if you'll accept.*

Orla looked at Nala and she knew . . . she *knew* this was the type of life she wanted. One where she could make art and music and be with others in the way that was right for her.

She didn't need to be lonely.

She blinked.

A haziness wrapped around Orla, and slowly she became aware of that staccato beat again, of Nala's singing, back in the real world—Orla's world. And Orla somehow managed to break through it, remind herself of what was important.

A shard of iciness filled Orla's body as she let go of Nala's hands, in both Orla's world and Nala's. The transition was abrupt, jagged. Orla's chest squeezed, and pain wound its way through her body, down her spine, settling in her gut. But she was back. The video was still playing on her phone, and for a moment, all Orla could do was gulp as she struggled to acclimatize.

Her breaths were ragged as she grabbed her tote bag, stuffing her art supplies back in it. "I'll be back soon, okay?"

But Nala didn't answer. She still sat there, on the Afghan rug, singing, her hands held high to the ceiling of Granny's house. And Nala's body . . . it was shimmering.

The fire alarm blared in LivXtra's complex. Orla was in the control room at the side of the arena once more. She'd stolen her father's ID card. Unlike when she had tried to sabotage her father's work, the temperature inside was sub-zero, and through the multilayered glass window, the whole herd of mammoths was screaming and stampeding. Blood was being drawn, smaller mammoths gored by the ivory tusks of older, frantic ones.

Maybe setting the fire alarm off wasn't the best idea, but it had given her time. While all the employees were evacuating, Orla could destroy the machine before the fire brigade arrived. She pressed buttons and pulled levers, but she hadn't a clue what she was doing, and no matter how many buttons she pressed or levers she pulled, nothing was actually happening. *Damn.* She plunged her sweaty hands into her pockets and—

Her eyes widened as her fingers found something.

Her breath caught in her throat, and she pulled Granny's lighter out of her pocket. When she flicked its switch, the flame burned brightly. The fire alarm was already on, and it was like it was goading her. She had her tote bag with her, with her sketches and erasers and pencil sharpeners and the half-used can of graphite fixative.

She might as well . . .

She pulled the can out. There was a hazard symbol on it: a flame inside a red diamond. She sprayed it liberally over the control panel, then lit the lighter and touched the flame to it. Orange flames licked along the buttons and switches, and the fire got bigger and bigger. It grew at an almighty rate, and Orla shrank back, part of her surprised that she'd actually done it.

She pushed open the steel door, coughing, her eyes smarting. The rush of fresh air fueled the fire behind her, but she slammed the door shut, breathing hard. She waited a moment to ensure that the control room was as fireproof as she believed and that no smoke was filling the mammoths' arena, and then she ran all the way back to Granny's house, not stopping to catch her breath until she arrived fifteen minutes later.

Finally, Orla heaved a sigh of relief.

Granny's house was empty.

Nala opened her eyes to the worried faces of her parents. Coldness wrapped around her, and then she was crying, and her mother was crying, and her father was crying. And everyone in the Clan was crying.

It worked. It worked.

Nala turned, trying to see everyone. Yes, there were her cousins, and her aunt, and the hunters were back.

"Is everyone safe?" Nala's voice broke. "Has anyone been lost?"

"No one has been lost," her father said, gently touching her shoulder. "You kept us all safe."

"But I went to the land of the Goddesses!" Nala cried, and a wave of exhaustion shook her. "And there are racing fires coming for us and—"

"Hush, my girl," her mother said. "You are safe now."

"But the racing fires!"

"Now we know, we can put up the wards," her father said.

"Can I help, too?" Was she truly a shaman now?

"You can," her father agreed. "But Tunaski took a lot out of you. Your mother kept your body safe until I returned, and until you were strong enough to come back to us. But you need to rest. Oh, my sweet girl, you've done so well. You did exactly as a good shaman should."

Nala's hand still shook with the energy, the impression of the Goddess's hand in hers. She turned her head, and more of the Clan neared her. Hands reached out, wanting her. Every person in a group had to touch the skin of a newly qualified Shaman—and that was what she was.

Her heart bloomed with warmth. *I did it.*

One Year Later

Hardly able to believe that any of this was real, Orla stared at the crisp white building of Arts University Plymouth. It was so geometric and refreshing—nothing like the LivXtra building—and she was *here.*

"We made it," she said, looking down at her dogs.

This was all she'd come with: Jasper, Teddy, and a suitcase full of everything they'd need for the next three years. She didn't have many of her original art supplies now; her father had disowned her the moment she'd been found responsible for the fire that had destroyed the most important room at LivXtra and had chucked out most of her belongings—but it was the best thing that could've happened. She'd moved into Granny's house, and it had hardly felt real when she'd applied for the BA degree in Painting, Drawing, and Printmaking.

But it was real.

"Are we ready for this?" she asked Teddy and Jasper, and both dogs looked at her with their beautiful eyes.

Orla nodded. *We're ready.*

And she thought of Nala, of the courage and vision that the Neanderthal had given her: a life that was different but acceptable.

Orla was finally ready to be herself.

INDULGE THE OTHER

LAURA POHL

The first time you hear that love will be your undoing is when you are beaten within an inch of your life. The laboratory is in shambles, glass digging against the heels of your palms as you bleed out on the linoleum. You will not die, of course. That is not how you were made. But it is your work on the floor, shattered, and so, it is the closest to losing your life you have ever been before.

The hero stands over you, their expression righteous.

"You lost," they say. "And it's because you do not understand love."

You do not, in fact, understand it, as you do not understand how your failure has anything to do with a feeling, or that elusive thing others have called *love.*

Someone takes you away. The wrecked body on the floor—

not yours—is all you can look at before the doors of the laboratory finally shut.

They put you in a juvenile detention facility, which amuses you, at least. You imagine the discussion between the hero and the authorities over what to do with you, whether to judge you by your face or what is inside your body. You are young and still look like a child that has not quite settled into adulthood—you will always look this way, although you stopped feeling weighted by that notion years ago. The pimples, if anything, are a sign that your skin still changes with the light of the sun, and that you are alive to feel bothered by them.

There is routine in detention. The waking, the exercise, the meals, the work. You do not cause any trouble, and you do not stand out. The other teenagers approach you with care—a hopeless companionship for a hopeless situation, like all of you are sharing the same lifeboat. With your good behavior, they let you work in the infirmary sorting the inventory.

That is their mistake.

You start taking things, but not ones that the wardens will notice. You collect people's scraps and the old electronic material the prison frequently changes out for new parts. Camera wires, batteries, circuit boards, diodes. They're not prime material, but they work for a coarse version of what you had spent so many years on before. You leave it hidden in the infirmary—dangerous, but easier to hide things within than your cell. You build it just like last time.

You remember your father's diagrams so well they might as well have been burned on the back of your eyelids. You do not know whether that is something he could have done. You have opened other parts of yourself, but never your brain.

You build the very thing that they locked you away for. It takes time. People forget what you are. Until, of course, your creation wakes.

You see the light behind its eyes. They are mismatched. One comes from a dead body, the other comes from a ward who had their orbit gouged out in a patio knife fight, and the doctor hadn't known how to reattach it. You know how, and so you have. It looks at you, a void behind those eyes. You wonder if that is what your father thought when he saw you the first time.

"Go," you tell your creation. "And satisfy yourself with living."

You learn of its fate soon after, because the hero comes back, slinging your creation's body through the detention door. It is destroyed once again, the brain—the brain you have meticulously crafted for it—has been wrenched from its head, and all that remains is an empty cavity. You feel something when you look at it, something that disappears a second later like it was never in your chest.

The hero throws what's left of your work onto the ground before you. You're sitting on the bench under the sunlight. The hero waits until you look up at them. They are older, visibly. White in their hair and wrinkles around their eyes. You had not realized it had been that long. Now they're the one who looks out of place. Everyone with matching uniforms to yours looks like they have a whole life ahead of them.

"You will not win," the hero says, as if they have to repeat it to believe it. "It is not human. It will never be human. It will never understand us."

Then they step closer and tear your arm off.

The older children on the patio gasp. One of them throws up. They break into a run and scatter back into the facility, but not before shooting a few looks toward you. A part of you wants it to be pity. They have shared your meals and dreamt the same dreams. You're not that different from them, except that the truth of you now lies exposed. They will know.

The socket sizzles where the arm's been torn off. It is not painful. You had turned the pain receptors off a long time ago. Still, the arm now lies next to your creation on the floor, half-flesh, half wire. The hole sizzles in static.

"You won't understand us either," the hero says. "If not me, my children will stop you. And my children's children. This I swear to you, villain."

You take your place in the narrative. The hero has called you villain, and so you are.

It is easy being the villain—everyone already expected it of you, and it is pleasing to fulfill expectations. You are already unnatural to the eyes of the world. Humans are organic, and they are mortal. You are neither of those things, although no one has asked you if you prefer it that way.

When the experiment fails a third time, when it comes back in ruins along with the face of the hero—not quite the same as before, a promise kept with a younger, fresher version—you are told the same thing. That what you want will never be achieved, for it lacks something every other human carries in their heart.

You remember your father saying he had done what he did for your mother. Love had not saved her, but to be fair, neither had science. Perhaps you, also, are an experiment that has gone wrong, and no one thought to inform you. But the only thing you have is the creation. The only thing left is to do it over and over again, to perhaps understand why a child made of coils and circuits could ever replace one of dead flesh.

It is no use making a living thing only of dead parts—your father's first lesson. Living pieces must be integrated, so perfectly that people cannot tell it apart from themselves.

It is an exercise in futility. They can always tell.

You do not comprehend how.

They now send the older children into the detention center to labor and you are sent to join them. You take up work with them in a mechanization factory. Ironic, in some ways, that you are allowed to build things that look like you. But that is all they are: *things*. And the thing you have been building was never meant to be an object.

You take things there too. They are better, newer things. Things that will last. One of the others notices and says, "You'll end up getting in trouble for that," but they do not stop you. You've seen the others take things, too, because they must learn to strive for themselves. And again that odd kinship is there, reluctant and hidden. You have all been found wanting in the eyes of society. None of you are good enough. You do not know whether you are truly alike, or if it's only the craving of your lonely soul.

You sneak out and dig up graveyards. You raid hospitals. You work on a brain and a heart, and you hope that this will be sufficient.

The next failure, the hero comes to you again. "Why are you doing this?" the hero asks. It's the first time you hear it raw in their voice. No, not truly the first time—there was once, before, when the very first of them offered their hand, a question yearning to be answered, and you had given out the wrong one. "Don't you ever get tired?"

"No," you answer sincerely.

"But it fails," the hero says. "It always fails. So why do you keep trying?"

They don't attack you, which you find strange. At this point, all their ancestors had already beaten you, exposed the wires on your arms, let the blood and the cooling liquid leak to the floor.

"Because I'll get it right eventually," you say, offering the truth. "I have to."

The hero sighs and knocks you out. That is the kindest death you have been given yet.

Not dead. You're not that lucky.

When it is once again made to the best of your abilities, when your creation's hand is almost as perfect as yours, then you tell it the same thing you have told all the others. *Satisfy yourself with living, for that is all there is to it.*

The hero still finds you and brings back your opus. Only its head, severed from the body, the wires cackling in electricity as they dangled from the neck where it once was whole.

"Enough," says the hero.

"I have outlasted your father, and your father's mother, and their mother's father," you say, although you might have gotten the order wrong. Gender has never been a concern of yours. "And I will outlast you too."

"Funny," says the hero, with a new quirk of their mouth. It is jarring. They are never supposed to be new. It's only a perpetual cycle—*your* cycle. But they have changed, and you still have not. "If you outlasted us, you'd have won already."

You cannot resist. This part is what you've come to expect—even look forward to. It's where your work culminates.

"Guess it comes to nothing," the hero finishes, picking up an iron rod from the debris, twirling it in their hands. This one's cruel, you realize too late. "Do you want to know why we last?"

The rod slams right into your stomach tip first, exiting out your back on the other side, and the hero twists it inside your entrails. You almost wish for a data processor in your mind to review the damage, if that would not make you less human and more loathsome.

"We do this," the hero says, taking the rod out and slamming it on the right side of your mandible, cracking bone and circuits, "because we have people to protect." You fall backward. "We do this"—the rod, sharp and terrible, sinks down into your right eye socket, and your vision blinks to black on that side—"because we are loved."

The iron rod—metal of your metal, part of your parts—comes down on you again and again and again, until all the receptors have blinked out, and you cannot see, hear, or smell, until you are reduced to nothing. Obsolete. A broken machine.

You understand, in a flash of clarity, what you are trying to achieve with the experiment. You understand what can happen if your creation finds the thing you've wanted to find all along.

You've seen now what love can do, what it has wrought.

You learn, then, to be afraid of love.

You begin again, with rage this time. You don't think you've ever known that feeling before, but now it burns through your blood vessels like a current, sizzling the nerve endings on your wires. It is rage that makes you build what you have never thought to build before. Why keep it to a predetermined shape, to the limits of a personage? It is not human. It will never be human.

You build a monster.

The monster, ironically, lives longer than the others. It survives like you—in feverish bitterness, in the savage spaces humans have created when they are so certain that everything they have built was upon kindness and acceptance. There is a place for the grotesque, the despised, but apparently no place to pretend you could be more than what you have been violently programmed to be. In this new and terrible world, you thrive.

You are no longer the villain by name but by choice.

You defeat the hero who comes to rise against you. They look older and more fragile, and their life is so easily taken by your hands that you almost let a laugh escape from your lips. You had never killed before.

You try to remember what your father said, when you first opened your eyes and knew yourself to be a living thing. It was not a command, like you are wont to do with the destitute replicas of yourself. Your memory is perfect, but those words were lost in the sensory overload. Next to the dead body, you try to recall that moment, of what it was like living without the weight of anything else.

Something stains your eyes as you think of the proffered hand, the promise you could not accept because you could not fulfill. You don't reach up to see if it's blood, fluid, or tears.

You have created many monsters, but they no longer interest you. They no longer seek the purpose you had started out wanting. They live among the humans, and the humans can no longer tell them apart from themselves. A part of you wonders if that means the work is finished. Another part of you is disgusted by the idea that humans only knew how to tell the robots apart when the machines' desires were greater than their detachment.

Love comes back to haunt you. You leave your monsters be. The world is dark looking out from the stark light of your laboratories. You watch the shadows as they dance across the grass and the tall buildings. You watch the people who walk by without ever raising their heads. A family of three, hand in hand with their toddler in the park. You don't remember if your mother stayed alive long enough for that to happen, or if her grief killed her before then. Couples stroll leisurely with their arms intertwined, smiling.

You come to a stop at a lake. You force a smile. All you see is yourself, standing solitary in the rippling water.

When the hero finds you again, you have almost forgotten about their existence. It seems far too long since anyone has decided to bother you or the army of inhuman things you have unleashed upon the world. They all carry your marks, and if anyone cared to look, they'd know the origins.

You can see the similarities on their face. They've diluted through the generations, but it was easy to know them not only for their features, but the fact that they always stood opposite you—they were the unstoppable force of nature, and you are immutable in your destiny. They are young, but not in the way you appear—your appearance is unchanging, and theirs is fresh like a bloom in spring. The eyes are the only thing that feel old. Sorrowful.

"It's been a long time," you say as you prepare. It's been a while since you killed, longer since you've taken a beating.

The hero sees you preparing. They notice the way you grip one of the screwdrivers in the laboratory bench hard with your fingers. "I'm not here for that."

"Then why have you come?"

The question rings through the empty laboratory space where no current experiment is housed. After the last hero died, you have not tried to create again. That decision should have been meaningful, but instead it's only the tedium of continuance, the pointlessness of repetition.

"I'm the last of my kind," the hero says, in what almost feels like resignation. "Whatever it is that we are, it ends with me."

The burning ardor of rage has left you, but there is still a spark in the dying embers. "One of your ancestors promised me that once, an ending. They did not succeed."

"I'm not here to kill you."

"That is because you can't."

A sardonic smile in reply is all you get.

The hero sits down on one of the stools and twirls around in a circle. One of your senses screams danger, but it has been dulled by recurrence. You know what comes next, so you need not fear it.

Except that the hero does not attack. They do not move against you.

"If I ever die," you say out loud, a thought you've had before but never voiced, "it'll be alone."

"Maybe," the hero agrees. "But you're not alone now."

The hero does not kill you, and more astounding yet, they return. They bring one of your creations along with them. Not destroyed—no wires exposed, no short circuits. It is almost intact, except that it no longer has a will of its own.

"They're starting to turn up like this," the hero says, although you have not asked for an explanation. "That's how I found out about you. My grandfather told me what it was."

The hero leaves the machine on the bench. It is from one of the last batches you made. Even the follicles arrayed along the skin are perfect. You touch the base of its neck, putting pressure in a specific point, and a panel slides off to reveal the workings inside.

"What exactly did you want to find?" the hero asks, and their voice grates on your nerves. You'd forgotten they were present. "Or did you just want company?"

Your creations were for the world, not for yourself. Or at least, not in the stricter sense of the word—they were, in a way, an extension of you. An extension of your desire to find out what was missing, a poor substitute for a soul.

The outstretched hand again, the one you didn't take, and whose fingers closed around nothing when you weren't able to give the right answer. The hand whose bloodied knuckles beat your creation; the hero who'd sworn that the rejection would be your downfall.

When you don't answer, the hero goes on, "Why did you stop?"

The question is in diametric opposition to the previous one. There was a time you could never imagine stopping.

"Because they're all failures," you say at last.

"They seem to live pretty well among humans."

"More insult to humans, then, that have come to rely so on machines." Your voice is vicious and cruel. "In the beginning, they could always tell the machines apart. How artificial they were. How unlike a person. My experiments were deemed repulsive, a corruption of human nature."

"And *were* you trying to corrupt it?" The hero quirks their eyebrow. You get annoyed again. It's such a young, childish feeling that you also get annoyed at yourself for feeling it, and then you wonder if being immortal is even relevant when the feelings of adolescence are the only things that truly stick.

You think of your mother, and the way she had looked at you. Never quite understanding how to truly see you for what you were. You wonder if she had the same questions for your father that all the heroes have asked before.

"No," you reply. "I was just trying to—understand."

"So what went wrong?"

You look at the broken piece of machinery lying on the table. The one that had been made in the image of the old hero—you see that only now, with years of clarity behind you. It was righteous and indifferent, which is worse than being cruel. You loathe the sight of your inadequacy.

"I stopped making them curious," you say at last.

INDULGE THE OTHER

The hero keeps bringing your creations back to you. Some have borne the trials of time, but others seem as intact as the day you made them. Your laboratory becomes a graveyard in reverse. It stores what can yet live, waiting in a state of suspension. You feel no urge to start again. The effort seems insurmountable.

"Is that how you plan to win?" you ask. "Not by beating me and locking me up in some dark cell, but by collecting every single waste I've left behind to prove my work has come to naught?"

"Is that how you think of them? A waste?"

The hero says it to provoke you. Science is never a waste, even when failing.

"Why are you here, then?"

"I have nowhere else to be," the hero says. They move to stand right next to you. You flinch. "Have you ever gone with them?"

"Gone with them?" you repeat, uncomprehending.

"Outside."

"I go outside."

"On your own, sure. But once you're finished with them, do you ever open the door and walk along with them?"

The question robs you of air, so much so that for a moment you forget you are not all machine, and you need it to breathe. What a terrifying reminder. You grip the table, trying to maintain your balance.

"What would be the point?"

"You tell me. It's a bit cruel, letting something so new find out everything by themself." There is no reprimand in the hero's voice, but the conversation takes another turn. "Do you love them?"

You stare at the hero, openly this time. You open and shut your mouth.

"What does love have to do with it?"

"Nothing," the hero says, "and everything."

If you knew how to love properly, you would have not wasted it on experiments. You would not have spent your years poring over creations who could not teach you anything that you did not know already.

"I'm not heartless," you say. You are deeply conscious of the thing you have in your chest, the one that constantly threatens to overwhelm. At this moment, it seems imperative that they understand this about you, as their ancestor did not.

The hero stares. They have such an open, honest face. It pains you to read it so well. You have severed yourself from humanity, but it slips through the cracks still.

"But . . ." you start again, because you now have the urge to be sincere too. "I do not understand love as you do."

"Who says I understand?"

It is said as a statement, not as a question.

"Love is a human thing," you say, because that is the only concept you have been able to grasp, for all these years of trying. "That is the reason your ancestors destroyed my experiments. They were empty."

"Do *you* think you're empty?"

You do not feel a need to answer that. It's implied. If your experiments are empty, they are no different from their creator. They could not become more.

"Is that why you've been doing this?" the hero asks directly, another unavoidable question. "To prove a point?"

You struggle with the question for a moment, but there is only one answer.

"Your ancestor, the very first one," you say, something you have never said out loud but have thought of it often, "had the right of me. They once offered me their hand, and I could not take it."

The hero frowns, drumming their fingers on the table. They're so restless. You were never able to reproduce anything that vibrant or alive.

"What did they ask in return?"

"Why do you assume there is something in return?"

"Because there always is," they reply, jaw set, eyes in turmoil. This is the angriest you've ever seen them, but it does not seem aimed at you. "So what was it?"

"They asked me to be theirs, and to put a ring on my finger to mark me," you reply. "They asked me to promise my eternity."

"You refused."

You stay quiet. Your creations do not breathe with you in the laboratory, their hearts completely still.

"Why?" the hero asks.

"Because I could not love them as they asked," you say. "I rejected the redemption someone was willing to give me."

"Bullshit," says the hero, and you startle like a cornered animal. "That wasn't redemption; that's just subjugation. My ancestor turned on you for that reason?"

You do not understand this anger. It is so similar to your own, when you had given up on understanding humanity, and now the world presents you with the very thing you despised in yourself. It is the rage that reflects equally in you, the anger at this thing that has followed you home. You never had to prove your love; it was always present in whatever you did.

But the hero had not deemed it enough, and you spent the rest of existence doubting it.

"What did you mean when you said you were the last of your kind?" you ask at last, a trepidation in your voice.

"That I'm more like you than you realize," they reply.

You think of the words all the heroes have called you before. Evil, unnatural. Greedy. You never understood why it was so wrong to want more than what you had. Wasn't that your most human trait? The one thing that could prove that you were exactly like them, despite the gears that made your arms move?

The hero offers their hand to you. "Come with me."

You blink, something akin to a laugh bubbling from your throat. "Where?"

"Does it matter?" they retort, unmoving.

You cannot stop asking the question. It is one you learned to ask early on, and it's always on the tip of your tongue. "Why?"

"Because I'm not making the same mistake my ancestor did," the hero tells you, voice nonchalant, their hand still outstretched. "I don't want more than you can give." They swallow. You see anger, still, but also hope. "And I know you won't ask for more either."

Love is not your undoing. It's in your creation.

You close your eyes and think of your father's kind hand brushing your hair away from your forehead. You remember him tinkering around your heart—the only part of you that was made purely of flesh. The one that should have decayed and never did. He had done it for love, and you thought you had understood that, but now you can scarcely imagine it. The sheer force of will it must have taken him to create you.

When you were born, he had given you a brain and a heart, but he had not given you a soul. You had to create it for yourself—out of all the things you learned, out of all the wishes you craved. Out of your inadequacy, out of the lack of understanding. In the hero's outstretched hand, you understand that your humanity has always been there. Whether others recognized it or deemed it enough does not matter. You have found what you had searched for, and it had always been within your grasp

The hero's promise to be the last of their kind remains until their dying breath. After many years, when their lungs stop dragging in air, you take their heart, and you put it in a cavity you had built just for them. You build another experiment, one last time. The creature opens their eyes, and you see yourself reflected in them.

You are wanted for what you can give. You give it freely, and it is enough.

ABOUT THE AUTHORS

Claudie Arseneault is an easily enthused aromantic and asexual writer with a never-ending cycle of obsessions but an enduring love for all things cephalopod and fantasy (together or not!). She writes fantasy stories that center platonic relationships and loves bright magic and heartfelt characters. Her most recent publications are *Painted Flock* and the Chronicles of Nerezia series. In addition to her own fiction, Claudie has co-edited *Common Bonds,* an anthology of aromantic speculative short stories with a sequel incoming. She is a founding member of The Kraken Collective, an alliance of self-publishing SFF authors, and the creator of the Aromantic and Asexual Characters Database.

Kemi Ashing-Giwa is an author and graduate student based in Palo Alto. Her work, which includes *The Splinter in the Sky, This World Is Not Yours,* and *The King Must Die,* has won the Compton Crook Award and has appeared on the *USA Today* bestseller list. Her short fiction, which has been nominated for an Ignyte Award and featured on the Locus Recommended Reading List, has been reprinted in collections including *Some of the Best from Tor.com: 15th Anniversary Edition* and *The Year's Top Tales of Space and Time.* She is now pursuing a PhD in the Earth & Planetary Sciences department at Stanford University.

Ian M. Carlisle has been writing various flavors of fantasy, science fiction, and more since he was in middle school. He graduated magna cum laude with his bachelor's degree in creative writing in 2024. In his downtime hours, Ian's either playing a favorite video game or watching a movie. But writing is never far from his mind; even while relaxing, he's probably thinking of a new story to write or an old one to continue.

Julie Sondra Decker has been a prominent voice for asexual and aromantic communities since 1998. She is the author of the book *The Invisible Orientation*, which was the first mainstream-published asexuality book for the layperson, and she also spreads ace and aro awareness through her popular YouTube videos, blog essays, and articles. Her interviews and reviews have appeared in print and digital media (*The New York Times, Salon, The Daily Beast, TIME Magazine, Marie Claire,* and *The Huffington Post*), on television, on the radio/podcasts, and in 2011's documentary film *(A)sexual.* She has published several asexuality articles with *Good Vibrations, Everyday Feminism,* and *The Toast,* and has given educational talks at the University of Virginia, Creating Change in Atlanta, Ryerson University, Wellesley College, and Princeton University. Julie is also a novelist, and she lives and works in Tampa, Florida.

ABOUT THE AUTHORS

Madeline Dyer is a novelist, anthologist, poet, and literary academic drawn to dark and monstrous stories. Her debut anthology *Being Ace* received a starred review from *School Library Journal* and was a finalist for a 2024 Lambda Literary Award, commemorating "outstanding LGBTQ+ literature from 2023." Her debut novel *Untamed* won the 2015 SIBA award for Best Dystopian Novel. She is currently pursuing a PhD in creative writing at the University of Bristol and also writes asexual romance and contemporary fiction as Elin Annalise.

Isa Fiel has never really stayed in one place for long, though she's currently debating the pros and cons of Southeastern US humidity. They're passionate about reading—and writing!—stories about the complicated nuances of being human. Growing up biethnic, religious, and queer, she's working on creating stories that catch the overlap of experiences that aren't often seen. When not wrangling plot bunnies, they can be found attempting to learn a third language, growing their plushie army, and enjoying older, underrated sci-fi shows that she argues should not have been cancelled.

Kalyn Josephson is a *New York Times*–bestselling author, sometimes-baker, and full-time consumer of too much tea. She lives on the California coast with two tiny black cats in a house in constant need of repair. She is the author of the Ravenfall series, The Storm Crow duology, the This Dark Descent duology, and *The Library of Amorlin.*

Taka Owen is an aroace writer based in Coventry, UK. They spend most of their time being exceptionally busy working at a castle, but still manage to find time to write whenever there's a spare moment. They mainly focus on writing scripts for the screen, but have recently branched out into short stories. Taka loves writing about identity, trauma, and nuclear waste management, and is looking forward to the day when there are less stories about romance and more about zombies. "Lovesick" is their first published work.

Laura Pohl is the *New York Times*–bestselling author of *The Grimrose Girls.* Her debut novel, *The Last 8,* won the International Latino Book Awards. Her work was featured in anthologies such as *Relit, Writing in Color, From a Certain Point of View: Return of the Jedi, Why on Earth,* and *For the Rest of Us.* She likes writing messages in caps lock, never using autocorrect, and obsessing about Star Wars. She will always be on the side of the villains—she will never change, she will never improve, that is a promise. A Brazilian at heart and soul, she makes her home in São Paulo.

Rukman Ragas is a Tamil writer of speculative fiction. A grateful alum of the Clarion West workshop through the Octavia E. Butler Memorial Scholarship, their work has appeared in venues such as *khōréō*, *Apex*, and *The Baltimore Review*. When not writing, he splits his time between diving into obscure legends of his heritage and playing D&D.

Soumi Roy is a writer born and raised in a small city called Midnapore in West Bengal, India, but chased her dreams to Seoul, where she pursued a PhD in biomedical engineering with a focus on the early detection of Alzheimer's. She mainly writes and reads SFF but adds more than a pinch of romance to all her novels. She has published several short stories and is a contributor to *These Bodies Ain't Broken*. A firm believer in the healing powers of tea and anime, she never says no to spirited discussions about her favorite shows. When not lost in her own imaginary worlds or catching up with deadlines, you can find her creating digital art of her favorite characters.

Rosiee Thor is the Pacific Northwest Indie Bestselling author of *Tarnished Are the Stars*, *Fire Becomes Her*, the *Dead & Breakfast* mysteries, and tie-in novels for franchises, including *Life is Strange* and *Firefly*. Their short fiction appears in anthologies across genres including the Lambda Award–nominated *Being Ace*, and they are the editor of *Why on Earth: An Alien Invasion Anthology* and *This Is How We Roll*. They live in Oregon with a dog, two cats, and an abundance of plants.

Ann Zhao is the Indie Bestselling author of *Dear Wendy*. When she's not writing, she works in youth and teen services at a public library, where she's always finding excuses to put her friends' books on display. Born and raised in Illinois, she lived briefly in Massachusetts for college but now resides back in the Chicagoland area.